Have a J... married life!

Laman's River
Mark Munger

Cloquet River Press
Publishing Stories from the Lake Superior Basin
www.cloquetriverpress.com

First Edition
Copyright 2012, Mark Munger

ISBN 978-0-9792175-3-1
Library of Congress Control Number: 20129011962

Edited by:	Scribendi
Published by:	Cloquet River Press
	5353 Knudsen Rd.
	Duluth, MN 55803
	(218) 721-3213
Visit the Publisher at:	www.cloquetriverpress.com
Email the Author at:	cloquetriverpress@yahoo.com

Printed in the United States of America
Cover Photograph by René Munger
Cover Art by: René Munger

Acknowledgements

Attempting to understand a faith, a faith wholly and completely and utterly American, when you've not been steeped in nor grown up in that faith, is a daunting, perhaps impossible task for a fiction writer. This novel is not a scholarly study of the inconsistencies, incongruities, or irregularities to be found in Mormonism.

Read this book for entertainment and the prompting of curiosity. If you're compelled to further investigate Mormonism, there are other resources, such as those I relied upon, which can assist your scholarship.

As usual, the piecing together of a story involves the assistance of others. The following folks contributed their time, comments, and skill to making this book a "better read": Renata Skube, Harry Munger, Rev. Cheryl Harder, René Munger, The Honorable Ken Sandvik, Anita Zager, Dylan Munger, Chris Munger, The Honorable Dale Harris, Rodger Cragun, Jen Claseman, Richard Pemberton, Gerry Henkel, and Rev. Stephen Schaitberger.

A special thanks to my father, Harry Munger, who has always believed. Thanks, Dad!

Thanks for all your help.
Mark Munger
2012

"At length the time arrived for obtaining the plates, the Urin and Thummim, and the breastplate. On the twenty-second day of September, one thousand eight hundred and twenty-seven, having gone as usual at the end of another year to the place where they were deposited, the same heavenly messenger delivered them up to me with this charge: That I should be responsible for them; that if I should let them go carelessly, or through any neglect of mine, I should be cut off; but that if I would use all my endeavors to preserve them, until he, the messenger, should call for them, they should be protected..."

The ancient record, thus brought forth from the earth, as the voice of a people speaking from the dust, and translated into modern speech by the gift and power of God as attested to by Divine affirmation, was first published to the world in the year 1830 as the Book of Mormon.

(The Book of Mormon)

Laman's River
By Mark Munger

ONE

It seemed to her that she was floating outside herself, watching and hoping that someone would interrupt her death. It was as if her soul, her eternal being, had been released from her earthly body. She had the sense that, though there was evil in what was happening to her, there was indeed a God: a God who would save her in the end. Though she had lost her faith, *this* was the time to rekindle the fervor she had felt as a young Saint so many years ago.

If anyone can save me from the Destroyer, it would be God.

Duct tape ensured that no air could seep through the clod of earth he'd stuffed in her mouth. She was only able to breathe by drawing in cool Minnesota air through her delicate nostrils. Despite having been born beautiful, her nose wasn't her own but the work of a plastic surgeon.

Her brown eyes, the ancestry of Korea plain in their angle and the depth of their color, teared.

"Don't cry, Sister," the man said softly, as if speaking to a small child. "But for your apostasy, I'd wager that your soul is free of blight, that your destiny is the highest level of the Kingdom."

The man's words only increased the flow of moisture from the woman's tear ducts. She was shivering. Her nakedness, normally a source of pride given her slender build, her athleticism, and her saline-enhanced breasts was distressing in the presence of a complete stranger. But the man's actions, his brief words, and the resolve with which he did his work made it clear he was not interested in raping her. Indeed: His gloved hands had passed over her with disdain, without the slightest hesitation, as if she was a package being wrapped for Christmas. He had effortlessly bound her wrists and ankles with white plastic zip ties and strapped her naked body to a northern forest spruce with blue nylon cord.

Pieces of earth worked towards the back of her throat. Her spine shuddered against the spruce. Flecks of blood appeared on her bare back where bark irritated skin: Her blood did not flow cleanly in the autumnal air but oozed slowly, as if suspended in time, as the man finished his work.

Maybe he's after money.

The dirt worked its way further to the rear of her mouth. To take her mind off choking, she thought of her husband, Mitch, and her daughter, Molly. They were at a Timberwolves game. Mitch would be sipping on a beer. He'd allow himself one and no more. Molly would be charged up on whichever caffeinated soda the Target Center served.

The woman considered her naked body. She had gone to the plastic surgeon before Mitch, before Molly; when she was a reporter at a Twin Cities television station trying to get airtime, trying to get noticed and move on to a bigger market. Though that had been her dream and the reason for her new nose and breasts, she wasn't a big-city girl. In fact, her love of wilderness had led to her predicament.

She'd shouldered her kayak and hiked a barely discernible portage off Seagull Lake. The sun was high and the sky was azure; the shade of blue that defines a great fall day in Minnesota's Arrowhead region. The temperature was in the low sixties. She carried a plastic refillable bottle of water complimented with hotel ice, a bag of trail mix, and an orange; all cached in the kayak's waterproof compartment. A single paddle—aluminum shafted and double-tipped with black plastic blades—was bungeed to the kayak's frame as she began the arduous trek up the trail to Lost Lake. She'd labored over the portage: a trail that hadn't been maintained in years. Deadfall and leaves concealed twists and turns in the path, forcing her to retrace her footsteps to make progress. She wore a life vest; a one-piece neoprene kayaking suit over her torso, her upper arms, and her thighs; and neoprene water shoes. A Fitger's baseball cap, a cap she'd picked up while staying at the historic brewery and hotel in Duluth, sat tight against her scalp; her jet black hair pulled into a pony tail and passed through the opening above the cap's adjustable strap. She left her wedding ring and other jewelry in the glove box of her Subaru in the parking lot of the Superior National Forest campground on the eastern shore of Seagull Lake where she'd launched the kayak.

She'd paddled Lost Lake by herself, ducking into the shallows of the irregular lakeshore, marveling at the fifty-foot-high cliffs that isolated the place from the outside world. She explored the narrow, winding lake, the watercourse running roughly east to west, in the company of a pair of soaring bald eagles. She'd watched a cow moose and her calf stand aloof and silent in belly deep black water, their heads methodically swiveling as they ate lily pads. When the woman grew thirsty, she pulled into a tiny rock cove, dragged the kayak onto an outcropping, and sat on stony ground, plastic water jug to her lips, praising whoever created the world she was privileged to occupy. She ate handfuls of trail mix: the raisins, peanuts, and M&Ms giving her nearly instant energy; and peeled and ate the orange before sliding the kayak back into the water and paddling across quiet stillness.

She'd been startled to see a motorized boat, a narrow aluminum rental with a ten-horse Honda four stroke, waiting at the

Seagull end of the portage. She hadn't considered that anyone would be interested in walking a half-mile through the desolation of northeastern Minnesota's boreal forest to arrive at a small lake that held marginal pike and scrawny perch. But there it was: a boat, loaded with fishing gear, at the trailhead, when she made her way back to Seagull.

A stranger, a man slightly older than her, had appeared from deep within the evergreen canopy. She presumed he'd been relieving himself because he seemed a bit sheepish when they met.

"Angelina DeAquila," she said firmly, offering her hand to the stranger.

The man was dressed for fishing; a khaki fly vest, the pockets bulging, flies and tiny spoons attached to patches of soft lamb's wool by their hooks; an Australian-style bush hat, the brim crumpled and distressed sat tight on his head. Shadow caused by the hat's brim concealed the details of the stranger's face. The man wore faded Levi's and a pair of Red Wing work boots, the brown leather of the boots oiled to shiny perfection.

"Aren't you a writer for the *Minneapolis Star Tribune*?" the man asked as he shook her hand. He didn't remove his canvas work gloves when returning her gesture. He chewed gum meticulously. A faint scent of licorice emanated from the man's breath as he spoke.

It hadn't struck her at the time, but came to her later, after the Taser took her down to the soft, leafy earth, that the fisherman hadn't offered up his name in response to her introduction.

"Yes. How did you know that?" she'd replied.

Her own question had a basis in fact. When she'd been on television, before accepting her present job, she'd been far more visible. Granted, a GIF of her face appeared alongside her column in the *Star Tribune*, but the picture was barely noticeable. The fisherman's insight caused her pause. Not alarm. Just pause.

By the time she regained her ability to move, it was too late. He'd already stripped her of her life vest, suit, and shoes, rolled her onto her bare stomach, and secured her limbs with zip ties. When she cried out, he rolled her onto her back, shoved dirt between her grimaced teeth, and duct taped her mouth. The man was efficient: he wasted little effort in dealing with her protests.

Why is this happening to me?

Her nostrils filled with the taste of moist earth tinged with the odor of decaying leaves. The connection between the dead foliage and her own situation caused her to resume sobbing.

"There, there, Sister. It will be over soon."

Over? What does he mean, "over"?

9

Her eyes widened as the man left her side. She tried to think of something, anything that she could do to free her mouth of the dirt and the tape so that her voice could be heard across the calm waters of Seagull Lake.

There are others out fishing. Maybe they will hear me.

But the man's thoroughness made any effort at speech impossible. She tried to swallow some of the dirt but the clod hung up in the back of her throat. She started to choke.

Maybe that would be better.

He dragged her kayak, clothing, and gear deep into the woods. When she struggled to breathe, the man hurried back. His gloved fists pounded her bare flanks until the dirt broke free and descended.

"That won't help," he cautioned in a soft voice, a voice at odds with his actions. "You'll just make matters worse. Focus on the Lord for He will deliver you from all travails," the man said in a delicate and caring tone. "Remember your scripture: '*Were the bands of death broken and the chains of hell which encircled them about, were they loosed? Yea, they were loosed, and their souls did expand, and they did sing redeeming love.*'"

It was then, as he studied her closely, that she realized how clear and purposeful the man's blue eyes seemed. Her hysteria lessened and she studied her abductor with false optimism.

He's going to ask for money and then, when he gets what he wants, he'll tell Mitch where to find me.

The suddenness of the filet knife slicing her throat, the searing pain as the delicate blade separated her carotid artery and disrupted the flow of blood to her brain, caught Angelina DeAquila completely unprepared for the Hereafter.

TWO

Sheriff Debra "Deb" Slater groped for the receiver of her remote telephone. The phone's annoying electronic ring had shattered what seemed to be a recurring dream: She and Rick exploring the Superior Hiking Trail above Manitou Falls, the sky gray and close, the forest lush with new spring. The fact that Rick was no longer ill, that his legs and arms rippled with the muscle of youth and the vigor of good health was a recurring aspect of her dreams.

"Hello," Slater said in a soft voice so as not to wake her husband as he slept in the small bedroom across the hall.

She was in the master suite of their compact home, a Craftsman-style house set back from the shoreline of Devil's Track Lake a few miles north of Grand Marais, Minnesota.

"There's been a murder."

Sheriff Slater recognized the voice on the telephone as that of Augie Olsen, the most senior deputy in the Cook County Sheriff's Office. Not most senior in terms of total time spent in law enforcement: that honor belonged to Deb Slater. She had more career experience—twenty-six years on the job—though only the last three had been spent in Cook County.

"Where?"

"Just off Seagull Lake. On the Lost Lake portage."

"Who's the victim?"

"Lady kayaker from the Twin Cities."

"How?"

"Throat was cut ear to fuckin' ear."

Olsen had a penchant for the colorful. As Slater sat up in bed, her flannel pajama bottoms barely touched the smooth pine planks of the bedroom floor. The cuffs of the pajamas disturbed dust and pillow feathers that Slater's indifference had allowed to accumulate beneath the bed. The sheriff held the receiver of the phone to her ear with her right hand: with her left, she restrained strands of untamed auburn hair dangling in her eyes. The hair color was vivid and youthful; straight out of a bottle; a subtle bow to vanity.

"There's more."

Across the darkened hallway from the small bedroom where Rick Slater slept, Deb Slater heard the repetitive rasp of an oxygen machine. Margaret Ann, "Annie", the couple's teenage daughter, whose room was also across the hall a few steps further towards the

11

guest bath, hadn't stirred. The only sound in the house, a two-story bungalow that Deb and Rick had bought three years ago, was that of Rick's constant mechanical companion. Even Duke, the ever watchful and ever present family black Labrador, his massive body curled at the foot of Deb Slater's bed, remained asleep, oblivious to the phone call.

"How's that?"

Slater placed her left arm over her head, folded her forearm around her neck, and stretched. The sleeve of her "Cook County Vikings Volleyball" T-shirt brushed a diamond stud earring she'd forgotten to remove after last night's dinner and silent auction in town. She'd attended the event, a fundraiser for the high school's athletic department, one of the few social engagements she allowed herself during Rick's illness. She'd bid on a few items: a signed first edition novel by local author Joan Drury; a John Peyton watercolor; a dog sled outing donated by Gunflint Trail Outfitters. She hadn't "won" anything; not that being the highest bidder on an item was really "winning" in the truest sense. At silent auctions, the "winner" often pays more for the item "won" than the item is actually worth. But she and Annie, who was in the ninth grade and had a shot at playing varsity basketball and volleyball next year, had enjoyed the evening. The earring reminded the sheriff of the laughter, the two glasses of wine she'd sipped over the course of the evening, and the quiet ride home in her Honda Passport through the dark October night with her rapidly changing, always challenging only child sitting utterly silent in the front passenger seat of the SUV.

"She was left bound to a tree. Naked. And it looks like she was Tased. Contact marks on her clothes and skin."

Slater shuddered at the vision Olsen's description painted in her mind.

"Raped?"

"Doesn't look like it. No visible fluids. No discarded condoms. No sign of trauma to…" Olsen paused, obviously trying to grope for an appropriate term to describe the dead woman's genitalia.

Slater spared the man the embarrassment.

"Her vagina. No bruising, no cuts, no scrapes?"

"No ma'am. None of the above," the deputy said agreeably, clearly relieved of having to provide further detail.

"Where is she now?"

"Stevenson and I photographed the scene. Bagged what little evidence there was. Really only her clothes. Life vest. Water shoes. Kayak and paddle. Couple short strands of blue rope. Brought her to the hospital. She's in the morgue, waiting for the medical examiner from Duluth."

"Any witnesses?"

"Nope. Found her car. Subaru Outback. White with brown leather interior; a custom kayak rack on the roof. Parked in the forest service lot on Seagull. The car was locked but the keys were tucked into the wheel well. Oldest trick in the book. Found her purse. Check book, wallet, credit cards and Minnesota DL all inside. Her jewelry was in the glove box. Overnight bag in the rear cargo area."

"Who is she?"

"Angelina DeAquila, a reporter for the *Minneapolis Star Tribune*. Her press credentials were in her purse."

"Anyone see her come or go?"

"Stevenson is still canvassing the Trail to see if anyone spotted her driving in or paddling the lake. Right now, all we have is her car, her belongings, and her body."

Slater glanced at the neon green numbers of the digital alarm clock on the nightstand next to her bed. It was six in the morning.

"It'll take me a half hour to get ready. I'll be in by seven."

"Sounds good."

There was a hitch in Olsen's voice.

"Somethin' else?"

Silence.

"Augie?"

Deb Slater discerned a buildup of courage on the other end of the telephone line.

"There is one other thing."

"Ya?"

"Don't really make any sense, given the situation and all."

Slater rubbed her emerald green eyes with her left hand before standing in darkness.

"For chrissakes, out with it, Augie."

"Her mouth…"

"Ya?"

"It was taped shut with duct tape and stuffed with dirt."

A lady newspaper reporter found dead, naked, bound, gagged, and her mouth filled with dirt. Some wake-up call.

THREE

The tires of a Chevrolet Tahoe, "Cook County Sheriff" stenciled on its white flanks, bounded over the pitching blacktop of the Gunflint Trail. Slater's hair dripped water onto the leather of the driver's seat. Her khaki uniform was moist under her arms and across her broad back from residual shower she'd missed when she toweled off quickly. Her rouge and eyeliner had been applied haphazardly.

At least I took the time to dab on some perfume, some Secret, and brush my teeth!

Slater's eyes searched the ditches and nether regions of the brush lining the roadway for white tail deer. She'd hit three deer in the past year, two of which died, the third, a big buck, his eight point rack magnificent against the headlights of her squad car, had bounced off the Tahoe's hood, causing serious damage to the SUV before crashing onto the pockmarked asphalt of the Trail. She'd stopped the Tahoe and exited the vehicle to deliver the coup de grace from her forty caliber Smith and Wesson M&P, certain the deer was history, only to find the buck standing in a shallow ditch, shaking his antler-weary head from side to side as if dealing with the after affects of a sucker punch. She'd watched the deer sway unsteadily for a few moments before he snorted indignantly and disappeared into undergrowth.

The sheriff encountered no deer as she approached the piedmont of the Sawtooth Mountains rolling towards Lake Superior. Deb Slater relaxed her grip on the steering wheel as the big V-8 adjusted its power to account for gravity. Then, as quick as a bat flitting at dusk, he was in front of her.

She dynamited the brakes on the big rig, spewing coffee from the sipping and air holes of the stainless steel travel mug she'd placed in the console between the SUV's front seats. The boar was enormous. Four to five hundred pounds. He loped from early morning darkness into the beam of the Tahoe's headlights, his agility and speed at odds with common assumptions of how black bears move.

"Shit," Slater muttered, though there was no one else in the vehicle. "He came outta nowhere."

The boar's haunches equaled the height of the Tahoe's hood as the animal straddled the centerline of the roadway. The animal's black fur undulated in the SUV's headlights as his massive hindquarters propelled him with lumbering grace. The bear veered off the road and crashed through a thicket of maple trees before vanishing in pre-dawn forest.

"That was cool."

Deb Slater had left her home on Devil's Track Lake without saying goodbye to Rick. It was Saturday. Annie would be home with her father until he was dressed, fed, and up and about for the day. Annie, unlike virtually every teenager Debra Slater had ever come across, was a consistent early riser; a young woman who slept only seven hours a night no matter how exhausted she was from her sports regimen. The girl would be there to make Rick his breakfast: a bowl of slow-cooked oatmeal with brown sugar, two slices of whole wheat toast with butter and honey, a glass of orange juice, and a cup of hot coffee. Annie would disconnect the stationary oxygen tank and help her father out of bed. Rick would negotiate the hallway leading to the guest bath to do his business. He'd carry a portable oxygen tank with him on his journey, the plastic tubing connecting the tank to his nose, his respirations shallow, his gait agonizingly deliberate; his refusal to rely on a walker or a cane witness to his fierce independence and fight.

The diagnosis had been nearly as slow and agonizing as the progress of the disease. Rick Slater was on the cusp of fifty. Debra Slater was forty-seven. Rick had been diagnosed five years earlier, after a lengthy period of deterioration. The symptoms started innocently enough; fatigue, an overall feeling of malaise. Trips to the Duluth Clinic followed by journeys to Rochester, to the vaunted Mayo Clinic, where Rick underwent days upon days of testing, consultations, EEGs, EKGs, blood draws, x-rays, and scans, none of which revealed an answer or explained why Deb Slater's high octane husband, a man who hunted, fished, canoed, skied, ran, and hiked with abandon was having trouble getting out of bed in the morning, stilled by an innate, creeping lethargy that had robbed him of his essence.

There were suppositions and guesses; leukemia, MS, MD, lupus, ALS (that one really scared the shit out of Deb when a young neurologist at the Mayo postulated it as a possibility) and similar auto-immune disorders. All were launched at the Slaters by well-meaning men and women in white lab coats; all of them proved false. It wasn't until Bob Thompson, their local family doc at the Cook County Family Medical Clinic in Grand Marais, spent a few hours on the Internet gleaning wisdom that anyone thought to order a muscle biopsy of Rick's thigh. Debra Slater thought about the moment their guessing game had ended. It was an instant, an event, in her life, she'd never forget.

Before their visit with Dr. Bob that fateful afternoon, Deb and Rick had never heard of mitochondria disorder. In retrospect, the diagnosis made perfect sense: Rick's mother, the person who'd passed on the genetic defect to her son through her maternal DNA, had died a painful and mysterious death in her late thirties. Betty Slater had apparently carried the cellular defect, the genetic mutation in her DNA, which had eventually stricken Rick.

Mitochondria disorder, Dr. Bob explained that terrible day under the extreme light of an exam room at the clinic, affects the mitochondria of the cells, sometimes at birth, often over time, as in Rick's case, when more and more cells are impacted by the defect, rendering the cells unable to deliver energy to propel the basic functions of the body. A build-up of lactic acid takes place because the mitochondria no longer efficiently turn food into energy. Over time, excess lactic acid causes muscle pain akin to what runners experience after completing a marathon.

"Unfortunately," Dr. Bob had said, removing bifocals curiously required for a healer in his late thirties, "there isn't a cure. We can use steroids for the worst flare-ups; modify your diet to reduce your digestive symptoms; prescribe oxygen for your shortness of breath. But that's about it. There's no cure."

"Will it progress?"

Rick had asked the question as his right hand massaged the site of the biopsy. A jagged line of knitted flesh had created a permanent scar on Rick's right thigh; though the wound had, over time, lost the color of indignity. He had been sitting on the edge of an examination table, his thick thighs, his muscular calves propped against the paper-covered curvature of the table, his torso rigid, his left hand clasped tightly, desperately to his wife's right hand. The conversation lapsed as the young doctor tried to find the words, words he didn't want to reveal to his friend and patient.

"Yes."

"How long?"

The doctor sighed.

"Hard to say. Years, for sure. How many, that's a tough nut to crack. There's a chance, as in cancer cases where chemo and radiation slow or stop the growth of a tumor, for a temporary remission. But there is no cure."

As the Tahoe rounded the last corner in the road before the Gunflint Trail merges with the city streets of Grand Marais, the vision of Rick's face, his rugged good looks, his innate handsomeness framed by neatly trimmed blond hair, his mouth held in a tight, unnatural grimace, his head nodding in appreciation for his newly-disclosed mortality, occupied Deb Slater's mind.

The sheriff had completely forgotten about the dead girl until she pulled the SUV into the parking lot of the Cook County Medical Center and turned off the engine. Debra Slater sat in silence. She watched the vehicle's headlights automatically dim, leaving her alone, in the dark, visions of the past her only companion.

FOUR

"All rise, District Court, Sixth Judicial District, the Honorable Elizabeth Prichard presiding, is now in session. Please remove your caps and hats; no coffee, juice, pop, gum, candy or food in the courtroom. Cell phones should be turned completely off. Not just on vibrate; completely off!"

Judge Prichard, a comely woman in her mid-fifties, stepped assuredly over the threshold between her judicial chambers and Courtroom No. 4 on the fourth floor of the iconic St. Louis County Courthouse in Duluth, Minnesota, the hem of her black robe swaying as she moved, her black hose shining in the artificial light of the courtroom, her slight physique reduced further by the robe's bulk. The judge paused briefly in front of the Formica surface of her bench and smiled before addressing the attorneys, court clerk, law clerk, court reporter, social workers, Guardian ad Litem, probation officer, family members, and the child standing at rigid attention before her.

"Please have a seat," the judge said in a rehearsed voice, her courtroom voice, years of practice having honed its tone and tenor to a fine pitch somewhere between a greeting and a command. At the judge's direction, the bailiff, Mrs. Brown, an attractive woman of indecipherable age, left her position near the judge's bench to secure the oak door leading from the public corridor into the courtroom.

Two lawyers, a St. Louis County social worker, the mother of the child at issue in the case, and the child all claimed antique oak chairs at the two counsel tables immediately in front of the court reporter, law clerk, and clerk stations in the cavernous courtroom. The room's high ceiling, originally of plaster and ornate terra cotta, replaced years ago by white acoustical tiles, soared above the space. The walls, partially original, partially reconstructed over the 100-year existence of the courthouse, were painted a sickly green. The floor, once bare Vermont marble, stone polished and shiny, but a perfect sounding board for echoes, had been covered and recovered with cheap carpet over the decades of the building's existence to deaden the noise in the room; a space nearly the size of a high school gymnasium. The present carpeting was a dull gray; made duller by the thousands of folks walking over it and depositing the residue of northeastern Minnesota's brutal climate (rain in the spring, summer and fall; nearly one hundred inches of snow in winter) on the frayed fabric. Save for the Minnesota state flag and the American flag standing motionless behind the bench, a reproduction of the state seal attached to the wall behind Judge

Prichard, and a vintage Regulator clock affixed above the entrance door, the courtroom's plaster walls were bare; the muted green surface, a vast field of mundane sourness. The only saving grace to the room was the woodwork; polished quarter sawn oak had been used to construct the judge's bench, the jury box, and the room's trim. The burled wood, polished by the county maintenance staff to effervescence, saved the space from terminal ugliness.

"We are here for court trial in the matter of *St. Louis County vs. Elsie Johnson*," the judge announced in a voice that carried across the distance between her bench and the counsel tables. "Is the county ready to proceed?'

Mary Simons, one of a myriad of assistant county attorneys working in the Duluth branch of the St. Louis County Attorney's office, rose to her feet. She was a large, straight necked, open faced woman in her late twenties. Dark, curly brown hair spilled across her shoulders, the hair firmly affixed and immobile as she rose; its stiffness the result of being tamed by inordinate amounts of hairspray.

"We are, Your Honor. But we believe we've reached an agreement. I'll leave it to Mr. Ashton to fill the court in on the details."

"Mr. Ashton?"

Lloyd Ashton, the public defender assigned to represent the child, rose laboriously from his seat. His client, a round-faced Ojibwe adolescent, remained seated, her nervousness evident as she nibbled the fingernails of both hands, her eyes lowered, not making contact with those of the judge.

From his body language, it was evident to anyone with even modest powers of observation that Lloyd Ashton was a tired man. Ashton's breathing was labored; his enormous pot belly protruded from beneath his cheaply tailored suit and threatened to burst through the meager security of the strained buttons of the white dress shirt he was wearing. A necktie was looped carelessly around Ashton's neck and was, here and there, visible beneath the collar of his shirt. Remnants of breakfast stained the tie. Ashton wasn't on the decline: He *had* declined.

The judges in the Sixth Judicial District, the four-county area to which Ashton was assigned by the district's chief public defender to provide legal representation to juveniles charged with crimes, to a man or woman cut Lloyd Ashton slack regarding his appearance. He was a kind-hearted soul, a man of integrity, if not one of personal hygiene. For that reason (and the fact that he was due to retire at the end of the year) the judges let the old man be. Lloyd Ashton was on the cusp of seventy and, once retired, what with the recent death of his wife of forty-three years, his diagnosis of Stage III lung cancer, and his

19

continued insistence upon smoking Camel straights despite his terminal disease, unlikely to see seventy-one.

"Your Honor," Ashton rasped, rising slowly from his seat, cane in hand to steady his wide girth against gravity and the spidery thinness of his legs, "we have indeed reached an accord."

The lawyer's propensity for speaking like a character out of a Dickens novel was another reason the judges cut him so much slack.

He's pure entertainment; a joy to try a case with, Elizabeth Prichard thought as she listened intently to Lloyd Ashton's remarks, studying the man over the rims of her retro-styled bifocals, the thick black plastic frames reminiscent of a prop from an Austin Powers' movie.

"Yes?"

"Ms. Johnson will be pleading guilty to one count of aiding and abetting Robbery in the First Degree, the other four counts of the petition will be dismissed by the county."

Judge Prichard turned her attention to the prosecutor.

"That right, Ms. Simons?"

Mary Simons rose in turn.

"That's the agreement, Your Honor. We've also reached an agreement as to disposition. There'll be a stayed sentence to AJC, the 90/120 day program. As part of the stay, Ms. Johnson will be placed at Elmore Academy in Elmore, Minnesota, where she can receive substance abuse treatment, an education, and, hopefully be placed, once she's done at Elmore, with her paternal grandparents in Grand Portage to attend Grand Portage Ojibwe School. That's the agreement, as I understand it."

Judge Prichard gave the teenager, who had moved on to fiddling with the edges of her sleek, black hair, a serious look.

"You understand, Ms. Johnson, that I am not bound by the sentencing agreement? That I will listen to your attorney, the county attorney, county social services, probation, Grand Portage social services, your mother, and you, but in the end, I have to make the decision as to what your sentence in this matter will be. You understand that?"

The girl nodded imprecisely.

"You need to answer out loud."

"I understand."

"Good. Counselors, I'll cover her rights with her. Who's going to cover the facts?"

Judge Prichard spent the better part of ten minutes going over the rights that Elsie Johnson was giving up by pleading guilty and taking advantage of the plea arrangement. Ms. Simons then questioned the girl regarding the facts of the crime. Elsie looked younger than her fifteen years as she struggled to understand the questions and provide answers to the county attorney. In the end, with some assistance from the judge, a factual basis was laid for the girl's participation in the offense; a robbery she'd been drawn into by her older brother, Darrell, and two of his friends; when the four of them were lurking in the shadows of an alley adjacent to Duluth's Lake Avenue, a Mecca for tourists visiting the city's newly-revived waterfront. Elsie Johnson hadn't really done much other than be there, and admit she would have alerted the police, while Darrell brandished a realistic looking toy gun in the face of an elderly couple on their way back from the Duluth Entertainment and Convention Center to their car, which they'd parked on Lake Avenue near the Ariel Lift Bridge to save the four dollar DECC parking fee. Elsie's role was that of reluctant lookout, which, given the level of the crime, placed her in jeopardy of having a felony record. The kids had used the twenty-seven dollars they took off their victims to buy a bag of poor quality locally grown pot, their dependence on grass being the main point for the robbery. It had taken the Duluth Police Department all of two days to track down the kids and lock up the four little hooligans at AJC, the local juvenile detention facility, where each of them sat, pending trial, because their home situations were so chaotic that the judges separately assigned to their cases could not, in good conscious, let the kids go home.

After hearing the sentencing recommendation, a recommendation in line with Ms. Simons's recitation to the court, Judge Prichard declared a recess to consider the options available for placement of the child. Twenty minutes after leaving the bench to mull over Elsie Johnson's fate in the privacy of her judicial chambers, the windows of which faced north towards the twin towers of Old Central High School and First Presbyterian Church, two ancient red sandstone buildings that have dominated downtown Duluth since their construction in the boom and bust days of the 1890s, the judge was back, seated behind her ponderous bench, ready to pronounce sentence.

"Mr. Oliver," the judge said quietly, her concentration keen as she addressed the probation officer assigned by Arrowhead Regional Corrections to the case, "have you considered the All Faiths Recovery Center in Minneapolis as an alternative to Elmore?"

Mark Oliver, the probation officer, rose to his feet. He was a non-descript young man, just beginning his career in corrections, uncertain in his manner, voice, and recommendations; the assuredness displayed by veteran POs likely years away.

"I have not, Your Honor. I am unfamiliar with that program."

"Well, Mr. Oliver, you should do your homework. Ms. Johnson's primary issue, it seems to me, other than the lack of parental

21

supervision," Judge Prichard said sternly as she eyeballed the child's mother sitting next to Lloyd Ashton at the counsel table, "is marijuana. By all accounts, she's a bright young lady who just can't get it together because of her pot use. All Faiths has a program similar to Teen Challenge, except that, unlike Teen Challenge, where the faith-based recovery program is limited to Christianity, All Faiths has folks on staff with training in virtually every faith tradition; from Islam to Hindu, from Pentecostal to Episcopal. As I understand it, they even have a counselor who deals with Native American faith traditions."

"Mr. Buckanaga," the judge continued, turning her attention to a Native American gentleman seated behind the child in the first row of the gallery, "are you familiar with All Faiths?"

The social worker from the Grand Portage Band of Ojibwe, thin as a reed, his thick gray hair tied in a pony tail, his bright teal shirt providing contrast to his dark features, rose to address the judge.

"I am, Your Honor. It's a good program. I think it would suit Ms. Johnson well."

"Any objection from you, Mr. Ashton? I would couple her time there with a Stay of Adjudication. So if she completes the program and one hundred and eighty days of probation without a misstep, she would leave this matter behind; she'd have no felony record. How's that sound?"

The defense lawyer conferred with his client before straining to rise.

"Ms. Johnson would have no objection to such a disposition," the attorney said as he stood unsteadily behind the counsel table.

"But Your Honor..." Ms. Simons interjected, annoyance clear in her voice.

The prosecutor had been engaged in a furious whispered discussion with the probation officer before sliding out of her chair and resuming her feet.

"The county is not in support of the Court's suggested disposition. Neither is probation. We feel that Elmore Academy is a better fit."

Judge Prichard scrutinized the female attorney.

"I trust the county's position isn't based upon the fact that All Faith's per diem is twenty dollars a day more than Elmore's," the judge quipped.

Ms. Simons balked. The judge had zeroed in on probation's unvoiced objection: the cost of programming. The Arrowhead Juvenile Center (AJC) was a regional correctional facility funded by five counties. No per diems were charged by AJC to Arrowhead Regional Corrections (ARC) for placement. Probation apparently felt it was being generous by offering to fund the girl's stay at Elmore Academy, a private facility located near the Iowa-Minnesota border, where a per diem would indeed be charged to and paid for by ARC. Money is always an issue in delinquency adjudications. Paying per diems that don't need to be incurred doesn't sit well with county commissioners.

Ms. Simons took a deep breath, weighed the consequences of candor, and fibbed.

"No, Your Honor. That's not the reason behind our objection."

Judge Prichard glared. She focused hard on Mr. Oliver. The probation officer seemed to shrink in stature as the judge glowered in his direction.

"That's good, Ms. Simons. I'd hate to believe that an officer of the court, whether a probation officer or an attorney, would allow money to dictate how we treat and rehabilitate children in trouble."

Gavel struck wood. Disposition was pronounced. Elsie Johnson was to be held at AJC until All Faiths Recovery Center could transport her from Duluth to the Twin Cities. Judge Elizabeth Prichard stood up, smoothed wrinkles from her robe, stepped down from the bench, and disappeared into her chambers.

Mary Simons collected her file and a legal pad filled with hastily scribbled notes from the counsel table and deposited them in a green canvas satchel, the informal briefcase a product of Duluth Pack, a local manufacturer.

"Is it just me, Mark," Simons whispered as the other participants cleared the courtroom and she fastened the buckle on the briefcase, "or is Judge Prichard using All Faiths more frequently than other judges?"

"Don't know. Like I told the judge, I haven't used it. I'm not familiar with it at all."

"She sure gave you *the look*, didn't she?"

"She sure did."

"I don't get it. I haven't had another judge send a kid to All Faiths since Judge Martin retired. And he only used it once that I can recall, at the request of the kid's parents. I think they were Seventh Day Adventists or something."

The lawyer and the probation officer walked through the doorway into an impressive lobby on the courthouse's fourth floor. The pair nodded to Mrs. Brown as the bailiff closed the heavy oak door to the courtroom behind them. Mary Simons stopped in the center of the polished floor of the impressive corridor. The probation officer stood quietly, waiting for the attorney to provide additional illumination as to what had just taken place in Judge Prichard's courtroom.

"It's a bit odd, is all I can say, this sudden need to infuse children with religion. I understand the judge is an evangelical. I get that. But I hadn't seen much evidence of religion coloring Judge

23

Prichard's decision-making until recently. Hell," the attorney said through a slight grin as she resumed walking, "far as I know, the kid doesn't even go to church."

The probation officer matched the lawyer stride for stride as they walked towards the stairwell. Mark Oliver had nothing to add; he could provide no insight into Judge Elizabeth Prichard's sudden need to save the souls of children.

FIVE

Gilbert Olson, MD, stood over the naked body of the victim. The cool air of the Cook County Hospital morgue slowed the decomposition of the corpse and bought the medical examiner time, time to uncover the mystery of Angelina DeAquila's demise. Though, in the case of the newspaper reporter, there was little guesswork involved in postulating the cause of death.

Vicious.

Olson, his hands protected by thin latex, gently examined the neck wound on the dead woman, a wound that had nearly severed Angelina DeAquila's head from her body.

Took out the carotid and the jugular, not to mention the larynx, the throat, and nearly half the spinal cord! Brutally efficient. Olson thought. *Efficient and well trained. I couldn't have done it better myself.*

"This wasn't some random killing by an amateur," Olson said, his words slightly muffled by the disposable white surgical mask he was wearing as he worked. "Whoever killed this young lady knew what he or she was doing."

Deb Slater stood a few feet from the body, her hands covered in the same latex gloves as the doctor, her eyes scrutinizing the nude body of the Asian American reporter.

She's such a little thing, the sheriff thought, *not much bigger than Annie.*

"Other than breast implants, a little cosmetic work on her nose, the dirt stuffed in her mouth, and the fact she's likely had kids," Olson added, "and this rather nasty gash across the her throat, there's nothing much else to see. From the direction of the cut, I'd say your killer is left handed."

"Murder weapon?"

"Ah. I'd guess a deer skinning knife or a fillet knife. The entry wound is thin, narrow; not much width to the blade. If I had to guess, I'd put my money on a fillet knife."

"Kids?"

"Or kid. The width of the hips suggests childbirth. And there are these," the doctor said, lifting the saline-enhanced edge of the dead woman's left breast to reveal minute striations. The nipple of the breast was small, the areola nearly identical in color to the pigment of the surrounding skin.

25

"Stretch marks," Slater whispered. "I know what those are."

The medical examiner turned his head towards Slater. Behind the mask, the sheriff could tell the ME was smiling.

"Of course. Annie, isn't it?"

"Yes."

"She's what, fourteen?"

"Fifteen."

"I'll bet things are just starting to get interesting around the Slater household."

"Not really. With Rick being sick and all, Annie's pretty much had to toe the line. She's a good kid."

Olson continued his examination.

"Well. No sign of sexual assault. There are these," the doctor said, lifting the stiffened left shoulder of the corpse to reveal two small burn marks on the woman's back.

"Taser?"

"Poor thing never knew what hit her. She'd regained her mobility, however, when her throat was slit. There are bruises on her wrists and ankles, as if she tried to break free of her restraints. But she didn't have a chance to put up much of a fight."

Slater raised her Canon digital camera and preserved the Taser marks on the dead woman's exposed back. The sheriff, or her deputies, had already documented everything else of importance. There was no need for her to linger as the body was dissected. There was no need for her to witness the final indignity that would befall Angelina DeAquila before the reporter's husband and daughter arrived later that day from the Twin Cities to claim the ice-cold corpse of their wife and mother.

"That's probably all I need," Slater advised reverently. "I'll take these photos back to the office and download them onto my laptop."

As Deb Slater turned to leave the room, the ME silently noted that the sheriff had gone through significant physical changes. Absent were the youthful curves that had always invited interest. Slater's girlish figure had been replaced by a thickened torso; not the sudden appearance of a paunch but the gradual rounding of shape which diminished the natural attributes that had made Debra Slater such a stunner.

Menopause.

Slater could feel Olson's eyes studying her as she walked away from the examination table, the nipples of the dead woman's artificially posed breasts aimed straight at the ceiling, her tiny mouth

26

closed in a permanent pout, and Angelina DeAquila's almond shaped eyes shut against the light for all eternity.

Slater knew that Olson was on his fourth marriage; eight kids between three families. The youngest was only a year or so old, a newborn the last time the doctor had occasion to be called to Cook County from his home base in rural Duluth, two hours away. Despite the ME's obvious failings in the fidelity department, Deb Slater liked the guy. She didn't want to like him; Olson had too many personal demons regarding women to make such admiration sensible. And yet, Slater found herself smiling at the knowledge that the doctor was watching her ass.

"There's one more thing."

Olson's comment caught Slater in mid-thought. The sheriff stopped and turned to face the medical examiner.

"How's that?"

"I did find this," the ME said quietly as he handed the woman a tightly wadded piece of paper, a label of some kind, its lettering obscured by wrinkles.

Slater accepted the paper and unfolded it.

"Where'd you find this?"

"The dead girl."

"Where?"

"She had one last surprise for her killer."

"Whatdayamean?"

"For all his or her thoroughness, I'm talking about the killer now, he or she must have gotten a tad careless and dropped the wrapper in close proximity to Ms. DeAquila. The victim somehow managed to curl the toes of her left foot around the paper. The wrapper was still in place when her body was brought in by your crew."

Slater straightened the wrapper with her fingers; her nails cut short, utilitarian and unpolished. She knew in an instant what she was holding: She had chewed the same licorice flavored gum when she was a child.

SIX

Elsie Johnson said her goodbyes to her mother, Jamie, and entered the waiting Astro mini-van in the sally port of AJC, "All Faiths Recovery Center" stenciled across the silver sides of the vehicle in bright purple lettering. A cross, a crescent moon, a Star of David, a beehive, and other religious symbols were displayed on the Chevrolet's exterior. The center's website address and telephone number, along with the center's slogan: "A Safe Place for Children of All Faiths", were neatly displayed across the rear doors of the Astro.

The Ojibwe girl found room on the middle bench seat of the van, sat down heavily, shoved a small Rage Against the Machine backpack beneath the driver's seat in front of her, strapped herself in, and proceeded to stare indifferently out the passenger side window, the glass obscured by fingerprints left by countless other teenagers who'd sat in the same spot, pondering the same reality; the reality of being displaced from home and family.

George Alder, a short statured, light skinned Native American of undisclosed tribe, his wide hips and heavy girth squeezed in tight behind the steering wheel of the van, nodded to his partner, Joyce Metzenbaum, as he turned the ignition key and started up the van's noisy V-6. Metzenbaum was a thinly configured Jewess; her stubbly black hair was cropped short to the scalp; her body was absent any curves or features of femininity. Her ears were devoid of earrings; she was free of jewelry save for a single stud pierced through her tongue, a solitary diamond shining like a bit of unmelted ice that clicked annoyingly against her yellow teeth each time she spoke; the stains on her teeth the result of years of chain smoking generic cigarettes.

In addition to the adults and Elsie Johnson, there were two other passengers in the van: Damien Newhouse, an African American kid from Cloquet, a paper mill city hugging the St. Louis River just south of Duluth on I-35; and Brenda Weems, a Caucasian girl from Floodwood, a small town located north and west of Duluth, a close-knit village primarily of Finnish ancestry. Newhouse was making his second trip to All Faiths, having failed to stay away from meth after he'd completed a six-month stint at the facility: He'd failed on his discharge back to his parental home in Cloquet. Weems, only twelve years old, was, like Elsie Johnson, a "newbie", a first timer, whose penchant for shoplifting to feed a crack cocaine habit had landed her in front of Judge Elizabeth Prichard in Duluth. Normally, shoplifting would be treated as a petty offense by the juvenile justice system. But

Brenda Weems was no minor thief: she, along with two female adult cousins conspired to steal in excess of two thousand dollars of clothing, jewelry, and cosmetics in an elaborate, if ill-fated, scheme. The three of them were caught by mall security loading stolen items into a pickup camper behind JC Penney in Duluth, where one of the adult women worked as an assistant manager. The adults, who had priors but weren't particularly dangerous, had received standard dispositions in court; stayed jail time, restitution, and small fines. Brenda, on the other hand, being salvageable in the eyes of Judge Prichard, was sent to All Faiths.

"What're you in for?" Brenda Weems, her small bright green eyes sparkling like a kid on her first trip to Disney World, asked Elsie Johnson as the van thundered south towards the Twin Cities.

"Robbery."

"Cool. I got caught shoplifting with my two idiot cousins. Their idea. Needed money for crack. I'm strung out like crazy. Haven't scored in a month, since the cops arrested me. How about you?'

"Weed. But I can do without it. At least, that's what I keep telling myself."

Newhouse sat behind the two girls, his shoes propped up against the side window in defiance. His eyes were closed. He'd started to fall asleep as soon as the van pulled away from AJC.

"What's your story?" Weems asked the boy.

"Meth," Newhouse hissed, annoyance at being prodded from sleep by Brenda Weems's scratchy voice clear in his reply.

"Awesome."

"Shut the fuck up," Newhouse responded, his voice rising in pitch. "There's nothing 'awesome' about it. I was clean for six months, almost off probation, and then my stupid ass sister took me to a party. Broke curfew. I used. Now I'm going back to that hellhole. Just shut the fuck up. You don't know nothin'."

Metzenbaum turned in her seat. Her black eyes flashed.

"Watch your language, Mr. Newhouse. As of right now, you're on All Faiths' time. You know the drill. Every time you curse will cost you an hour of good time."

After a three-hour jaunt down the freeway, with a bathroom break at the state wayside rest just south of Hinckley, the van pulled through the front gate of the All Faiths facility in Minneapolis' posh Kenwood neighborhood.

When the treatment center was first proposed as a use for the old Bedford Mansion, the home long fallen into disrepair, the sprawling lawns and gardens reduced to weeds and tumble after decades of neglect, the white paint of the Corinthian columns of the expansive front porch of the Greek revival-style three story monolith peeling, exposing the underlying white pine lumber to weather, the neighbors, mostly childless couples embedded in Kenwood with old wealth, had risen up en masse to object. But the city council had passed the requested rezoning by a narrow margin. The liberal traditions of Minneapolis politics overcame the arguments of the well to do. The only caveat to the council's approval was the express preclusion of juvenile sex offenders from being housed and treated at the facility.

True to the philanthropic heritage of George Harrison Bedford, the 19th century founder of Bedford Windows and Millwork along the then-wild and untamed Mississippi River, the mansion, once there were no little Bedfords being raised in the house, had been deeded to George Bedford's church for use as an orphanage. The Unitarians operated a home for orphaned boys in the mansion from the late 1890s until the late 1970s, when orphanages became passé. The house sat vacant. Efforts by the church to sell it in its diminished and abused condition were unsuccessful until the newly formed board of All Faiths visited the site and declared the building "perfect" for the new juvenile chemical dependency and behavioral treatment center that was being planned. With twelve bedrooms, multiple living areas, a ballroom on the first floor, two kitchens, a billiard parlor on the fourth floor, and unlimited space for programming, the old mansion was exactly what All Faiths had been searching for. After extensive renovation and remodeling, bringing the old structure into the 21st century in terms of electrical, plumbing, fire suppression and a commercial kitchen, the facility opened to its first clients in January of 2006 and was an instant success. Most of its clients came from the Twin Cities, with the exception of a few isolated referrals from northern Minnesota. Judge Elizabeth Prichard had sent six children to All Faiths, three of which, including Elsie Johnson, were Native American girls.

Elsie's bedroom, a large space on the third floor of the mansion she shared with six other girls, offered a view of ancient oak trees and a gazebo in the process of rehabilitation across the south lawn of the premises. Newly installed Bedford steel clad windows, energy efficient but appropriately styled with muntins, overlooked a green yard sloping to a shallow pond, the water choked with cattails and sedge grass; another project on the grounds awaiting funding.

Elsie was designated a member of the girl's Novice Group. During her ninety-day minimum stay at All Faiths, she would, if she followed the rules of the house, completed all her schoolwork, and behaved herself, progress after thirty days to the girl's Seeker Group, ultimately completing her stay as a graduate of the Believers. The curriculum for each client was customized to fit his or her faith heritage. Each child was assigned a spiritual mentor, the one person who remained constant during the resident's stay at All Faiths as the child moved through the three peer groups towards graduation.

Elsie's mentor was Edward Big Hands, an Ojibwe whose family hailed from the Turtle Mountains located between North Dakota and Manitoba. Big Hands had been raised in the traditional Ojibwe religion, his ancestors having resisted the efforts of successive Methodist, Congregationalist, and Episcopal clergy to convert the family.

Big Hands received a scholarship to attend the University of Utah by virtue of his jump shot (having been named All State and the Most Valuable Player in the North Dakota state basketball tournament as a senior) where he obtained a BA in sociology and a minor in history. He stayed on at Utah after receiving his BA to work on a doctorate in Comparative International Sociology, but left the program when his youngest sister Amanda died, the victim of an execution-style drug slaying. The tragedy brought Big Hands to the Twin Cities for the funeral, where he decided to put down roots and attempt to dissuade other young Native Americans from falling into drugs and alcohol.

That Edward Big Hands was one of the first Native Americans to be converted by The Prophet to The Principle following a chance meeting of the two men at a fundraising event for the University of Utah's basketball program a year after Big Hands began his work at All Faiths was a testament, not to Edward's ongoing grief and religious ambiguity, but to the power of The Prophet's charismatic charm. One chance meeting had not completed Edward's conversion. It had taken months of correspondence, emails, telephone discussions, and visits by local Twin Cities' missionaries affiliated with The Colony to convince Edward that the true and purposeful path for young Native Americans was assimilation into the fundamentalist Mormon faith, where they too could achieve the highest level of Paradise. The most convincing argument for conversion, in Edward's opinion, was the Mormon focus on sobriety and abstinence from caffeine, tobacco, drugs, and alcohol. Having witnessed the destruction of his beloved little sister and many other friends, relatives, and family members occasioned by substance abuse, the Mormons' strict prohibitions against the use of drugs and alcohol struck a nerve with the young Indian. He had long ago sworn off alcohol. He'd never personally used any drug stronger than aspirin. And other than as an adjunct to traditional Native American ceremonies, Big Hands had never used tobacco.

What remained for Edward Big Hands to reconcile was the complete banishment of caffeine from his life. As a four-cup-of-coffee-a-day man, this was a sacrifice that took somewhat longer than Edward had anticipated. But in the end, Edward Big Hands was able to break

31

free of caffeine as well, purifying both his mind and his soul from all addictive influences.

When Elsie Johnson was assigned to Edward Big Hands for spiritual mentoring, the process of her conversion was predestined. It was the singular task Edward was charged with as an emissary of The Prophet to the Native peoples and it was a task that Big Hands embraced with enthusiasm and tact.

By the time Elsie Johnson had been at the facility two months and completed the Seeker level of her stay, she was familiar with the basic tenets of the Mormon faith. She was not aware, and would not become aware, of the specific attributes of The Principle or The Colony, until she disappeared from the facility near the conclusion of her delinquency sentence.

"Where's Miss Johnson?"

The question was asked on a sunny December morning by Meg Applewick, the program director at All Faiths, as classes were beginning in the girls' section of the treatment center's educational wing. Newly appointed with Apple iMacs at every learning station, the classroom occupied the mansion's former ballroom on the ground floor. The high ceilings, antique crystal chandeliers, and ornate plasterwork made the room expansive and elegant. The girls, who nearly always made up the majority of the clients staying at the facility, benefited from their numbers by being assigned the best classroom. The boys were relegated to the former billiard parlor on the fourth floor for their classes. The billiard parlor was an impressive space in its own right but far less ostentatious than the ballroom.

Edward Big Hands had called in sick. He was not present to teach his first hour social studies class of young women. Applewick noted the man's absence. She had addressed her question, as she stepped inside the ballroom to take attendance, to Beverly Thomas, the woman who normally taught English but who could, in a pinch, teach social studies on a substitute basis if need be.

"She didn't come down for breakfast," Jane Preston, a fourteen-year-old alcoholic volunteered before Ms. Thomas could respond.

"Has anyone checked on her?"

Beverly Thomas left the lectern at the front of the classroom to speak with the program director.

"I sent one of the girls up to the dorm a few minutes ago," Thomas said guardedly. "It appears she's taken off. Her backpack, suitcase, and personal items are gone. As soon as I found out, I notified security."

"I was in a board meeting," Applewick replied with obvious annoyance. "No one bothered to alert me."

"The police and her probation officer have been notified. Starr took care of that."

Thomas' reference was to the Dean of Students, Starr MacDonald, who was in charge of discipline, attendance, and physical education classes for residents at All Faiths.

"Do we know when she left?"

"Interviews with other girls in her dorm indicate Miss Johnson left sometime between lights out and five this morning. No one is 'fessing up to having seen or heard her go."

"I'd expect that to be the case. These kids won't snitch. If this keeps up, our license is going to be pulled. How did this happen with the doors locked and security on duty all night long?"

Beverly Thomas shook her head.

"I have no idea. But it's clear she's gone. Nothing good can come of a fifteen-year-old girl walking the streets of downtown Minneapolis on her own."

The implication in Thomas's words—prostitution, drug use, child porn, or worse—stung the director.

"Let's hope the police find her before too long," Applewick said tersely.

Ms. Thomas nodded and walked back into the classroom intent upon discussing the Reconstruction of the South with her students, leaving Ms. Applewick the task of calling the girl's mother and giving her the bad news.

SEVEN

Brooke Talmadge walked through a native grass field, the heads of prairie flowers open but wilting under the sharpness of the day. The field overlooked the east bank of the Smith River in central Montana. The meadow she walked through sloped quickly from piney woods (marking the limit of the Lewis and Clark National Forest) to stony ground demarcating the river's edge. Cattle and horses grazed casually on the brittle, drought-impacted grass of an adjacent pasture. The pasture was located just north of the wild meadow the girl was crossing. The hem of the teenager's peasant dress, the thin cotton fabric decorated in a faint calico print, caught the wind and threatened indecency. The girl freed the fingers of her left hand from the handle of the stainless steel feed bucket she was carrying, shifted the bucket's weight to her dominant right hand, and pressed the dress firmly against her thighs with her left palm as she marched with determination towards the lambing station. At a stock fence, she lifted a loop of wire free of a cedar post and opened the gate just enough to shimmy through before sliding the wire back into place. A pensive sigh escaped her lips as she studied the dry, barren ground of the pen. A ewe lay in the dirt panting in the October heat. Tiny lambs suckled at her swollen teats. The ewe's fat belly undulated with each pull at her nipples. The ewe's white wool was caked in gray powdery dust, which also covered the lambs. Blue bottle flies buzzed the air. At the far end of the pen, another ewe, pregnant and ready to lamb, stood watching the young woman with steady eyes; feet splayed, the excess weight of pregnancy distributed evenly against the hardpan ground.

Brooke stopped at the feed tray—an old cast iron pressure tank that had been cut in half with a torch, the rounded bottom of the tank resting in dirt—and slowly emptied the bucket of feed into the trough. The ewe nursing her lambs remained prone while the pregnant ewe meandered towards the feed. The girl stood up and stroked the sheep's soft wool as the animal gobbled grain.

Standing next to the ewe as it ate, Brooke Talmadge quietly watched the play of silvery water against open sky. Across the Smith, limestone towers, the yellow rock turned gray by weather, interrupted dense lodge pole pine forest. The spires, cliffs, wilderness, and trees afforded protection against prying eyes.

"You about done loafing, Sister Brooke?"

Abby, their husband's first wife, approached the lambing pen from the main house, her stride purposeful, her tone commanding, as she addressed the younger woman.

Brooke nodded. The gesture was an acknowledgment that Abigail held the power in their relationship. Standing in silhouette against the sun, the younger woman's distinctive undergarment was visible beneath the calico; the expectant arc of her body was restrained by cotton from her ankles to her breastbone. The telltale cut of the garment's neckline, the ever-present smile of cloth, peeked out from the dress, accenting the lovely line of Brooke's chest and neck. The girl's pale chestnut eyes blinked at the approach of the older woman but she did not speak.

"I asked you a question," Abby repeated, her thick body echoing with authority.

The first wife stopped at the fence and placed both hands on the top wire of the confining perimeter. The fence was constructed of squares of steel wire to ensure that lambs did not wander out into the main pasture where they would be trampled by cattle and horses. Abigail Talmadge's dark brown eyes fixed hard on her sister wife. A faint breeze tossed a strand of the older woman's graying black hair across her cheek. Abby reached up with her left index finger and brushed the offending hair back into place behind her left ear, the remainder of her long hair secured in a tight bun.

"Yes, ma'am."

"Good. Charles has been looking for you. He needs help in the barn. He's re-arranging the bales of alfalfa we put up last week. Some of the stacks got a bit off kilter. You can give him a hand."

Brooke nodded.

Girl's a bit too quiet for my liking, the older woman thought. *And a bit insolent as well. But that will change. She'll learn to be more compliant, to follow directions. She seems to please Charles. And there's the child growing inside of her to consider. Another Talmadge to join us in Zion. I hope it's a boy.*

The girl walked slowly across the dusty pen towards the older woman. The noon sun reflected off the dark skin of Brooke Talmadge's face, her Native coloring attractively set off by the calico.

She's as dark skinned as I am light, Abby Talmadge thought. *What a world! Fifteen years ago, if you would have told me Charles was going to take a Lamanite as his second wife, I would have laughed. But The Prophet's vision changed that. Brought our people a clear understanding of The Principle.*

The fixed edges of Abby's face softened as Brooke opened the gate and joined the older woman outside the lambing pen.

"How're you feeling?"

The girl, though only seventeen years old, didn't demure, didn't look at her bruised brown leatherwork boots in answering, but stared defiantly into the eyes of the older woman as she responded.

There's that spirit, that insolence. She will be a project. But she's worth it. If she can carry babies to term, if she can return some peace to Charles after what we've been through, she will be worth the extra effort.

"I'm fine. Tired, but fine."

"And?"

They had spoken sparingly of the girl's pregnancy, Brooke's first. The signs had been obvious. Without discussion, Charles ceased taking the girl to the main bedroom of the big house. He was content to mitigate his desire with Abby, regardless of how tired and shopworn Abigail Talmadge might appear. Abby was witness to the morning sickness and the sudden increase in appetite that had afflicted the girl in the early stages of gestation. Though Brooke tried to conceal these things from her sister wife, the older woman, who herself had given birth to seven children (only three of whom had survived infancy) knew full well the signs of burgeoning life.

The Crow girl looked away, towards the splash of river slicing through the rippling foothills of the Little Belt Mountains.

"I hope it's a boy," Abby interjected, not allowing the girl to respond. "Charles deserves a son."

Brooke Talmadge blew warm air through thin lips. She didn't speak. She simply picked up the empty bucket and moved her weary feet. There was hay to be stacked. Even in her condition, there was hay to be stacked and more work to be done than she had ever imagined when she accepted Charles Talmadge's offer to share a cup of hot cocoa two years earlier.

They'd first met in Pinesdale, Montana, in a disintegrating greasy spoon, three days after her fifteenth birthday. She'd left the Crow Reservation in south central Montana, having been born and raised in Pryor by her mother and having been abused by her mother's boyfriend in all the ways an adult man can abuse a young girl; her Caucasian daddy gone, gone, gone to some far off village in northern Alberta before her first birthday. The last time Julius Black Leggings (her mother's boyfriend) came after her in the bathroom of their rusty old travel trailer outside Pryor, Brooke had kicked the wobbly drunk in the crotch, grabbed her knapsack, a change of clothes, one book (her favorite book, *Wide Sargasso Sea*), some tampons, a tube of tooth paste, a bottle of her mother's cheap perfume, a can of spray deodorant, a bar of soap, a wash cloth, and a wad of Julius' cash before hightailing it out to 416. Brooke Benson had no plan. She simply walked north, along the shoulder of the highway, towards Billings. Just outside of Pryor, she caught a ride with DeJesus Chaco, an Apache (the older brother of one of the boys she went to school with) and his girlfriend, Jamie Redhorse, a Crow girl who once babysat Brooke. The couple stopped DeJesus' battered white Suburban on a dime when they recognized the girl. They welcomed her into the SUV, all the while asking what the hell a fifteen-year-old Indian girl was doing out on the lonely road by herself. She didn't tell them much; just enough to convince Jamie (who'd had her own run-ins with Julius when she came over to babysit) of her need to get the hell out of Pryor, Montana. Brooke rode with the couple all the way to the Flathead Reservation, home to the Bitterroot Salish, the Pend d'Oreille and the Kootenai tribes, where DeJesus was scheduled to start a job as an ironworker on a new health care center the tribes were building. After a few days of hanging around Indians she didn't know, Brooke drifted south, accepting a ride from a rancher and his wife who happened to be driving to Salmon, Idaho, for a family wedding. It was in Pinesdale, Montana, as she was spending the last of the hundred dollars she'd pilfered from Julius Black Legging's stash of drinking money, where fate matched her up with Charles Talmadge.

Wary of white men, she ignored the tall, thin, boney man with the beaming smile and quick wit until he cracked her rigid demeanor with stupid jokes and bad puns, sat down in her booth, and changed her life forever.

EIGHT

The Tyler drove the silver Taurus nonchalantly south on I-35W, the music of Felix Pappalardi blaring from the rental car's cheap speakers, the Taurus's cruise control set at sixty-nine miles per hour. Semi-tractor trailers, trucks, cars, and the occasional late season Harley passed the Taurus without changing lanes.

"Theme from an Imaginary Western", a tune not Pappalardi's own, dominated the interior of the sedan. Pappalardi's multi-faceted bass, his high tenor, juxtaposed against lead guitarist Leslie West's gravely blues vocals, left The Tyler nearly inconsolable with joy.

"Damn," The Tyler muttered, his words lost in the cascade of music, "those boys could play."

The Tyler's faith prohibited the enjoyment of such music; music that followers of the Angel Moroni, Joseph Smith, Brigham Young, and the one *true* modern-day Mormon Prophet, Obadiah Nielsen, would abhor and condemn as blasphemy; the Work of the Destroyer. But, as a close confidant to President Nielsen, closer even than the First and Second Counselors, who, along with Nielsen, made every serious decision for The Colony, The Tyler, whose true name was never spoken, a man known only by alias or title—"The Tyler" being a reference to an archaic Masonic office applied to the assassin by First Counselor Ezra Pratt originally as a slight—was granted certain "privileges" in return for his loyalty.

The Tyler's fidelity required that he (from time to time) eradicate those who posed a serious threat to The Principle. In return, The Prophet overlooked certain of The Tyler's personal habits, including his devotion to Felix Pappalardi's music.

The Tyler considered his most recent assignment as he drove south through an autumnal landscape defined by barren trees (save for the persistent oaks whose brown leaves hung on stubbornly against the changing seasons). Thick blankets of gray hid the sun. There was no rain, only defuse light; the light of death and dying, a quality of light with which The Tyler was well acquainted.

After his honorable discharge from the United States Marine Corps (where he'd served as a reconnaissance sniper), The Tyler had fallen upon hard times and into criminality: the occasional assault; a robbery here or there gone bad; stupid decisions that eventually landed him in a jail cell, which he shared, for a brief time, with notorious forger,

38

murderer, and fallen Latter-day Saint, Mark Hofmann. Hofmann was eventually convicted of killing folks who'd discovered he was taking the Mormon hierarchy for a ride by selling forged historical documents to church authorities. It was while sharing a cell with Hofmann (a man whose Mormon beliefs had evaporated, replaced by Hofmann's unfailing belief in himself) that The Tyler's own Mormon heritage was rejuvenated. Hofmann's skepticism was the manure that enriched the roots of faith within The Tyler; faith ultimately transformed into Mormon fundamentalism after The Tyler read a pamphlet he'd borrowed from the jail library recounting Obadiah Nielsen's prophetic vision.

"Funny how the Lord brings folks together," The Tyler mused, re-setting the cruise control on the Taurus to an even seventy-three, not wanting to draw attention to the car but needing to make time. His flight from Minneapolis to Great Falls was due to leave in an hour. The Taurus was just passing Forest Lake when he accelerated. He was a cautious man; preparation was essential to his chosen profession. The Tyler's schedule did not allow him to miss his flight, a flight booked under one of his numerous aliases. His false identities were backed up by drivers' licenses and passports produced by contacts inside The Church of Jesus Christ of the Latter-day Saints.

In vaults carved into the stone foundation of the Wasatch Mountains, records concerning virtually every living human being, together with records memorializing the Earth's dead, are preserved for genealogical research and for temple ordinances by the Mormons. Despite having been excommunicated by the mainstream Mormon Church, President Nielsen maintained ties with the folks working in these vaults and passed along his associations to The Tyler. The connections enabled The Tyler to be someone he was not.

Pappalardi's bass thumped out the rhythm line to "Yasgur's Farm." The Taurus blew over the I-35W bridge spanning the Mississippi River as The Tyler considered his love of Pappalardi's music.
As a teenager, The Tyler had chanced upon an old newspaper clipping describing Felix Pappalardi's death at the hands of his wife, lyricist and artist Gail Collins. The date of Pappalardi's demise had caught the youth's eye: April 17, 1983, the day The Tyler was confirmed in the Mormon faith. This discovery convinced the boy that he and the musician shared something ethereal and spiritual. What this connection *was* exactly was something The Tyler had never nailed down. But it was there. He knew it, as surely as he knew that there was

a God and that Joseph Smith was a great prophet and not some charlatan trickster from upstate New York.

As the Taurus plunged ahead, The Tyler marveled at the new span. The bridge had been erected in less than a year's time following the unfortunate and disastrous collapse of its predecessor.

"People died here," The Tyler lamented. "Innocent people, who never had the chance to reconcile with God, died here."

The thought of men, women, and children amiably driving over the old bridge, construction equipment in place for a rehabilitation project, the combined weight of the equipment and the vehicles too much for the distressed concrete and steel of the structure, the platform cracking like a saltine broken into soup, cars, trucks and vans filled with innocents spilling into the broiling river downstream from St. Anthony's Falls, piqued The Tyler's interest.

The Tyler's blue eyes were riveted on traffic. His bush hat sat on the front passenger seat of the Taurus. His fishing vest and fishing equipment were piled neatly on the car's rear seat. The Taser and a thirty-eight caliber Ruger LCP (a dependable automatic he'd purchased at a premium on the streets of Minneapolis before his journey north) were tucked under the clothing. The arrangement of his personal belongings was evidence of the man's innate carefulness.

As he drove, The Tyler also mulled over the death of Angelina DeAquila.

Unfortunate but necessary.

He recalled that he'd spoken this same truth before. The memory stung him like the barb of a hornet.

I will make sure a baptismal ceremony is held for her. She will have the option, through the ordinance, of accepting redemption. I'll give her name to the intercessors. They'll pray for her, conduct the necessaries. It will be fine.

There had been a time, after his first assignment, the first occasion when he'd been asked to invoke blood atonement to protect The Principle, when he trembled with fear; fear that he was doing not the work of God, but the work of the Destroyer. It took daily prayer, constant meditation, and consistent reading of *The Bible, The Book of Mormon, The Doctrine and the Covenants, The Pearl of Great Price,* and President Nielsen's seminal revelation (and the foundation of The Colony and The Principle) *Nephi's Letter to the Lamanites,* to reconstitute The Tyler's evangelical zeal.

"He was so young," The Tyler murmured, remembering back to the Idaho social worker who had stumbled into The Colony in search of a missing Nez Perce girl, Bethany Comes to Ride, who'd been reported "on the run" to the authorities and who'd been sighted in the company of The Prophet outside The Colony.

The social worker, Elwood Jones, was only twenty-two; fresh out of college and newly on the job when his supervisor sent him snooping around Montana's Smith River, the place chosen by The Prophet for The Colony; the place consecrated as Laman's River; paradise on earth, the New Zion.

The young social worker had disappeared in the forest. Elwood Jones' naked body had been cast over a ledge into an abyss, his arms and legs bound, his mouth sealed with duct tape and clogged with Montana earth. The Tyler had, before pitching the young man over the side of the canyon wall, placed one precise 9mm round in the center of the social worker's forehead. Despite the victim's clean and immediate death, that first kill had troubled The Tyler for months.

Perhaps it's the redundant mutilation of his body that continues to plague me.

Though the social worker died instantly when the bullet shattered his skull and tore apart his brain, The Tyler had seen fit to slit the dead man's throat.

Did not Nephi kill Laban by the blade of Laban's own sword, cleaving Laban's head from his shoulders? Did not Prophet Brigham Young, the Moses of the Mormons, the man who brought polygamy out of the dark recesses of shame, did he not describe in great detail a dream of using his Bowie knife to "cut the throats of apostates ear to ear"?

Even with scripture clearly in support of his actions, the assault on the social worker's corpse seemed duplicative and perverse to the killer.

"Still," The Tyler considered, an acoustic tune by Leslie West playing unobtrusively in the background as the Taurus made its way over the viaducts and ramps of the Crosstown, "it had to be done. He made contact with the girl and obtained an understanding from The Principle and the reasons why the girl had been sealed to The Prophet. If that information had gotten out, if the tenets of the Reconstituted Brotherhood of Latter-day Saints, especially the doctrine of sealing Caucasian men to underage Lamanite women, were exposed to public scrutiny without appropriate theological explanation, all hell would have broken loose," The Tyler mused. "The revelation that came to The Prophet on the mountaintop near Pinesdale, that the blood of the Lamanites needed to be washed clean, purified by the blood of the chosen in order to advance the souls of the Lamanites to the Celestial Kingdom, must, at all costs, be protected. The man's voice had to be stilled. It was, after all, God's will."

Pinesdale, Montana, is the site of an obscure community of fundamentalist Mormons affiliated with the Apostolic United Brethren

(AUB), a polygamist group that forbids its members from entering into plural marriages with female relatives, or marrying girls under the age of eighteen, or forcing a woman into polygamy against her wishes. The community has existed peaceably near the Idaho-Montana border for decades. The Western philosophy of "Leave me alone and I'll leave you alone" has prevailed in Pinesdale, where the AUB controls the schools, the city government, and the police. It is postulated that the AUB's constraints on polygamy protect Pinesdale from outside forces.

But, as revealed to one of Pinesdale's leading citizens, Obadiah Nielsen (who, at the time of his prophesy, was serving as First Counselor to the President of the AUB), the limitations placed upon the AUB members were, in a word, apostasy given the certain and swift need to save the Lamanites from perdition. After a whirlwind of revelatory mania, which struck when Obadiah Nielsen spoke with the Angel Nephi on the barren peak of an unnamed mountain in the Bitterroots (a spire that was later named "Nielsen's Peak" and dedicated as such by the National Forest Service; one of Nielsen's adherents being the chief cartographer of the Bitterroot National Forest), Nielsen put fingers to keyboard and completed *Nephi's Letter to the Lamanites,* a 20,000 word epistle delivered directly to Nielsen by the Angel Nephi and attested to by four AUB members—all male and all bearing the surname "Nielsen"—in two weeks. Within six months of the prophesy being edited and distributed in Pinesdale, Nielsen was excommunicated from the AUB, the Reconstituted Brotherhood of Latter-day Saints was formed, funds were collected and pooled, and Obadiah Nielsen, his family, and his closest friends (including Charles Talmadge, whose wife, Abby, was Obadiah Nielsen's younger sister) purchased one hundred thousand acres of remote ranch and forest land situated on the east bank of the Smith River in central Montana.

The group (which incorporated as a non-profit religious organization under the laws of Utah) obtained the property as the result of a foreclosure sale involving the estate of a well-known Hollywood actor. There was only one gravel road in and out of the parcel; a road that came to be guarded by sentinels armed with automatic weapons and barred by a steel gate; a road that was closed to public traffic because The Prophet's vision included a caution from the Angel Nephi to limit outside access to The Colony, as the former ranch came to be known.

The seventies, The Colony's advisory council, with direction from the First and Second Counselors and The Prophet, administered the property, holding thousands of acres of land in reserve for future converts after providing each original family with three hundred acres of pasture and two hundred acres of timber upon which they could ranch, farm, log, and build homes. The families did not own the land;

they were granted fifty-year leases renewable for successive ten-year extensions, though any member of The Colony could have their lease terminated for "violating the tenets and spirit of The Principle." The goal was to have two hundred families living and praying together in the valley, producing as many mixed-race children from plural marriages with young Lamanite girls as God would ordain; children whose blood, generation by generation, would, as revealed in the correct and original editions of *The Book of Mormon* eventually be purified of evil:

Their curse was taken away from them and their skin became white like unto the Nephites."
(3 Nephi 2:15)

Once the two hundred families were established, President Nielsen prophesied that the colonists would spread their faith "throughout the lands of North and South America, and thence to the distant corners of the Earth, eventually cleansing darkness from all the peoples of those lands, making mankind white and delightsome in God's eyes" (*Nephi's Letter to the Lamanites* 3: 30).

Such were the moral and theological underpinnings of The Tyler's faith. Because of his beliefs, beliefs The Tyler held before him in wonderment, he was confident that the death of Angelina DeAquila was justified, necessary, and welcomed by God.

The Tyler pulled the Taurus into a garage stall in the Avis section of the rental car ramp at the Minneapolis-St. Paul International Airport, shut off the engine, and pulled the keys from the ignition. He didn't wear gloves; he wasn't worried about fingerprints. Fingerprints, if they were found, would lead to a fiction, a person that existed only in the imagination of a worker in the deep recesses of the hall of records beneath the Wasatch Mountains. Successive name changes across three states made The Tyler confident that he was impervious to discovery.

Even so, I wish I'd been able to account for that last caffeine-free Coke can I lost while dealing with the reporter. Can't figure out what happened to it. Tossed the other five empties and the plastic ring in a dumpster on the Gunflint. But that last can may have prints on it. In fact, I know it does. I opened it when I had my gloves off. Stupid. Still, it's unlikely the authorities can sort out my true identity, much less find me. God will cloak me, protect me. God is great. God is good...

The trail of The Tyler's existence was so clouded, twisted, and confused that it was unlikely fingerprints lifted from the soda can could be traced back to him. Indeed, the fingerprints he'd been required to

43

provide the Marines upon his enlistment and the fingerprints various law enforcement entities had gathered from him during his former life all led to a person who no longer walked the Earth.

The Tyler smiled as he put on his hat, gathered up his gear, his fly pole carefully stored in a fiberglass rod tube, his fishing vest packed in an old military duffle bag, someone else's name stenciled across the green canvas. He picked up the .38 and the Taser and deposited them in a paper sandwich bag, closing it against scrutiny.

Never can be too careful.

Walking briskly but without apparent hurry, The Tyler merged with the passengers, well-wishers, and airport workers entering the terminal. Just inside the door, he dropped the sandwich bag containing the Taser and the gun into a garbage can before joining a line of passengers waiting to print e-tickets. No one noticed The Tyler as he moved through the security line and entered the gated area of the facility. He'd done what The Prophet had asked and now, he was on his way home.

NINE

Jennifer Bick Nielsen washed dishes in the porcelain triple sink of the kitchen, her wrists deep in sudsy water, as she scoured egg, fried potato, and syrup from the earthenware surface of the household's daily plates. Her long blond hair was tied in a neat bun. Silver pins kept the silky waves of gold in place as she worked furiously to clean the breakfast dishes, pots, and pans. Every so often, her hazel eyes would focus on the scene outside the big bay window over the sink and allow her moments of glory. Beyond the frosted limits of the window glass, the terrain of Keystone Ranch, her home and the home of her three sister wives, rolled out before her like a panoramic photo clipped from a Montana tourism brochure.

The Prophet and President of the Reconstituted Brotherhood of Latter-day Saints had built the eight bedroom sprawling ranch style log home in stages; from modest beginnings the house now enclosed more than ten thousand square feet of living space, with separate bedrooms for each of the women and two dormitory style bedrooms, thirty feet long and fifteen feet wide for their children. The children (save for the infants who stayed with their mothers until their second birthdays) were divided by gender and housed together in the spacious dormitory bedrooms in military style bunk beds. Eight children, three boys and five girls, none of them carrying Lamanite blood, had been born into the Nielsen family with many more anticipated.

The Prophet and his wives occupied one wing of the massive home. Each of the women's bedrooms was located across the hall from the master suite: a room equipped with a four-post king-sized bed, an in-floor Jacuzzi tub, a sauna bath, and a steam shower. A fifty-inch flat-screen LCD Samsung television, the only television in the house, dominated one wall of the suite. The women's rooms were arranged like a wheel around the master suite, The Prophet's bedroom forming the hub, the spiritual center, of the plural marriages between the man and his four wives. The design was practical and worked well. Rather than rotating their wifely duties on a weekly or monthly basis, the sister wives rotated each night. It was rare that The Prophet missed a night, save for illness on his part or the part of one of the women. When a wife was having her monthly, the other women simply shortened the rotation, with the caveat that no amorous activity took place on Sunday. Sunday was a day of rest for The Prophet; a day reserved for reflection, physical rejuvenation, and spiritual contemplation. Though it was well

45

known around Laman's River that, Sunday aside, Obadiah Nielsen had an insatiable appetite for women.

But it would be a mischaracterization to say that The Prophet's embracement of plural marriage had anything but an ancillary connection to sex. Desire and physical ecstasy were merely collateral benefits of The Principle. Nielsen's belief in plural marriage was theological; based upon an understanding that polygamy had been practiced by the founders of the Mormon faith, including Joseph Smith and Brigham Young. The fact that the conception of Mormon children, children whose premortal souls (souls floating about in the primordial cosmic ooze, waiting for conception) needed Mormon men and women to conceive and birth them as fast as humanly possible, and the fact that sealing ceremonies involving Caucasian men and young Native American girls (preferably virgins) were mandated and prescribed by the Angel Nephi's prophetic revelation, all compelled The Prophet to preach and practice polygamy.

Obadiah Nielsen had not set out to become an apostle, much less The Prophet. Raised in a traditional Mormon home in a prosperous suburb of Las Vegas, Nevada (a city originally populated by Mormons), Nielsen had been a tall, athletic, square jawed, quick thinking boy who boasted an enormous head as a child, a head topped with flaming red hair, whose curiosity of all things spiritual, at least as they concerned Mormon history and theology, saw him enter Brigham Young University on a full academic scholarship. Not that he needed financial assistance. His recent ancestry, the Nielsen line on his father's side and the Paulson line on his mother's, had joined to amalgamate and consolidate immense wealth; wealth built through connections to the gaming and prostitution industries in Nevada. Though neither family owned casinos or whorehouses, both families provided the casinos and legal brothels with services (food service, laundry service, non-alcoholic beverage service, and janitorial service) and had done so since the advent of legalized gaming and prostitution in the state. After graduation from BYU with an MBA, a degree that astounded those who had predicted Obadiah would study theology and join the hierarchy of the Mormon church as a professional administrator (preachers and most church officials generally being volunteers; the administrators being the only paid staff in the faith), Nielsen went to work in the family business, New Trends Services, Inc., and within five years of working his way up the ladder, became CEO of the company. Obadiah Nielsen was on holiday at his cottage in the Bitterroot Mountains when he fell in love with Pinesdale native Evelyn Fremont. Six weeks after the couple's first date, Obadiah and Evelyn sealed their relationship for eternity by marrying in the local temple.

Pinesdale was also the place Obadiah Nielsen cast off his traditional Mormon faith, adopted The Principle, and became a member of the AUB. After several years of commuting from Las Vegas (where he and Evelyn had settled) to western Montana, Obadiah Nielsen resigned as CEO of his family's company, sold his shares of stock, and moved his growing family to Montana, his coffers full and his mind open to new experiences and new prophesies from God.

Jennifer Bick, a young runaway twenty years Nielsen's junior when they met, was sealed to him and to Evelyn as their sister wife three years after Obadiah and Evelyn moved to Pinesdale. In time, Amanda Promise, a seventeen-year-old daughter of one of the AUB's seventies, and Joyce Billington, a widower in her early thirties and the best cook of the lot, joined the family.

Bethany Comes to Ride, the young Nez Perce maiden (whose indiscretions had caused the death of Idaho social worker Elwood Jones), had once been sealed to the family. But the clandestine contacts between Mr. Jones and the Indian girl had necessitated a call to The Tyler and the disappearance of the two from memory.

Though Jennifer Bick did not know the details of Bethany Comes to Ride's demise, she had acquiesced to the result after a family conference was held between The Prophet and his three other wives; Evelyn, Amanda, and Jennifer. The vote for expulsion was unanimous. One dark night while she was in the arms of The Prophet, Jennifer heard the sounds of struggled panic from the unfortunate Nez Perce girl's bedroom. The next day, when Jennifer went to wake the Indian girl to do chores, Bethany Comes to Ride was gone. So were her clothes and all her personal affects. Bethany's name wasn't mentioned again except for a brief period after the girl's disappearance when the Nielsen children asked "What happened to Sister Bethany?" The answer from the sister wives and The Prophet was always the same: "She returned to her people."

Shortly after the disappearance of Bethany Comes to Ride, Joyce Billington, a woman whose quiet demeanor, barren womb, and plain features made her an unlikely choice to be the successor wife to the vibrantly beautiful Nez Perce girl, drew the attention of The Prophet. Burdened by Bethany's unfortunate but necessary death, Obadiah Nielsen struck up conversation with the matronly Joyce as she worked the lunch counter of Pete's Eats in White Sulfur Springs where The Prophet routinely stopped in for lunch when he was in town checking on various accounts at the local branch of the Security Bank of the Rockies, a Mormon owned bank where some, not all, of The Colonies' accounts were held.

"You're new here, aren't you?" The Prophet had asked.

"Yes, I am. More tea?" the sturdily built woman with the great smile and interesting age lines had replied.

Their conversation had started innocuously; with small talk and The Prophet ordering his traditional plate of ham, eggs, American fried potatoes, tomato juice, and hot herbal tea. Over a series of visits, they formed a friendship. Their relationship blossomed until Joyce agreed to visit The Colony. An avowed Mormon, Joyce Billington had a pedigree that intrigued Nielsen.

Her heritage, having been born of the union of Mary Strang and Joseph Strang (distant cousins and descendents of James Strang, who founded the polygamist Mormon sect on Beaver Island in Lake Michigan after splitting from the mainstream Mormon Church following the death of Joseph Smith), and having been the wife of Rudolph Billington, a traditional Latter-day-Saint who died on a fishing trip in the remote reaches of northern Minnesota, impressed The Prophet.

The fact that Joyce indicated she was seeking "new experiences" to rekindle her spirituality after the tragic death of her husband suggested to The Prophet that Joyce Billington was open to The Principle.

Revealing her life story to The Prophet, Joyce explained that the couple had remained childless after five years of marriage; a circumstance that had compelled Joyce and Rudy Billington to consider plural marriage as a means of bringing children into their home. Adoption didn't appeal to the couple. So, as they struggled with Joyce's infertility, a condition she attributed to chemotherapy occasioned by childhood leukemia, plural marriage entered into the conversation between husband and wife. But before the couple could investigate polygamy as an option, Rudy Billington had fallen out of his canoe in the middle of Lake Kabetogama and drowned.

"You should live here," The Prophet had proposed as the two of them walked a path in The Colony along the eastern bank of the Smith and watched a pair of mallards swing across quicksilver water.

"But it's too far to town, to get to work, I mean," Joyce had replied. "My car isn't very reliable."

Nielsen's shining eyes had looked down upon the woman with kindness, an emotion, despite his ability to order the deaths of innocent people who stood in the way of his vision, he seemed able to summon at will.

"There'd be no need for you to work. You misunderstand what I am saying. If...", his voice trailed off as they stopped and sat down on a wooden bench overlooking the Smith.

"Yes?"

"I get the sense that your husband was your one great love."

"He was."

"Well, then please take nothing untoward, of a sexual nature, in what I am about to propose," the tall, thin man said as he placed his right hand on the demurely clothed knee of his companion.

"Alright."

"If you and I were married, there would be no need for you to work in town. Come here, to be my cook and my wife, to help care for all the children of Laman's River."

Joyce's eyes had opened widely at the suggestion. They had only known each other for five weeks, hardly a suitable period of courtship for The Prophet to announce his intentions.

"We hardly know each other," the woman said, her face flushing with color.

The Prophet smiled.

"You take my intentions wrongly," Nielsen had said quietly. "I am not, with all due respect, interested in you in that way. As in the days of Brother Young, I would like to be sealed to you for time only. It would be a marriage of convenience. There would be no obligation, on your part, to share yourself with me, to take my bed. As I understand it, you've already been sealed for eternity to your departed husband. I have no wish to disturb that bond."

Joyce's eyes had closed hard

"Can I have some time to consider your offer?"

"Surely. Take all the time you like. My thought is that you would run the kitchen, under Evelyn's direction of course. Be in charge of procuring food, preparing meals, stockpiling canned goods for the larder. And help care for the children. That's all I would expect. Anything else you wish to involve yourself with in the home, with the church, in The Colony, would be up to you."

"I'll think about it. You're sure there would be no claims upon me, no demands for intimacy? Because, I must tell you, that's a road I no longer wish to travel. When Rudy died, that part of me, I'm afraid, died as well."

The Prophet had looked closely into Joyce's eyes as he reiterated his pledge.

"That is not why I want you to be my wife. I have three other women with which to occupy that part of my life. I enjoy your wit, your company. And, Lord knows, we could use a good cook at Keystone Ranch! If I don't figure out something soon, to appease the children, who complain daily about the food Evie has been serving up, I may be forced to put down an armed rebellion!"

They had resumed their walk. Three weeks later, Joyce Billington had telephoned The Prophet and accepted his proposal. Within the month, Obadiah Nielsen and his three wives were sealed in marriage to Joyce Billington Nielsen for time only, after which Joyce, who was a hard working, non-complaining woman, immediately pitched in and installed her authority over the kitchen at Keystone Ranch.

Though Obadiah Nielsen formed The Colony in response to the Angel Nephi's prophetic visit to Pinesdale, The Prophet's marriage to Bethany Comes to Ride ended in disappointment. It was this failure, this loss that troubled Jennifer Bick Nielsen, and soured her mood, as she studied the bounty of Keystone Ranch through the frosted glass of the kitchen window and waited for another runaway Lamanite girl to join the family.

TEN

"Blake Ellingson caught a glimpse of the guy," Deputy Augie Olsen announced as he poured coffee into a Little Store travel mug, the container's hard yellow plastic chipped from years of abuse.

Olsen stood in the conference room of the Cook County Sheriff's Office, a new facility constructed against tradition. Instead of simply expanding the existing Sheriff's Office (which had been attached to the Cook County Courthouse), the county had built a new, state of the art jail and law enforcement complex further up the hill and tucked in tight against the footprint of the looming Sawtooth Mountains, the ridge that traps the diminutive tourist town of Grand Marais (the last vestige of civilization in northeastern Minnesota before Highway 61 disappears into Ontario wilderness) between forest and lake.

Sheriff Debra Slater sat at a big polished pine table in the center of the room, the furniture brand new, an expense that, five years ago, the county board was willing to make. It was an expense that, in hindsight, with the downturn in the nation's economy, now seemed extravagant. Slater's coffee mug, "Shut Up and Let Me Think" stenciled across the white porcelain surface of the cup in red, sat to her right, steam escaping the mouth of the container.

A thin manila folder, the file containing the office's investigation into the death of Angelina DeAquila, was open in front of the sheriff as she reached across the paperwork, grabbed the mug, and drew hot coffee between ungarnished lips. She wore no lipstick, just a hint of rouge and a trace of eyeliner as she studied the documents and photographs in front of her.

"Do you have a report or statement memorializing what Ellingson saw?" Slater asked, replacing the mug on the blond wood of the table.

"Yup. It's in the file. Sylvia typed it up yesterday."

Augie Olsen's reference was to Sylvia Emmons, the department's one and only secretary, a woman of stern demeanor who had worked for Cook County in various secretarial roles for over forty years. At seventy years of age, Sylvia (who had once commercially fished Isle Royal, the largest island in Lake Superior) was leathered by the sun, sinewy as rope and boasted language as salty as a sailor's. There was little in life that surprised or challenged Sylvia Emmons, including photographs of a beautiful dead Korean American reporter bound, gagged, and tied naked to a spruce. She'd typed the reports with little emotion or fanfare, though Augie Olsen had detected, as the old woman finished listening to the microcassette of the deputy's investigation, a hint of upset creeping over the old woman's solid countenance.

In the three weeks since Angelina DeAquila's murder, little had changed in terms of the information Deb Slater and her deputies had gathered. The fact that Blake Ellingson, a local contract logger (who cut and delivered balsam and aspen to Sappi, a paper mill located in Cloquet), had recently come forward was the first break the sheriff's office had caught in the case.

Slater located Olsen's typed report and read its contents.

To: Angelina DeAquila Homicide File
From: Augie Olsen, Badge #3
Re: ICR: 183765CC
Date: November 9, 2009
Today at 0634, I, Deputy Olsen, interviewed Blake Ellingson (DOB-4/5/62) at the Pickled Herring Café in Grand Marais, Minnesota. Ellingson had telephoned the sheriff's office on 11/8/09 and indicated that he might have information relevant to the death of Angelina DeAquila, whose body was discovered near Seagull Lake on 10/10/09 at approximately 0430. Investigation by the medical examiner revealed that the time and date of death was likely 10/09/09 sometime after 1500. At approximately 0945 on 10/09/09, Mr. Ellingson recalls seeing a silver Ford Taurus with Avis rental car stickers on the windshield and rear bumper in the area of Seagull Lake. There was, according to Ellingson, a male driving the vehicle. Ellingson had interaction with the driver when the vehicle made a wrong turn onto a road leading to the section Ellingson was clear-cutting. The Taurus became stuck as it attempted to turn around and Ellingson used his skidder to pull the Taurus out of the mud. Ellingson was able to give the following description of the driver: white male, approximately early to mid-thirties. Blond hair, blue eyes. Average build, approximately 5'10" and 180#. The vehicle had fishing equipment in the back seat, including a rod container, which had airline tags attached to it (airline unknown), as well as a tackle box, fly fishing vest, and a duffle bag or knapsack. Ellingson noted that the occupant of the Taurus requested directions to the National Forest campground on Seagull Lake and also inquired about a place to rent a fishing boat and motor. Ellingson advised the driver to try Brule's Resort and provided directions to Seagull Lake. The Taurus then drove away. Ellingson did not see the vehicle again that day.

Note: Follow up included an interview with Sally Brule at Brule's Resort. The resort's rental records confirm that a 14' aluminum fishing boat with a Honda 10hp four stroke was rented to "Dave Petters" for cash at approximately 1035 on 10/09/09. Sally doesn't recall the denominations of the bills used to pay the $50.00 half-day rental fee. Her description of the individual renting the boat and motor is identical to that given by Ellingson except she believes the individual driving the Taurus and renting the boat was closer to 6' in height than 5'10." A South Dakota driver's license was left as security for the boat and motor and was copied for the resort's files. A copy of the DL, in the name of Dave Petters, is attached to this report. Sally was not in the resort office when the boat was returned and the driver's license was retrieved by Mr. Petters. Examination of the boat revealed fragments of duct tape consistent with that used to bind the victim; fibers of blue cord, again consistent with the rope used to bind the victim; and a partial fingerprint on a caffeine-free Coke can found wedged beneath the rear seat of the boat. Sally confirmed that the occupant of the Taurus and the renter of the boat and motor purchased a six-pack of caffeine-free Coke with cash along with a package of Black Jack chewing gum before renting the boat and motor. The Coke can has been sent to the BCA for fingerprint identification. Sally confirmed that Petters was driving a silver Taurus, Minnesota License #345-789. She did not see any rental stickers on the vehicle.

A.S.O.

Slater finished reading. The last page of the document included a color laser copy of Dave Petters' South Dakota driver's license. Studying the photo, the sheriff was struck by the man's eyes.

    Haunting.

    There was little doubt in Sheriff Debra Slater's mind that David Edward Petters was the man who had taken Angelina DeAquila's young life.

    I doubt that Petters is his real name.

    Silence occupied the conference room.

    "Ya. I know," Augie Olsen said, "his real name isn't likely 'Petters'. This was carefully planned. He messed up leaving the soda can in the boat. It was wedged under the seat, likely got stuck there as he moved his gear around. But beyond that, the guy was pretty smooth. I doubt the partial print will be of much use. The victim's husband was vehement that the victim didn't have any enemies and wasn't seeing anyone outside their marriage. The motive, that's the thorny thing here. I just don't see what the hell the guy's motive was."

"Stalker?" Slater offered, fixing her eyes on the deputy. "She was a beautiful young woman who'd been on TV and was writing for the largest paper in the state."

"Checked with both the station and the *Tribune*. Nothing on the radar. Plenty of letters to the editor about her, though. She wrote a column about religion and politics. But none of the letters seemed remotely threatening or raised alarm, at least in the opinion of her editor."

Slater nodded.

"Religion and politics: two topics you're not supposed to talk about amongst friends. Check out some of her more recent columns. Maybe she touched a nerve, pushed the killer into taking action because of something she wrote."

Olsen scribbled notes on a legal pad. Deb Slater managed a tired smile.

"Do we know why DeAquila was in northeastern Minnesota?" the sheriff asked.

Olsen took a seat across the table from his boss. His broad shoulders slumped, as if defeated by his lack of knowledge about the woman, her story, why she had come to the northern forest to die.

"Not really. Her husband said it was for work, for a story she was researching. No real details. Somethin' to do with the Ojibwe. That's all he knew. The paper had no clue. Her editor thought she was up here just to kayak and clear her head. With all the layoffs at the *Tribune*, her job was iffy. Took a personal day. Remember, the tenth was a Friday. She could've just zipped up from the Cities for a little breather. She stayed at Fitger's in Duluth on Thursday night. She and the hubbie had plans for Sunday morning. She rented a room at the Lutsen main lodge for Friday night. Never checked in. Appears she was alone, at least until her killer found her. No evidence of a tryst or anything remotely suspicious."

Slater pondered the killer's photograph before placing Olsen's report back in the manila folder and closing the file.

"She have a laptop?"

"It's missing. Her husband gave us a description, right down to the serial number and carrying case color. But it wasn't in her car."

"Cell phone?"

"iPhone. But it's gone too."

Slater stood up and flipped the edges of her auburn hair away from the collar of her tan uniform shirt. The sheriff's eyes focused on Olsen as she spoke.

"Anything on her computer at the *Tribune*?"

Augie Olsen shook his head.

"Hadn't thought to check. I'll have someone from Minneapolis P.D. stop in and talk to her editor and maybe take a peek at her workstation. Might be something on the hard drive."

Slater closed her eyes to mere slits, her mind searching through the information she'd received.

"The rental car agency?"

"License plate tracks to the Minneapolis airport. We'll need a search warrant. Avis won't give us much without one."

"Talk to the county attorney. Maybe there's something there. Though, as careful as this boy is, I doubt we'll find anything beyond a bogus credit card. Include DeAquila's computer and her cubicle at the *Tribune* in the warrant. Make a trip to the Cities as soon as the judge signs the paperwork. Coordinate your visit with Minneapolis P.D. Sooner than later, Augie. Sooner than later."

Deb Slater paused to consider the absence of any serious motive in the case.

Why would someone want Angelina DeAquila silenced?

"I don't think we're dealing with a random act, here," the sheriff observed. "No rape. No defacing the body beyond what it took to kill the poor woman. This was planned. The duct taped mouth. The dirt shoved down her throat. Someone was sending a message: 'Shut the fuck up.' This probably isn't the killer's first rodeo. Let's see what we can find out from the FBI."

Olsen nodded.

"You want me to call Herb?"

"I'll do it. Herb owes me," Slater said, calculating the many favors she had done for Agent Herb Whitefeather over the years.

Now that FBI Agent Herb Whitefeather was in his last year with the Bureau and sliding towards cushy federal retirement, it was time for Deb Slater to call in a marker

ELEVEN

The Tyler's blue Dodge Dakota 4x4 was parked next to a log cabin in a small gravel parking space overlooking the north bank of Sixteen Mile Creek to the southwest of White Sulfur Springs, Montana. Though he was a follower of The Prophet and the chosen protector of the Principle, The Tyler did not live at Laman's River, preferring to remain in the shadows, away from people.

The cabin, a building that took The Tyler the better part of two years to construct by hand, was hidden in a dense forest of lodge pole pine; trees that had survived fire, drought, and heavy snows in the valley of the Big Belt Mountains through which the creek flows clean and wild. The two-track logging road running into The Tyler's forty-acre parcel, land he had purchased with an inheritance from his grandfather, was passable in the summer, fall, and winter; when The Tyler plowed snow with his Dakota or, in a pinch, an old Oliver tractor equipped with a snow bucket.

Spring caused the most difficulty for The Tyler. The annual thaw reduced the road to a quagmire of yellow mud. Even with a heavy-duty winch mounted to the frame of the old Dakota, a truck that had seen many miles between The Tyler's cabin and places far distant, there were occasions when The Tyler could not make it out during March and April. But he was a patient man. He relished such moments of respite. The time off allowed him to read fiction, his favorite pastime when he wasn't doing the bidding of The Prophet. The Tyler was partial to Hemingway. Though he no longer possessed the temptations of manhood, The Tyler enjoyed analyzing Hemingway's machismo.

After embracing Obadiah Nielsen as a prophet of God, The Tyler came across the story of Boston Corbett, the Union soldier who shot and killed John Wilkes Booth. Booth fled Washington, D.C. following the assassination of President Lincoln. Boston Corbett was one of the Union soldiers assigned to hunt down Booth. Cornering Lincoln's killer in a barn, Corbett disregarded orders to bring Booth in alive and shot the assassin through a thick plank wall. The wound was a mortal one and Booth died the next morning. Though in line for discipline by the Army for his insubordination, Corbett's disobedience was thought to be heroic by many and he became a celebrity.

There is scant information available about Boston Corbett's early life. But the one historical fact that all scholars seem confident of is Corbett's status as a eunuch. Corbett, having lost his young wife at a young age, sought solace with prostitutes. In a moment of unrelenting guilt over his transgressions, Corbett, who was an evangelical Christian, castrated himself with a penknife, nearly bleeding to death in the process.

Approximately six years before the death of Angelina DeAquila, The Tyler chose to emulate Boston Corbett's self-surgery. It was a decision The Tyler had once lamented, but, in the afterglow of hindsight, came to accept as having been inspired by God.

The Tyler walked into the great room of his cabin carrying his duffle bag, fishing equipment, the reporter's computer, and her iPhone. He deposited his gear on the smooth pine floor and placed the woman's belongings on the kitchen counter. There were no walls between the great room, which was dominated by a Russian soapstone fireplace (the main source of heat for the home) and the kitchen containing a hand pump, sink, LP gas refrigerator, and wood cook stove. The Tyler's bedroom, the solid pine door to his personal space closed to scrutiny, was the only other room in the cabin. The facilities were outside; a small outhouse stood a short distance from the back door.

The great room's ceiling soared without restriction. The air in the cabin was cool despite the fact that it was sixty-five degrees outside; a warm day for November in central Montana.

The Tyler walked deliberately to a MacBook resting in its docking station. The computer was attached to an LCD monitor and a laser printer located on an old kitchen table serving as a desk. The table, its blue-flecked porcelain top chipped from hard use, was placed along the south wall of the cabin beneath two large double hung windows overlooking Sixteen Mile Creek. A cow elk stood fifteen feet from the window, munching contentedly on grass, her smooth tan flanks heated by the sun. The Tyler stood in front of the keyboard, hit the spacebar, and watched the monitor come alive. Wallpaper displaying cover art from Mountain's *Nantucket Sleigh Ride* album filled the screen. A live rendition of "Southbound Train", captured at Woodstock when the band was in its prime, played softly in the background as The Tyler placed the computer's mouse on an icon and clicked. The cover art disappeared, replaced by an office email program. There were two messages from The Prophet in The Tyler's mailbox.

The man needs to learn patience.

The Tyler opened the first of the messages.

To: *disciple13@fastercomp.com*
From: *thework1@fastercomp.com*

Date: October 11, 2009
Re: Problem in Minnesota
I attempted to reach you via Blackberry but apparently either the device was off or you were not in an area where there was service. Please advise whether you have taken care of the spiritual issue we discussed. I am looking forward to hearing that your efforts were successful.
O.H.N.

In truth, The Tyler knew that The Prophet would be attempting to contact him *while* he was engaged in his craft. That had been the pattern in similar situations in the past; Nielsen's curiosity getting the better of him, sending text or email inquiries that could, if latched onto by the authorities, make things dicey for both men.

The Tyler mulled over a response. Rather than replying immediately, he opened the second email.

To: disciple13@fastercomp.com
From: thework1@fastercomp.com
Date: October 12, 2009
Re: Problem in Minnesota
Still haven't heard from you regarding your visit to Minnesota. Also, be aware that a package is being secured and will be arriving at the Great Falls airport sometime before Christmas. I would like your assistance in retrieving the package and delivering it to my attention. Please reply at your convenience.
Kindest regards,
O.H.N.

The Tyler had checked his Blackberry on the flight back to Montana and found the same messages. He didn't reply during the flight because he was exhausted by the weight of taking the young reporter's life. She had been surprised at her death, a circumstance that caused him great pause when he considered the event. He had hoped she'd known what was coming before the knife was drawn, before her stay on Earth had ended. But, from her eyes, the stark reality of it all confined in those pools of dark brown, he knew that it was unexpected, that she had not been prepared.

He had first considered her surprise when he knelt on the shoreline of Seagull Lake and drew the filet knife's blade through sand to remove blood from steel. A thousand miles away and days removed from the murder, The Tyler found he could not erase Angelina DeAquila's face from his memory: Her expression at the moment of reckoning was impossible to forget.

To: thework1@fastercomp.com
From: disciple13@fastercomp.com
Re: Pick up
Date: October 13, 2009
  The trip to Minnesota was extremely taxing but fruitful. The issue has been completely resolved. I am available to pick up the package. Please send details.

Within moments, an email indicating the flight number and arrival time of the Montana Air connection bringing Elsie Johnson and her steward from Minnesota to Montana was sent by Nielsen and displayed on The Tyler's computer. The girl's handler, a woman The Tyler had not met, a missionary of The Principle who lived in the Twin Cities, expected The Tyler to meet them at the gate. It would be his job to protect the future wife of The Prophet from the temptations of freedom. But the young Indian woman's arrival wasn't imminent: The Tyler had time to discover what Angelina DeAquila had learned about The Colony and time to prepare his cabin for winter before the young Lamanite arrived.

  The Tyler opened a leather satchel containing the reporter's laptop, removed DeAquila's computer, situated it on the table, connected the external power cord, and plugged the unit into the wall. Solar panels on the roof of the cabin provided all the electricity The Tyler's Spartan lifestyle required.

  Knowledge is power.

  The assassin was curious, incredibly needy of knowing what the young woman knew about The Colony's connection to northeastern Minnesota. He'd purloined the reporter's computer and iPhone from her car after the murder, using keys DeAquila secreted in the wheel well of the Subaru to gain entry without force.

  The Tyler's fingers manipulated the computer's keyboard. He waited for a prompt. The device was password protected. He reached into a drawer, located a USB cable, and connected the dead woman's computer to his Mac. The Tyler clicked the Mac's mouse. Leslie West's version of "Master's of War", the guitarist's ragged vocals competing with the aging pipes of Ozzie Osborne, exploded into the room like a hurricane. The Tyler smiled. Though the song lacked the support of Pappalardi's bass, there was still an essence, an undercurrent of familiarity to the new cover of the old Dylan tune.

  The Tyler touched the keyboard of his Mac. He initiated a search of the dead reporter's computer using a CIA program that, somewhere along the line, an acquaintance had provided to him. Instantly, the program demystified the meager password protections embedded in the reporter's notebook. What The Tyler found on

Angelina DeAquila's computer convinced him that her death was indeed ordained by God.

TWELVE

"What's the Cook County Sheriff need help with this week?"

Herb Whitefeather's expansive Lakota face broke into a smile as he spoke. The FBI agent greeted Deb Slater in the doorway to his cluttered third-floor office in the Gerald R. Heaney Federal Building in the Civic Center, a grouping of four granite buildings tucked into the significant bosom of Duluth's downtown hillside. Whitefeather chewed the eraser end of a No. 2 pencil, his cocoa brown eyes affixed on Deb Slater's smooth face.

"Nice to see you too, Herb," Slater replied from outside the agent's office.

"Come on in, sheriff. You know I don't stand on formality, especially when an old friend comes to call."

In truth, the two law enforcement officers had a complex and longstanding friendship dating back twenty years. They'd shared one infamous case during that timeframe; a double homicide involving a Yugoslav operative named Jack Kobe, a case that cemented their professional relationship. They'd solved that case, though not without significant drama. There had been other occasions when Slater, whether as a St. Louis County deputy, Lake County undersheriff, or Cook County sheriff, touched base with Whitefeather, seeking advice, forensic assistance from one of the FBI's crime labs, or simple mentoring. Murders. Kidnappings, Bank robberies. With Herb Whitefeather's retirement looming in August, their connection was drawing to a close. Slater wanted to bring the FBI man one last problem, one last intractable mystery: The ritualistic murder of a Twin Cities newspaper reporter.

"Have a seat, Deb."

Slater passed on the obvious hug that, in a less professional setting, would have been her natural response to Whitefeather's invitation. The sheriff nodded and with quick strides, her former athleticism apparent even in middle age, claimed the one chair in the messy office that wasn't stacked with files and bundles of paperwork.

"What's on your mind?"

"Murder a few weeks ago. Young newspaper reporter by the name of Angelina DeAquila. Up off the Gunflint."

"Read about it in the *News Tribune,*" Whitefeather acknowledged, removing the pencil from between his yellowing teeth, the enamel stained from a three-cup-a-morning coffee habit. His love of cigars was a casualty of his marriage to Susan Salminen. Susan had been the agent's live-in girlfriend for the better part of a decade before the acknowledged bachelor finally "popped the question." Susan had reformed the big man in ways that were both obvious, as reflected in her edict against smoking, and subtle as in the healthy foods she inspired him to eat. Susan's near-religious nutritionalism didn't stop the Native man from purloining the occasional Whopper or Big Mac whenever he was on the road. But the effect of his wife's healthy lifestyle had an impact on the old Minnesota Muskie forward: Thanks to her intervention, Herb had slimmed down to his playing weight.

Herb Whitefeather had loathed the day he would turn fifty-seven. Born in 1950 to two full-blood Lakota parents living in Bismarck, North Dakota, the Indian was a stellar high school athlete, both as a defensive end in football and a high scoring power forward in basketball, attributes which found him sought after by every D-2 college in the Midwest. After spending two years tearing up the court for North Dakota State University in Fargo, Whitefeather bypassed his junior and senior years to play professionally in the old ABA for the Minnesota Muskies, and a year later, for their successor, the Minnesota Pipers. A torn ACL sent Herb back to school, where he graduated from NDSU with a sociology degree with an emphasis on criminology. He worked as a beat cop in Fargo until the Bureau recruited him.

The big man passed the Bureau's "official" retirement age of fifty-seven in August, 2007. But due to a lack of Native American agents in the FBI (42 as of the date of Angelina DeAquila's murder; less than 1% of the bureau's active field agents) the Director had granted Herb Whitefeather annual extensions of tenure until age sixty; the last possible date Whitefeather could carry a shield and sidearm for the Bureau.

Slater studied the walls of the agent's office as she considered how to approach her suspicion; that the reporter's death wasn't the result of random murder, but the result of a serial killer, the sort of specter the FBI was well equipped to profile.

The sheriff's focus was interrupted by the room's appearance. Plaques, photographs, and commendations that would ordinarily be on display after four decades in law enforcement were absent from Whitefeather's office. In place of the missing accolades and mementos, rectangles of starkly yellow paint, paint untouched by the impotent Duluth sun, created a pattern against the dirty manila background.

He's getting ready to retire. A bit premature, I'd say. He's got nearly a year to go.

Slater's inventory completed, she returned her attention to the enormous man seated behind the desk in front of her. Whitefeather placed his pencil on a paper calendar covering much of the oak writing surface of the desk.

"How can I help you?"

Deb Slater bit her lip as she considered the dead woman's naked body on the steel gurney of the hospital morgue, DeAquila's Asian features distorted in death, flecks of native Minnesota earth discoloring her cold lips. The sheriff opened a satchel and laid five color photographs of the woman's head and neck, shots the sheriff had taken before the autopsy was conducted, on the agent's desk.

"Remarkable."

Slater frowned.

"That's it? That's all you've got? I bring you a beautiful dead newspaper reporter with her mouth duct taped and stuffed with dirt, her throat slit from ear to ear, found naked but not raped, in the middle of goddamned nowhere, and the best you can do is, 'remarkable'?"

Herb Whitefeather's worn Native features beamed.

"Well, it is, Sheriff Slater. However you slice it, pardon the pun, the fact that she, as I understand it, wasn't raped, given the trouble the killer took to strip her, bind her, shove dirt into her mouth, and gag her, is remarkable, don't you agree?"

The sheriff considered the agent's point.

"I guess."

Whitefeather feigned incredulity.

"You guess? You can do better than that, sheriff!"

Deb Slater considered the agent's prompt.

"Thing is," Slater offered quietly, "we're at an absolute dead end in terms of motive. She wrote a column about religion and politics for the *Minneapolis Star Tribune*. We're looking into that as a starting point. Olsen's on his way down to the Twin Cities with a search warrant to take a look at her office computer, workspace, home computer, and such. I have a gut feeling that her murder *might*, and I say might with caution, have something to do with whatever she was working on for the paper."

Whitefeather handled each photograph with deliberation. Slater held her tongue as the FBI agent scrutinized the images.

"Find anything of forensic value?"

Slater nodded and provided Whitefeather with other photographs: a shot of the caffeine-free Coke can wedged beneath the seat of the fishing boat and a shot of the Black Jack gum wrapper found protected by the dead woman's curled toes.

"Remarkable."

Slater couldn't withhold her annoyance.

63

"Damn it, Herb. Is that the only word you know?"

The Indian's narrow lips formed a weary smile.

He's tired, Slater thought. *He's pushing sixty. He's had enough of this crap. Susan's what? Fifteen years younger? He's looking forward to hanging it up, finding a beach in Florida where he can sip Red Stripe and think nasty thoughts.*

Deb Slater's relationship with Rick, the bonds of intimacy once taut and strong, now sagging and weak due to Rick's illness and her own menopausal decline, disquieted her as she ruminated on Susan Salminen's forty-five year-old body. Susan retained the elusive aura of youth. The younger woman's body remained firm and slender, the benefit of never having carried a child and spending two hours a day at the gym. Slater considered her envy as images of Herb and Susan cavorting on a white sand beach played in her mind.

"Don't be so sensitive," Herb said. "It's all, at the very least, 'remarkable'. Maybe more than that. But how does one know, at this early stage, whether the evidence is relevant or not? That's a determination better left for another day. But, at the very least, Sheriff Slater, the possibility that the killer enjoys caffeine-free Coke and chews licorice-flavored gum, must be considered 'remarkable'. Don't you agree?"

Slater nodded acquiescence.

"Can you do some digging? See if the Bureau has run across anything like this in the past? Maybe we're dealing with a serial killer, maybe not. If we are, it's possible he's left similar evidence at past crime scenes."

"'He'? Being a bit sexist, aren't you sheriff?'

"Just playing the percentages, Agent Whitefeather. How many murders of this type, where the killer is a stranger, and that again is a presumption on my part, are committed by women?"

"You're likely right. Odds are it's a guy. The question, as you so aptly ask it, is 'why?'"

Deb Slater gathered up the photographs and slid them into their folder. She replaced the file in her briefcase and stood up.

"Can you help? Make a few inquiries inside the Bureau. See if anything clicks?"

Whitefeather diverted his gaze out a window, the only window in his office. Three stories below, late November blustered. Pedestrians walking west on Second Street turned their uncovered faces away from the gale as they staggered into the teeth of an Alberta Clipper.

"I've got some folks in Quantico I can call. See if there's anything like this on our radar. It would help if Olsen can come up with a plausible connection between the woman's death and whatever she was working on for the paper. Short of that, maybe it's just a garden variety crazy stalking beautiful women in secluded places."

Slater grasped the handle of the briefcase in her left hand and extended her right towards her mentor.

"I've a gut feeling that it's related to her work, that it's not some isolated bit of bad luck. I don't see it as being tied to her home life. Things there seem copasetic. No hint of another man," Slater said as she shook Whitefeather's hand, "or woman," she added with a wink.

"You catch on quickly, Sheriff Slater," Whitefeather replied through a toothy grin. "Things aren't always as they appear."

Slater stopped short of the threshold and looked back at the FBI agent.

"That a new philosophy you've come up with, oh wise sage of the prairie?"

"Funny girl. Nope, just something I've learned along the way."

Slater laughed, gave a perfunctory wave, and left the man's office.

THIRTEEN

"You shall be delivered from the sins and travails of this world," The Prophet announced from the open stage of the rudimentary meetinghouse, a cavernous pole barn constructed at the very center of The Colony.

Two narrow gravel lanes met at the exact point where Obadiah Nielsen had commanded his followers to erect the building. Early winter sunlight flooded the worship space through a line of skylights in the meetinghouse roof. Additional illumination was provided by two small windows, one on either side of the pulpit standing on the stage in the front of the sanctuary, crank-out casements lining the walls, and utilitarian fluorescent fixtures. The congregation sat in rows of austere pews, the seating retrieved from innumerable antique shops throughout central Montana, the wood painted white to instill a sense of Celestial order, and listened to The Prophet with rapt attention.

The sacrament, a simple ceremonial gesture composed of bread and water reminiscent of Jesus' last meal with his disciples, had already taken place. Occasionally, the sound of a small child fidgeting would interrupt the cadence of The Prophet's speech but the distraction was momentary and did not undercut the message.

Obadiah Nielsen, wisps of graying red hair slicked against his broad skull, his jaw thrust forward in a prophetic pose, towered behind the pulpit and thundered out his message of love, reverence, and salvation in a deep and confident baritone. His eyes darted amongst his flock. The Prophet riveted his attention upon individuals who, during the past week, had slackened in their work ethic or who had grumbled too much when asked to contribute food to The Colony's communal food larder, an essential sacrifice given Mormon scripture. For, as *The Book of Mormon* chronicles, life and human existence are all about being prepared for and weathering catastrophic floods, storms, wars, and famine. Each family was called upon, and expected to deliver without gripe, grouse, or complaint, food for the communal larder. Those who acquiesced with muted protest were known and they received the "eye" as parishioners of the meetinghouse liked to call it: the steady, individual, unspoken scrutiny of The Prophet during Sunday morning meetings.

"And it shall come to pass that you will be chosen, said the Lord God," Nielsen continued. "But such is not certain unless you do as you're bidden. Then you will reap what you've sown, so long as you follow the paths of righteousness and fortitude, demonstrating

66

steadfastness in The Principle. There shall be, in that final day of beauteous reckoning before the Almighty, a gathering of all of our loved ones, young or old, weak or strong in the Lord. And you shall be counted amongst them unless you fall into sloth and morose promiscuity, unless you fail to protect this precious River of Laman, our way of life, our Gospel. Stand now with me, oh pioneers of Zion, oh citizens of the Promised Land, and sing with Sister Jeanette that old and sacred song, 'Come, Come Ye Saints.'"

A tiny woman in a muted green dress trimmed with white Irish lace strode purposefully from the third row of pews, the first rows on either side of the wide aisle being reserved for young men being raised to the priesthood, and sat on the burnished surface of a maple bench. Her right index finger flicked a toggle. The electric organ hummed to life. Adjusting a microphone on a stand, Jeanette Albrecht, third wife to the Second Counselor, Micah Albrecht, began to play the old Mormon hymn. Her tremulous soprano hit pitch and led the congregation. Voices joined in. The metal roof of the meetinghouse shook with holy joy as the congregation's unified pride swelled to God.

Come, come, ye saints, no toil nor labor fear;
But with joy wend your way.
Though hard to you this journey may appear,
Grace shall be as your day.
T'is better far for us to strive our useless cares from us to drive;
Do this, and joy your hearts will swell -
All is well! All is well.

Why should we mourn or think our lot is hard?
T'is not so; all is right.
Why should we think to earn a great reward if we now shun the fight?
Gird up your loins; fresh courage take.
Our God will never us forsake;
And soon we'll have this tale to tell-
All is well! All is well...

The service concluded with the last chorus. The congregation left the church, each adult in turn shaking The Prophet's hand as they exited the heated meetinghouse to confront the chill of early December. Obadiah Nielsen engaged each of his flock personally, with genuine appreciation; from the most ardent adult supporter to the least aware infant, playfully tousling children's hair, amazed and encouraged by their presence, showing particular favoritism and attention to the children born to Lamanite mothers and Caucasian fathers within The Colony. The winding column of sturdy, self-assured Mormon husbands and their sons dressed in clean white dress shirts, neatly pressed suits or sports coats, and narrow ties, their Sunday best dress shoes polished to sheen; accompanied by their wives, the long hair of the women and their daughters piled into buns, their calico, denim, and chiffon dresses swaying with each step, the mothers carrying babies in their arms; reverently passed the prophet in parting.

"Good Sabbath to you, Brother Pratt," Nielsen said, shaking the hand of his First Counselor with vigor.

Ezra Pratt, short, bald headed, dead eyed, fat bellied, and thick bodied, stood next to The Prophet. Pratt's family, three children and three wives, waited patiently for the First Counselor. The women engaged in small talk with The Prophet's wives, the children of the two families peeling off, seeking places to run, hide, and play free from adult scrutiny.

"Fine talk this morning, Brother Nielsen. I especially liked the reference to the solid foundation of our faith, the ties between Isaiah and Nephi. Can't go wrong reminding the people of where it all started, now can we Brother?"

Pratt spoke methodically. There was nothing careless about the man, from the alignment of his tie to the sheen of his black Doc Martins, the gleaming surfaces of which repeated the clear blue sky, the rugged cliffs surrounding the valley, and the adjacent pine forest as if the shoes were made of glass.

"I thank you kindly for your support, as always, Brother Pratt. It will be a fine day, will it not, when we can raise up a proper temple here in Laman's River, a place to properly pray for unbelievers, a sacred sanctuary for the sealing of marriages and blessing the dead?"

"All in good time, Brother. All in good time. Remember, 'patience is a virtue'. Let us be patient and all good things will come to us."

"Amen, Brother Pratt. Amen. It's good the seventies have approved the design submitted by the architect and that the first spade of dirt to build God's temple will be turned come spring."

"Provided the economy continues to recover and our stock portfolio continues to rebound," Pratt added with caution.

"And it shall. God's hand is in it, don't you see? We were tested but didn't panic, didn't sell off like the other fools. Now our riches are increasing once again. A year from now, the spires of a holy temple will touch the blessed sky of this bountiful valley and God will smile. Praise the Lord!"

"Yes," Pratt replied. "Praise the Lord indeed."

Pratt observed the departing crowd. His eyes followed the exodus of parishioners as they walked in small family groups towards their vehicles parked on the hard gravel of the meetinghouse parking lot. Cars and pickup trucks roared to life. Tires spun and shot rocks as vehicles departed. Nielsen smiled broadly. Pratt studied The Prophet's face before addressing the man.

"I hear there's a young Lamanite on her way to join your family," Pratt offered.

Obadiah Nielsen faced the smaller man and smiled.

"Indeed."

"I hear she's a handful."

Nielsen's mouth opened but he said nothing. He refocused his attention on his wives as they clustered in front of the family Denali.

"Isn't that the case, Brother Nielsen?" Pratt asked. "Isn't your betrothed, as they say, a 'spitfire'?"

The Prophet returned his eyes to the smaller man, fixing his gaze on the blood red bulb of the First Counselor's nose, a nose that had been broken innumerable times in innumerable spats.

"That's what I've been told. She'll have enough time, waiting to restore her purity over the next six months, to come to a place of peace."

Nielsen's reference to the six-month period was due to Elsie Johnson's impure status. The girl was not a virgin. Before she could be sealed to The Prophet and taken to bed as his wife, she would need to refrain from any corporal satisfaction for a period of six months, after which, she was presumed to be pure in the eyes of the church. Obadiah Nielsen knew that, in some instances, male members of his flock who had taken fallen women or women of divorce in as plural wives had failed this test. It was a stern test, no doubt, one at odds with the natural curiosity of man; to take a new woman into your home and remain celibate with her for half a year. Some men could pass the test. Some could not. But, given that he was in dire need of converts to The Colony in order to fulfill Nephi's prophesy of two hundred believers living in harmony along Laman's River before The Principle could grow beyond the soaring peaks of the Big and Little Belt Mountains, The Prophet chose practicality over piety. He had cast a blind eye to the shenanigans of his male parishioners who could not abide by the six-month rule. He had allowed unclean women to be sealed, silently acquiescing to the transgressions of man in order to achieve God's higher purpose.

Clouds quickened over the valley. The two men stood on the parched grass of the meetinghouse's front lawn. A storm loomed in the rapidly approaching weather.

"Best get on home and button up the barn, the sheds, and the house," Nielsen observed, shading his eyes with a massive paw as he watched dark sky advance above yellow rock. "The horses will be getting riled up and anxious. There's a storm brewing. Can't tell if it means snow or rain, either of which, the Lord willing, we surely do need."

Pratt nodded significantly. His cheeks jiggled from the gesture.

"Dry as flat bread on a Swede's plate," the shorter man observed. "Ranching's a tough way to make a living."

"Maybe you should stick to accounting," The Prophet joked, slapping the smaller man on the back.

Pratt retained his CPA credentials and was the treasurer of The Colony. The accountant's ranching exploits were meager at best, bordering on out and out failure at worst. Ezra Pratt didn't respond to The Prophet's lighthearted criticism.

"Well, take care, Brother Pratt. Stay dry."

Nielsen turned to lock the meetinghouse door. A snowflake touched his cheek. The flake was strikingly cold as it slid down the significance of The Prophet's jaw.

"I will, Brother, I will. And you," the fat man added as he walked towards his waiting family, his children and wives gathered expectantly near their own black Denali, their hands covering their ears against the wind, "stay away from that young Indian girl until you two are sealed. Wouldn't want the sins of the flesh ruining our Prophet, now would we?"

Nielsen grinned as he extended a key and locked the church.

"Not to worry, Ezra. I've got other wives to keep me busy with the Lord's work."

FOURTEEN

"What's this J-drive on Ms. DeAquila's desktop?" Deputy Olsen asked.

Cook County Deputy Augie Olsen and Detective Samantha Byrnes of the Minneapolis Police Department Homicide Division were seated at the dead reporter's desk in her work cubicle at the *Minneapolis Star Tribune*, DeAquila's Dell desktop monitor illuminated, the LCD screen displaying the computer's various drives. It was quiet in the newsroom. It was Sunday afternoon and most of the newspaper's staff had the day off. Albert Richards, the editor who supervised DeAquila's work, stood behind the two cops, offering suggestions, answering questions as Olsen and Byrnes made their way through various applications, programs, and files. The network administrator had logged them onto the reporter's computer. In a matter of an hour, the officers had opened and closed hundreds of files, none of which seemed to be the least bit interesting or revealing. The J-drive was the last unexplored niche; their last hope to link information on the computer to the woman's death.

Detective Byrnes possessed a short, square stature. It was apparent from first glance that the woman was not interested in men. Her brown hair was shorn close to the scalp. She wore a solitary ruby stud in her left ear and no make-up to speak of. Her pale skin fairly glowed beneath the florescent lighting of the newsroom as she craned her neck, allowing her eyes to focus on the flat screen over the rims of her cheaters.

Olsen guessed she was in her early thirties, but the woman could have been several years on either side of that equation.

"Never seen that before," Richards remarked. "I have no idea what's on her J-drive."

Olsen, the Cook County Sheriff Department's expert on cyber porn and all things computer related, double clicked on the drive's icon. A prompt for the Cloud 9 website appeared. The site required another password.

"Shit."

Byrnes turned her milky face towards the deputy.

"Excuse me?"

"Sorry. Richards, you know her password?"

"Like I said, deputy, I didn't even know there was a J-drive. Maybe she wrote it down somewhere."

The officers rummaged through Post-it notes taped up around DeAquila's workspace. They considered notes and memos tacked to a small bulletin board hanging on the wall behind the desk.

"Try this," Byrnes said, pealing a faded Post-it from the bulletin board. A photograph of the dead reporter, her husband, and their daughter at a zoo occupied the space above the post-it retrieved by the detective.

"Cute kid," Byrnes opined.

"Love of her life," Richards replied.

Olsen typed in the numbers from the post-it note.

"My guess is that the password is her daughter's birthday," Byrnes observed as the computer processed the input.

The screen changed. Information DeAquila had saved on the Cloud 9 website appeared as a series of folders.

"She used the program as a backup," Byrnes observed. "To keep data safe from bugs or hard drive crashes. The site transfers the information to an off-site server."

"I use cloud computing myself," Olsen added, scrolling through the folders listed on the site. "Just in case we have a catastrophe, I won't lose all my work, have to start over. But these folders also include original research of some sort," Olsen said before dragging the mouse to a folder. "They're not just duplicates of what's on her computer's hard drive."

"I think you're on to something."

Byrnes pointed her thick left index finger at a folder labeled "Mormon Polygamists."

"Click on that."

"What the hell," Richards muttered. "I never asked her to look into the Mormons. And she never mentioned she was working on anything like that either."

Olsen clicked the mouse. Files appeared under the main folder bearing headings such as "Research", "Colonies", "Articles", "Links", and "Leads."

Olsen opened the file labeled "Articles."

The first item cataloged was a newspaper clipping copied from the website of the *St. Paul Pioneer Press*.

Juvenile Authorities Hail Opening of All Faiths Recovery Center

At a bar association meeting yesterday, Judge Omar Constantine, head judge of the Second District's juvenile division, applauded the opening of a new juvenile delinquency residential treatment program in Minneapolis.

"All Faiths will fill a void, providing faith-based chemical dependency treatment, safety, classroom learning, and cognitive skills

training for at-risk youth throughout the State of Minnesota," the judge said, speaking at the monthly meeting of the Ramsey County Bar Association held yesterday at the Minnesota Club in downtown St. Paul.

Recently opened in an old mansion in the trendy Kenwood neighborhood of Minneapolis, Judge Constantine stressed that, though the per diem rates charged by All Faiths were higher than those of other local juvenile residential facilities, the addition of faith-based rehabilitation "will guaranty that the success rate of the new program will exceed existing delinquency education and detention facilities."

"This program," All Faiths's Board member and State Senator Elmer Barnes added when called for comment at the State Capitol, "will mimic the programming and success of the Teen Challenge facilities in the Twin Cities and Duluth. That program has a low rate of recidivism, is extremely safe in terms of the public, and is considered to be one of the most innovative in the nation."

All Faiths is expected to house approximately fifty residential students of both genders and will offer access to councilors from most major faiths, including The Church of Jesus Christ of the Latter-day Saints, Native American spirituality, Islam, and Buddhism, as well as mainstream Christian and Jewish denominations.

Similar articles had been saved by DeAquila in the same file folder. Olsen located and opened more recent newspaper pieces from around the Midwest chronicling the progress of the All Faiths facility. Another article piqued Olsen's interest. The dead reporter had highlighted portions of the article.

"Check this out," Olsen said quietly as he read an article copied from the *Bismarck Tribune.*

Teenage Girl Sent to Juvenile Facility Found Dead

J.L.K, a fifteen year old Lakota girl sent by Judge Ed Hansen of Bismarck to All Faiths Recovery Center, a program located in Minneapolis, Minnesota, which specializes in treating chemically dependent, at-risk children through adherence to the child's choice of faith, was found dead in a field near the Minneapolis-St. Paul International Airport after having run from All Faiths. The body, located in a remote area at Fort Snelling (a section of abandoned housing slated for rehabilitation) was found by a couple walking their dog last Sunday.

According to the Bloomington Police Department, foul play is suspected but details are being withheld pending further investigation.

Officials at All Faiths did not return phone calls placed by the Tribune.

Funeral arrangements for the young woman are pending.

"According to the Bloomington Police Department, foul play is suspected..." was the portion of the article highlighted by Angelina DeAquila.

"Richards, you know anything about this?" Olsen asked.

The editor stared at the screen.

"I had no idea she was researching All Faiths. But what the hell does the death of an Indian girl from Bismarck have to do with the Mormons?"

"Your guess is as good as mine," Byrnes said, re-reading the article. "Anything stand out in DeAquila's background that might've compelled her interest in the topic?"

Richards, a tall, razor thin man with thick blond hair, bushy blond eyebrows, and nondescript eyes that retreated in shadows cast by his beaked nose, shook his head.

"No clue. Her husband might know something about this. I have no idea what her religious beliefs were. Obviously, with what went on down in Texas with Warren Jeffs and his clan, there's significant interest in the media regarding Mormon fundamentalism. Sex—and certainly polygamist sex—sells papers. But I have no idea what she was up to."

Olsen scrolled through additional pieces in the "Articles" file but found nothing further of substance.

"Try the file marked 'Contacts'," Byrnes suggested.

Olsen complied. A single name appeared.

"What the hell..." Olsen muttered.

"You know that name?" Richards asked, his innate reporter's curiosity aroused.

"I sure do."

"Who is 'Elizabeth Prichard'?" Byrnes asked.

Olsen pushed himself away from the desk, stood up, and wagged his head slowly from side to side. The deputy allowed air to slowly escape over his teeth as he stared hard at the monitor.

"She's a judge...In Duluth."

"A judge...in...Duluth," Byrnes repeated in identical cadence.

"That's right. A judge."

Olsen reclaimed his seat. The officers reviewed other files in the "Mormon Polygamists" folder. In the "Leads" file, they found another newspaper article, an excerpt from the *Duluth News Tribune* regarding Judge Prichard.

Judge Urges Use of Faith-Based Juvenile Facility to "Correct' the Sins of Youth

Speaking to the Minnesota Churches of God Convention held this past weekend at the Duluth Entertainment and Convention Center, District Court Judge Elizabeth Prichard stated that she was encouraging evangelicals working in courts, corrections, probation, social work, and law enforcement to use the All Faiths Recovery Center as a "first choice" for cases involving chemical dependency-related juvenile "misbehaviors." Judge Prichard, a member of the Good News Council, which directs and operates Good News Chapel in West Duluth, said that the advent of a faith-based treatment model for teenagers, particularly teenage girls, is long overdue.

"We've had Teen Challenge in Minnesota, for years," the judge told the 300 delegates in her address to the convention, "but despite the name, that program is primarily directed towards young adults. And," the judge added, "Teen Challenge relies solely upon Christianity as its model."

Though a practicing evangelical Christian herself, Judge Prichard went on to point out that, while conversion is the number one goal on her personal faith agenda, by not allowing at-risk children to receive treatment in a facility that recognizes their own faith heritages, "we are losing kids to drugs and alcohol. All Faiths," Judge Prichard noted, "while not exactly in line with my personal belief in Christ as Savior and Risen Lord, is certainly a great addition to our treatment tool box."

A fund raising auction and dance for All Faiths is scheduled to coincide with the closing ceremonies of the convention on Sunday afternoon.

"Why was DeAquila so interested in this subject matter? And how the hell does Judge Prichard fit into whatever it was that DeAquila was looking at?" Olsen asked.

Byrnes shook her head.

"I have no idea. But I think we need to pay Mr. DeAquila a condolence call. Maybe there's something in his wife's background that will ring a bell."

Augie Olson nodded in agreement.

His fingers touched the keyboard. Under the "Links" section of the Cloud 9 files, Olsen found hypertext links to dozens of websites dealing with Mormon polygamy, polygamist sects, and polygamist communities. Some of the websites lauded polygamy, but most lambasted the practice. There were dozens and dozens of links; too many to review in-depth while DeAquila's editor stood over Olsen's shoulder.

Be much easier to take the time to go through these back at the office.

"Pursuant to Judge Sandvik's search warrant, we'll take Ms. DeAquila's computer and other personal papers with us," Olsen said as he closed the J-drive and shut down the CPU. "I'll list everything on an inventory sheet and leave a copy for your legal beagles. I think Detective Byrnes is right. It's time to go pay Mr. DeAquila a visit."

FIFTEEN

Lizzy Joy Kittridge was fifteen when her father, Edward Baines Kittridge, announced that she was to be sealed in plural marriage to her uncle, Jeremiah Kittridge. Educated at the Academy of The Principle on property owned by the family in rural Tooele County, Utah, Lizzy had a brilliant mind, a sharp wit, and possessed an even sharper tongue despite the strictness of her upbringing in the fundamentalist traditions of the Latter Day Reformed Church of Christ, an offshoot of the once powerful Blue Cliffs Arizona polygamists.

As a direct descendent of the Reformed Church of Christ's founding patriarch, Norman Kittridge, had Lizzy been a young man, her keen mind and inquiring disposition would have been seen as blessings. Instead, her strong personality and intellect required, at least according to her father's view, frequent beatings and whippings; and, when corporal punishment proved ineffective in curbing Lizzy's individualism, an arranged marriage to her Uncle Jerry, a man in his late fifties, was pronounced as the cure for her mischief. Her interest in politics and the law, interests that remained stunted due to her gender and the isolation of her family, would have, had she been blessed with male instead of female genetics, likely prompted her father to encourage her to attend Brigham Young University in Provo. But such was not Lizzy's fate. Her fate, as dictated by *The Book of Mormon* as interpreted by Edward Kittridge, was marriage to her paternal uncle as she turned the corner of puberty. At least, that was the plan.

May 1st, 1973. The sealing ceremony was to be held at the Tooele County Temple in the presence of Lizzy's extended family, her seven prospective sister wives, and her future husband. But Lizzy Kittridge did not attend her own wedding.

Instead, Lizzy, fully dressed in the pristine white garment her mother had been sealed in, had vanished from the world of Mormon polygamy forever. Her father's 1971 Jeep Wagoneer disappeared as well, stolen by a fifteen-year-old girl desperate to escape a life of brutality, incestuous sex, and fear; the common and ordinary lot of women who remained in the Church of Christ as sister wives to the patriarchs of the church.

Edward Kittridge's Jeep had sped through the barren, dry land of northern Utah, kicking up dust as it blew through mile after mile of rural gravel road before hitting pavement. A few days later, the

77

Wagoneer was located by the Utah Highway Patrol in a parking lot at the Salt Lake City airport no worse for the wear. But the girl was gone. No trace was left of Lizzy Kittridge, or the two thousand and sixty-eight dollars she had liberated from a coffee can secreted beneath her mother's bed. This was household money allotted by Edward to his most senior wife to care for his family; the three sister wives and eighteen children he was charged with providing for as the CEO of Kittridge Investments, the financial arm of the cooperative businesses instituted by Nicholas Kittridge, the son of the sect's founder.

The money and the girl had disappeared. The church elders decreed excommunication as Lizzy Kittridge's punishment for her apostasy. But, with no clues as to where the girl had gone, no understanding of the life Lizzy Kittridge sought as her own personal resurrection, the decree remained an empty threat against a ghost.

SIXTEEN

"By the power of the Holy Spirit and Jesus Christ our Lord, I unseal you as Celestial husband and wife."

The words, which had been spoken in the Laman's River meetinghouse by First Counselor (and Priest of the Reconstituted Brotherhood of Latter-day Saints) Ezra Pratt, were not uttered in the presence of the entire Nielsen family but said in secrecy; hidden from both the public and the sister wives and children of Obadiah Nielsen. Bethany Comes to Ride, dressed in her best white dress, her coal black hair clean and luminous in the artificial light of the meetinghouse's sanctuary despite the darkness of the Montana summer night outside, had stood next to her husband, shaking with nervous tension, her thin pubescent stature markedly in contrast to the towering frame of The Prophet.

The couple had stood slightly apart, near the preacher's lectern at the front of the cavernous sacred space, as Pratt had performed the ceremony that cast the Lamanite girl out of the Nielsen family and out of The Colony forever. Her unpardonable sin, speaking to an outsider in confidence about the tenets of her faith and The Principle, meant that she could no longer be trusted. Her time at Keystone Ranch had, she knew that night despite her young age and inexperience, come to an end.

After the ceremony had been completed (the First and Second Counselors acting as witnesses; the only other person in attendance a thick shouldered, strong armed man with stark blond hair and clarion blue eyes), Bethany Comes to Ride had been escorted in tears from the meetinghouse, her manner agitated, her fears increasing, into a waiting black Denali where she was firmly lodged in the rear passenger's seat behind the driver before being whisked away from the meetinghouse down The Colony's main road.

"Where are you taking me?" the Indian girl had asked pensively after the blond stranger, a man she had never seen before that night, activated the vehicle's child proof door and window locks, effectively imprisoning her.

"To your people."

The girl had stared silently out the passenger window and considered the man's response. Outside the SUV a moonless night emphasized distant stars. Only vague shapes, shadows, and defuse suggestions of geography were visible as the Denali accelerated through the Smith River valley.

"That's a long way."

The Tyler had smiled at the girl's misconception. Indeed, it was a long way from central Montana to the Nez Perce Reservation on the Idaho-Washington border, an area defined by the Snake River to the west and the Clearwater Mountains to the east.

"Yes it is."

"Thumbsucker," a Mountain tune featuring blues licks and Felix Pappalardi's vocals, had played softly in the background as the SUV followed Zion's Way. After stopping momentarily at the security gate, where The Tyler had a brief conversation with the two male Colony members manning the checkpoint, the Denali headed west until it reached US 12.

The SUV had followed the highway into Helena but did not stop in the city. The Denali turned right on State Highway 141, continued on blacktop, and then followed a gravel road into the Nevada Lake Wildlife Management Area. The Denali skirted the north shore of Nevada Lake, a pristine reservoir formed by damming the Blackfoot River, before entering a campground; the big wheels of the Denali spitting rocks as the vehicle braked to a stop.

"I need to take a leak."

The Indian girl had considered the stranger's statement as he exited the vehicle. Cool night air entered the Denali as the man opened the door and stepped into wilderness.

"Gross," the girl had whispered.

The man walked to the edge of a thicket under a canopy of scraggly pines and spread his legs. Bethany Comes to Ride had listened as the man's urine sprayed undergrowth. When he had completed his business, the man walked back to the car, his hands freely swinging in cadence to his stride, his blue jeans tightly pressed to his muscled legs, his square chin prominent even in the darkness of the isolated, lonely campground.

"Please get out of the car."

The girl's eyes had grown wide under the dome light of the Denali as The Tyler opened the driver's side passenger door and motioned for her to exit.

"Why?"

"I want to show you something."

Having lived in a Celestial marriage with The Prophet after meeting him in the Helena gas station and convenience store where she'd worked after running from a foster home in central Idaho (where she'd been placed after failing school), Bethany Comes to Ride was no longer a virgin. She understood a man's lust; his need to be satisfied.

She had seen that need in The Prophet's eyes and had attempted, as best she could, to comply with his demands. The Colony had been the first place she'd ever lived that seemed safe; that had met her need for security. She had accepted The Principle, accepted the tenets of the faith as true. She was attempting to reform herself, to become a better person, a better wife, when she had been snatched from her bed to attend the unsealing ceremony.

When The Tyler commanded her to exit the Denali, she had searched the man's handsome face, his kindly blue eyes, for evidence of lust. Reassured by what she thought she saw there, Bethany had stepped out of the SUV.

"Come with me."

She had followed the stranger down a lonely path to the shoreline of Nevada Lake. Standing on a concrete boat ramp sloping towards the lake, the two of them looked out across placid water. In the distance, Bethany could distinguish the far shoreline rising above the flatness of Nevada Lake as a silhouette against the night sky. No cries of coyotes, no calls of loons, no croaking of frogs had disrupted the solitude of the wilderness that night.

"Beautiful."

The man had been standing to her left as Bethany Comes to Ride spoke her last word. His left arm, hard muscled and taut, drew the fillet knife across her throat faster than the word could be uttered. Blood spurted, flowed down her meager chest, and soiled her dress. The Tyler's left hand brought the blade of the fillet knife back across her jugular, ensuring complete severance of the vessel and the near decapitation of the girl's head.

The Tyler had gently lowered the slight, juvenile body, the girl's womb secretly carrying The Prophet's child, onto cool ground. The Tyler's right hand remained tightly pressed to the Native girl's thin lips, stifling her last cry, restricting the last gurgle of air from her lungs as she died.

Rest in peace, Bethany Comes to Ride. Thee are now with the Alpha and the Omega. May God give thee a home and a family in His Kingdom. Amen

He had stripped the girl of her clothes, admiring God's handiwork as he removed the white dress and Mormon undergarment from the reposing corpse. He placed a clod of Nevada Lake soil in the girl's mouth before lifting the dead Indian girl and carrying her into deep woods. After covering what had been Bethany Comes to Ride with deadfall, The Tyler retrieved the girl's blood-stained dress, her traditional Mormon undergarment (so diminutive in size as to prompt tears from The Tyler), the girl's white leggings, and her finely polished shoes from the edge of Nevada Lake and carried them to an isolated campsite. His pace slowed by angst, The Tyler had retraced his footsteps, opened the rear hatch of the Denali, retrieved a one-gallon red plastic gas can, and returned to the campsite's fire pit. He had placed the clothing in a neat pile within the stone perimeter of the pit, his fastidiousness obvious in his attention to detail, and covered the garments with dead branches and pine boughs. Dousing the wood and clothing with gas, The Tyler lit a match and tossed it towards the pyre.

Whommppp.

Within moments, evidence of the unfortunate girl's existence had been reduced to ash.

SEVENTEEN

Joyce Billington became the fourth wife of The Prophet after the disappearance of Bethany Comes to Ride. Joyce's place in the Nielsen family was secured by her being sealed to The Prophet and his three surviving wives in a private ceremony at the Laman's River meetinghouse.

There was little physicality in the marriage. It was, as Obadiah and Joyce had agreed, a marriage of convenience between an old man and a widow; a circumstance not at all unusual at the stage of life they each occupied. The Prophet, true to his word, did not make untoward demands upon the woman; he contented his carnal needs with the other three fillies in his stable. Joyce, it was understood amongst the sister wives, was exempt from the rotation that saw each woman occupy the master bedroom of the complex in satisfaction of their spiritual obligation to procreate; their religious duty to bring new souls into the Earthly realm so that those souls could, once having been baptized into the Mormon faith, reach eternal bliss upon their own deaths. There was, given Joyce's barren womb, no reason for her to participate in relations with The Prophet; sex, purely for pleasure, Mormon theology teaches, has no place in human existence, which is why even the mainstream Church frowns upon birth control of any sort and labels abortion a sin.

Snow drifted down over the open water of the Smith River. Weightless flakes waltzed to the ground. Sheep grazed morosely near the rocky shoreline of the watercourse. Joyce Billington Nielsen, her thick red hair tied in a bun, a bright blue wool stocking cap, the cap knitted by her sister wife, Evelyn, tight to her scalp, a brown storm coat wrapped around her sturdy frame to keep out the cold wind racing through the valley, wandered towards the open water of the Smith, retracing a trip to the water's edge she'd made the first of each month since she'd come to live at Keystone Ranch.

"Why do you feel compelled to seek out communion with the river?" The Prophet had asked after observing one of Joyce's treks.

"It helps me remember Rudy's face. He died on the first of the month. It calms me to think that he's not gone but lives on with our heavenly father."

"For now, you're sealed to me," The Prophet had reminded the woman tersely. "You're sealed to me on Earth. You can reclaim your beloved later on, in the Hereafter."

She had smiled when her new husband pointed out the obvious. Her history, such as it was known to The Prophet, included the fact that she had been sealed to Rudy in a temple wedding.

"I know that, Obadiah. But you also know he was my first. I will always love him in a way different and apart from how I respect you."

The Prophet had, in time, come to accept her explanation, come to respect the private time she spent along the banks of the Smith.

Joyce pulled up the left sleeve of her coat and glanced at her watch, a cheap waterproof Casio that had been on her wrist for years.

Fifteen minutes. They should be here in fifteen minutes.

She brushed snow off a yellow sandstone boulder worn smooth by flood, sat on the rock, and shivered as she scanned the landscape with hazel eyes. Snow continued to fall. The wind drove icy flakes into Joyce's face. There were no trees shielding her from the weather; pasture having been brought to the river's edge years before regulations were enacted requiring a buffer between livestock and trout. The woman was completely open to the advancing storm as she waited.

Twenty minutes after beginning her vigil, Joyce's eyes averted from the contemplation of the unknowable to a yellow raft rounding a bend upstream. The inflatable drifted from fog into view, riding low on the river's diminished current, the aft sweep oar manned by a male guide. Two anglers, men by their posture, cast streamers towards eddies and pockets as the boat floated towards her. Joyce removed a mittened hand from a pocket of her coat and waved.

"Nice day to be on the river," she offered sardonically as the boat landed near her. "How's the fishing?"

"Slow. Only caught two small brookies," the guide replied from the aft of the boat.

"How's it going?"

A bald-headed fisherman standing in the boat's prow, the man nearest Joyce Nielsen, asked the question as his eyes carefully searched the shoreline.

"About as well as can be expected. I'm a bit tired of cooking for a tribe of Mormon zealots," Joyce related. "It's not the sort of duty I signed up for, you know?"

The bald-headed man chuckled.

"I can imagine," another voice said.

The second man smiled as he spoke. He was a large, heavily built man with a full beard, his black whiskers turning to gray, his oval face flat as a pan and red as a beet from the cold. His words conveyed a hint of sympathy, of understanding.

"I doubt that," Joyce retorted. "You don't have to wear these ridiculous clothes. I'm no fashion model but these dresses..." She stopped and adjusted her Mormon undergarment as she spoke. "And this goddamned underwear. I wish you had to wear this outfit for a day. I swear: You'd go crazy." The woman tightened the wool coat around her body against the rising wind. "Let me be clear about this, Agent Stevens. Perfectly fucking clear. This is the last undercover assignment I'll ever work!"

Stevens, the heavily built man with the beard, nodded again.

"There's been a development," the bald-headed man interjected.

"How's that?"

"Another murder. Woman reporter in Minnesota, Got too close for comfort. At least, that's what we think. Same M.O."

"Throat?"

The bald-headed man nodded again.

"Dirt in the mouth?"

"Yup."

"Damn. That makes what, three?"

"Four, if you count the social worker."

"I'd forgotten about him. M.O. was slightly different."

"True. The killer used an automatic. One shot to the noggin. But the rest of it, including the redundant slashing of the poor guy's throat after he was already dead, seems to fit."

"Anything else?"

"There may be more we haven't discovered. And never will." Stevens hesitated before continuing. "Gibbons thinks it's time for you to come in."

Joyce Nielsen stood up and glanced behind her.

"Not yet. There're a few more things I'd like to figure out."

Stevens shook his head.

"You've done as much as can be expected. We've got enough on these clowns to take the whole lot of them down for child molestation, welfare fraud, and conspiracy. Corrine, it's time to come in, to get safe."

The use of her given name visibly upset the woman.

"Don't use my real name! Never use my real name!"

"Sorry," Stevens said in a hushed tone. "After ten years together in the Bureau, old habits are hard to break. But what I said still stands."

"Plesha," the woman said quietly to the bald-headed man, her confidence restored, "you tell Gibbons one more month. Next month, on the first, you guys can pick me up right here and get me the hell out of this nightmare."

The bald-headed man nodded. He reached beneath a wooden seat in the inflatable.

"Here," the agent said in a whisper, handing her a small silver-plated automatic. "Gibbons said you'd be stubborn. He wants you at least to be able to protect yourself, now that we're getting closer, putting on some pressure."

"What the hell is this for?"

"Take it. Whoever Nielsen has doing his dirty work is one sick, perverted fuck. A .38 under your pillow is just a little insurance."

Corrine Faith McDonald, for that was Joyce Billington Nielsen's full given name, the name on her certificate from the FBI Academy at Quantico, considered the handgun before extending her mittened hand and accepting the automatic.

"Here's an extra clip. Just in case," Plesha added, handing the female agent a loaded magazine crafted from the same shiny chrome as the handgun.

The woman slid the automatic and the extra magazine into a pocket of her coat.

"Thanks."

The guide pushed the boat away from the shore with a sweep of the oar.

"Stay safe," Stevens urged as he regained his feet, stood gingerly in the center of the raft, stripped fly line from his reel, and lofted a streamer into a silver pool behind a craggy sandstone boulder in the middle of the river.

"Always. One month. Don't forget me."

"Not likely," Plesha said firmly.

The Smith caught the bow of the boat. A sudden flurry of snowflakes obscured the raft as it began to drift. A golden eagle soared above the water, riding the wind, gliding effortlessly upstream.

"Good luck fishing," the woman called out above the gale.

"You too," Plesha replied as the raft became enveloped in fog.

EIGHTEEN

"So what's the deal, Augie?" Sheriff Deb Slater asked.

Olsen, who'd just returned from his excursion to the Twin Cities, sat across the conference room table from his boss, Angelina DeAquila's office computer, monitor, and keyboard plugged into an outlet in a wall of the carpeted room. File folders retrieved from DeAquila's cubicle at the *Tribune* and from her home were stacked in front of the deputy as he negotiated his way through the cyber files stored on the computer and on the Cloud 9 site.

"Seems that DeAquila was raised Mormon, though she left the church in her second year of college, when she met her husband at the University of Utah. He's Methodist, or at least was, and they were married in a Methodist church. But both sort of fell off the religious wagon, so to speak. Became agnostic," Olsen said quickly, the pace of his words threatening to overwhelm Slater's ability to comprehend what the deputy was saying. Olsen realized his own excitement and tried to put the brakes on his enthusiasm. "Got this all from the husband, Mitch. Seems to be a regular guy. No motive at all for wanting his wife dead. A tax lawyer at a big downtown Minneapolis firm. Nothing on the radar in terms of irregularities at his work or in his personal life. Stand up guy, from all appearances."

Slater sipped tepid coffee and considered the information.

"So she was researching Mormons after leaving the church. Any clue as to why?"

"Know anything about the story of Lehi and his sons?"

Slater shook her head.

"That some sort of Biblical story/"

"*Book of Mormon*," Olsen advised, "according to Mitch DeAquila, who studied theology before switching to law. That's how he met his wife. They sat next to each other at a lecture on the University of Utah campus when an evangelical Christian debated an elder from the mainstream Church of Jesus Christ of the Latter-day Saints. The Mormons. Anyway, after the debate, they started dating. She became vehemently anti-Mormon. She was obsessed with revealing the faith's fallacies, including inconsistencies between the tenets of the Mormon religion and *The Book of Mormon* itself. One of those discrepancies was the practice of polygamy."

Slater scratched her forehead as she thought.

"Didn't the Mormons get rid of polygamy, like a hundred years ago?"

"Had to or Utah wouldn't have been admitted into the country as a state. But pockets of 'true believers' have remained dedicated to what they call 'The Principle'. Mormon fundamentalists, according to Mitch DeAquila and the research his wife was doing, believe that the original position of the church, belief in what they call 'plural' or 'Celestial' marriage; one man, multiple wives…"

"What, no 'one woman, multiple husbands?'"

Olsen smiled.

"Funny, boss. The dictionary definition of 'polygamy' applies both ways; a person with multiple husbands *or* wives. The term's been corrupted over the years. The term that actually fits the fundamentalist Mormon beliefs is 'polygyny'; one man, multiple wives. But the Latter-day Saints aren't into equal rights. I also uncovered the fact that Utah, with its huge Mormon population, proved to be the undoing of the Equal Rights Amendment when it was voted on."

"Mr. Trivia."

"But," Olsen said with a wink, "I digress. Anyway, Angelina DeAquila was obsessed with fundamentalism in the Mormon faith. Couldn't get away from it. Ate it. Slept it. Drank it, according to the husband. With her contacts inside the church—her parents and extended family remained active after she left the faith—DeAquila had access to leads and inside information regarding fundamentalist sects. She used the approach that she was trying to bring polygamy to light for the betterment of the greater Mormon faith. But in fact, she was after the whole kit and caboodle. She had no use for any form of Mormonism. Period. But she didn't share that position with her informants. Mitch said it bugged the crap out of her that, despite the fact that their own 'bible', *The Book of Mormon,* considers polygamy a sin, the early prophets and leaders of the church ignored the supposed word of God, *The Book of Mormon,* Jacob 2:26, 2:35, and Jacob 3:6. Here, take a gander."

Olsen handed Slater the scriptural text already bookmarked to the relevant passages. Her eyes studied the verses.

Wherefore, I, the Lord God will not suffer that this people shall do like unto them of old…For there shall not any man among you have save it be one wife; and concubines, he shall have none…

Behold, ye have done greater inequities than the Lamanites, our brethren. Ye have broken the hearts of your tender wives, and lost confidence of your children, because of your bad examples before them…

(T)he Lamanites…are more righteous than you; for they have not forgotten the commandment of the Lord, which was given unto our fathers—that they should save it were one wife, and concubines they should have none, and there should not be whoredoms committed among them.

"You thinking of converting?" Slater quipped after reading the text.

"Seriously boss, this woman was damned obsessed when it came to the issue of polygamy. She went on and on with her husband about how the church's holiest book, *The Book of Mormon,* could absolutely view plural marriage as a sin, and yet prophets of that very same church, men who supposedly had a direct revelatory relationship with the big guy upstairs, violate this prohibition, essentially sinning at will, marrying underage girls, other men's wives, and their female cousins. Guys like Brigham Young and Joseph Smith, the founding fathers of the church, took multiple wives in direct contradiction to the word of God. Angelina DeAquila was incensed by the church concealing this hypocrisy from its membership and its refusal to acknowledge that its earliest believers and leaders were, in essence, frauds."

"Interesting background, Augie. But what the hell does that have to do with DeAquila getting her throat slit in my county?"

"Can't tell you that yet, boss," Olsen said apologetically. "But there's more to the back story. And it might give us something to go on in terms of why the woman was killed."

"Do tell."

Olsen moved his fingers over the keyboard of the dead reporter's work computer.

"The files she stored on a cloud website, Cloud 9, contained references to two other murders. A young Lakota girl from North Dakota ran from a treatment center in the Twin Cities and wound up dead on the grounds of Fort Snelling. Same M.O. as the DeAquila murder. We'll come back to that one in a second. And there's also a clipping from the *Independent Record.*"

"What's that?"

"Helena, Montana, newspaper. Seems another young Native American girl, who'd been missing for quite a while from a foster home placement in Idaho, turned up dead near Helena."

"Let me guess. Her throat was slashed?"

"Yup."

"The body was naked but she hadn't been raped?"

"Bingo."

"And there was dirt stuffed in her mouth?"

89

"Three for three."

Slater stood up and walked over to a window overlooking Grand Marais. The picturesque fishing village was neatly arranged below the hillside occupied by the law enforcement center. From the window, Slater had a clear view of Lake Superior. Ice had formed on the lake in response to below zero cold. Lake Superior's solid blue-gray surface extended from the town's harbor east towards the distant Wisconsin shore. A weak winter sun shone above the frozen desolation. Only the heartiest souls moved through the village, desperate cold forcing most residents of Grand Marais indoors where they were safe from the penetrating depth of winter. The sheriff continued to study the scene below her while she considered Augie Olsen's story.

"Go on. What do dead Indian girls and a dead reporter have to do with Mormons?"

"Don't know the whole of *that*..." Olsen said. "At least, not yet. But Minneapolis P.D. believes there's some sort of connection. The detective I was working with down there—Sam Byrnes—pulled the murder investigation on the Indian girl killed at Fort Snelling. A dead end; just like the murder in Montana, no pun intended."

Slater ignored the gallows humor as she turned and retraced her steps. She didn't sit down at the conference table, but reached for the coffee pot, poured another cup of strong brew, raised it to her lips, and sipped while Olsen reviewed his notes.

"The passages you read from *The Book of Mormon*..."

"Yes?"

"Byrnes and I think there's something connecting DeAquila's fascination with polygamy and the Lamanites."

"The what?"

"Indians. Native Americans. Originally, the Mormons were taught by their prophets and their scriptures that Lehi...Remember him?"

"From *The Book of Mormon*?"

"That's the guy. He appears in the very beginning of the book. He and his sons, Nephi and Laman. Well, according to the story, Nephi is the favored son and Laman is literally the family's black sheep. When Lehi and his family, including Laman and Nephi, who are all Jews, leave Israel and come to the New World sometime before the birth of Christ, Nephi's followers and Laman's followers split apart. Great wars and battles ensue. The followers of Laman, the Lamanites, eventually win out, slaughtering the Nephites. It's more complex than that but essentially, the Lamanites end up ruling North America. They're the forefathers and foremothers of present-day Indians. At least, that's the original doctrine, though, because of genetic testing, the church now says the term 'Lamanite' encompasses all the peoples of the New World, including those of Asian origin; folks who have a DNA cocktail linked to immigration over the Bering Sea. There's not one shred of evidence, according to DeAquila's research, that Native Americans are in anyway related to the Jews, which is another huge hole in the Mormon view of the world."

"Augie, you're giving me a headache. Get to the point."

Slater's tone revealed that her patience was being tried by the theology lesson.

"Deb, this is important stuff. It'll help you understand what was going on in DeAquila's head."

Slater relented.

"Okay. Just try to get there a bit faster. I'm getting older by the minute and this case isn't getting solved by you and me jawing about Mormons."

Olsen's mouth opened in a wide grin.

"But that's the point, Sheriff Slater. Theology is what may solve this case."

"On with it, Augie!"

"Sure thing, boss. So we have two dead Indian girls, both from troubled backgrounds, both on the run apparently at the time they were murdered. And a reporter digging around the edges of not only polygamy within the Mormon fundamentalist communities, but also looking at the Lamanite aspect of things. Why?"

"That's the million dollar question, I'll wager, isn't it?"

"Sure is. Looking at all the websites and links and resources DeAquila pulled together, it seems that the notion, as contained in *The Book of Mormon,* that the Lamanites were given dark skin due to their apostasy—their disbelief, their straying from God—is also something that the church has downplayed or revised over time. Originally, the Mormon doctrine was as quoted in 2 Nephi 5:16:

And he had caused the cursing to come upon them, yea, even a sore cursing, because of their iniquity. For behold, they had hardened their hearts against him, that they had become like unto a flint; wherefore, as they were white, and exceedingly fair and delightsome, that they might not be enticing unto my people the Lord God did cause a skin of blackness to come upon them.

"Downplayed?"

"The original versions of *The Book of Mormon,* 2 Nephi, 30:6, stated that the Lamanites, after coming to Jesus, would have 'their scales of darkness fall from their eyes; and many generations shall not pass away among them, save they shall be a white and delightsome people.' Modern versions of *The Book of Mormon* redact 'white' and

91

insert 'pure' in what DeAquila, in her notes, calls 'a disturbing trend of revisionist political correctness'; an attempt to make mainstream Mormonism more palatable to a wider audience."

"Interesting. But the point being…?"

Olsen stood up and stretched his arms above his head before leveling his gaze on his boss.

"We think DeAquila was on to something. Something to do with what Mormon critics call the 'bleaching of the Lamanites.' In certain circles of Mormon fundamentalism, and that's the rub here, Byrnes and I haven't been able to pinpoint which sect or sects actually subscribe to this theory, there's a belief that, to bring the Indians back into God's fold, they have to be 'bleached'. This goes back to the teachings of Joseph Smith, the guy who originally found the plates containing the writings that became *The Book of Mormon* on a hillside in upstate New York, teachings that have been suppressed by the church hierarchy for the better part of a century. Like the polygamist doctrine of the early church founders, the 'bleaching' doctrine continues to exist as scripture but is suppressed by today's church. DeAquila found documents and commentary that confirm Smith absolutely taught and believed that, in the early 1830s, before the church really got going, it was essential that Mormon men take Indian wives so as to 'purify' or 'whiten' the blood of the offspring of the Lamanites."

"You've got to be kidding me," Debra Slater said thoughtfully. "I've never heard that doctrine espoused by any Mormon I've ever come across. Certainly not by the Mormon missionaries who used to show up on my parent's doorstep in little Glenwood, Minnesota. I'd let 'em in just to talk. It was interesting, hearing their perspective, at least for a Presbyterian girl like me. I remember that they didn't consider me to be 'saved'. I had to accept the Angel Moroni to be considered a true believer. I always told them 'thanks, but no thanks'. They were polite, easy to talk to. But not a one of those young boys, boys I caught staring at my bare legs more than once when I was wearing shorts during the summer, I might add, ever said a word about 'bleaching' the Indians."

"And they wouldn't have. Like I said, modern church hierarchy has suppressed Smith's less, shall we say, 'politic' revelations. Just like polygamy, which came to Smith in a revelation and was written down as scripture, but is now in disrepute; so too is the 'bleaching' of the Lamanites espoused by Smith now conveniently ignored by Mormon leaders."

"I understand why Angelina DeAquila left the church. She was Korean, right? A person of dark skin."

"Race and Mormonism is more complex than black and white. Even though God disfavors the Lamanites, they've always been considered destined for salvation. The Asian equation isn't even mentioned in *The Book of Mormon*. Asian men have always been allowed to attain the priesthood, whereas blacks, up until the 1980s, were considered impure due to their skin color. Though blacks could join the church, African ancestry of any quantum was a bar to a man reaching priesthood status. But we're off topic. The focus of DeAquila's research was locating fundamentalist groups that both *believe* in polygamy as gospel *and* promote intermarriage between white males and Native American girls to 'bleach' Lamanite bloodlines. I think she zeroed in on these facets of Mormonism after she came across newspaper articles detailing the murders of the Indian girls."

"She ever find a link to a Mormon sect or sects that met her parameters?"

"Not that Byrnes and I could uncover. But DeAquila did find something else of interest."

Slater tilted her head. Her mind was racing from too much caffeine and no breakfast. She'd left Rick asleep at home with his morning oatmeal cooked and ready on the stove, his toast buttered and sitting on a plate on the kitchen table. But in her haste to meet with Augie Olsen, Slater had skipped breakfast.

Stupid move. Should have at least grabbed a bagel on the way in.

"How's that?" Slater asked, her mind returning to focus.

Olsen printed copies of the articles mentioning All Saints and Judge Elizabeth Prichard from a laser printer connected by a wireless link to DeAquila's computer.

"Here."

Olsen handed the articles to his boss. Slater scanned the headlines and briefly reviewed the clippings. The sheriff gulped air before continuing.

"You think Judge Prichard knows something about the murder of Angelina DeAquila?"

"Not necessarily. But Byrnes and me think she may know something about sending Indian girls to a treatment facility that seems to have a way of losing them. One girl sent to All Faiths turned up with her throat slit. That's not good publicity for a place that has such a highly regarded reputation. It's curious, at least to me and Byrnes, how only one judge in the Sixth Judicial District, one out of sixteen, uses All Saints for juvenile dispositions. DeAquila got the stats from Arrowhead Regional Corrections. It's clear that Prichard has some sort of weird predilection for sending kids to All Faiths. What makes it more interesting is that an Indian girl Prichard just sent there vanished from the place a week ago."

"Christ."

Augie Olsen leaned back in his chair and turned off the dead woman's computer.

"Amen."

NINETEEN

The presence of a uniformed female officer and a Native American male the size of a refrigerator knocking on the glass door to Judge Prichard's chambers on the fourth floor of the St. Louis County Courthouse in Duluth gave the judge pause as she walked hurriedly towards the ruckus. It wasn't the fact that an officer and a big Indian were there: Judge Prichard entertained any number of city cops, county deputies, and agents from the Minnesota Bureau of Criminal Apprehension over the course of an ordinary work day, all of whom knocked patiently on the glass door for admittance to her private space. The criminal justice system is, first and foremost, about paperwork. Search warrants. Arrest warrants. Complaints. All signed by law enforcement, by a prosecutor, and, ultimately, by a judge. So the fact that Slater and Whitefeather were paying the judge a visit wasn't what threw Prichard for a loop: It was the fact that she'd never met either officer before.

FBI special agents don't routinely navigate state courts; their purview is federal, where they interact with United States District Court Judges and U.S. Magistrate Judges. It's a rare occasion when an FBI agent crosses the threshold of the St. Louis County Courthouse other than to pay his or her personal real estate taxes in the assessor's office on the second floor. And because Debra Slater's jurisdiction was over one hundred miles away from Duluth in Cook County, which has its own courthouse and its own long-serving resident judge, the only times Slater found herself in the Duluth courthouse were when her department was short-staffed, there were prisoners in custody who needed to be run through the first appearance process, and Judge Sandvik wasn't available in Grand Marais or Two Harbors, the two courthouses he serves on Lake Superior's North Shore. In those instances, Deb Slater would appear in Duluth, prisoners in tow, for hearings.

Judge Prichard paused as she reached for the brass doorknob and studied the woman and the big man before opening the door to her inner sanctuary.

"May I help you?

• • •

Slater had called Whitefeather after concluding her meeting with Augie Olsen. There was more—much more information—contained in

95

Angelina DeAquila's computer files regarding the mysterious murders of the two Indian girls; one in Montana and one in Minnesota, which Olsen and Byrnes had retrieved. There was, as an example of additional material, a file folder assembled by the dead reporter regarding a young male social worker from Idaho, a man sent to investigate the disappearance of the dead Nez Perce girl in central Montana where she'd last been seen. The young man vanished as well, his whereabouts unknown, further complicating the picture. But these matters, Slater surmised, where distant, ancillary details to her investigation into the murder of Angelina DeAquila. Slater was charged with solving a heinous crime in her own backyard; the brutal death of a young woman who had, at least as revealed in her research, an incredible fascination with Judge Elizabeth Prichard.

Buried deep in DeAquila's handwritten notes regarding Mormon fundamentalism, the reporter had recorded the following annotation:

Elizabeth June Prichard → *Lizzy Joy Kittridge?*

The entry was penned in beautifully anachronistic script on the same sheet of paper as other equally cryptic notes, all of which appeared to be directed towards establishing a link between Judge Prichard and a person by the name of Lizzy Kittridge. But there was little detail connecting the judge with the other woman; only tenuous, preliminary suppositions once held by a dead reporter, who was no longer able to fill Slater in on the gaps left by scanty notes.

"Dig up anything that can help us in our investigation, Herb?"

Slater and Whitefeather had arranged, a few days before their meeting with Judge Prichard, to meet for lunch at the funky Greenwich Village-inspired Amazing Grace Bakery in Duluth's trendy Canal Park district. The eatery, founded by folk music fan Chip Stewart, is a haven for college kids, artsy types, and would-be fiction writers and poets. The bakery boasts the best homemade soup and bread in Duluth.

Slater wasn't a fan of folk music, the usual fare at the bakery when live music was being offered; her tastes were more in line with Kenny Chesney and Clint Black. She liked Tim McGraw's voice despite his liberal political bent and his support of Obama against her man, McCain, but couldn't bring herself to admit she was a McGraw fan out loud. It puzzled her that, despite proclaiming himself to "be a good old country blue-dog", McGraw supported an über-liberal guy from inner city Chicago against a war hero.

Still, the fact that the sandstone brick walls of Amazing Grace contained publicity stills of some of the best-loved and unfailingly liberal folk singers in America wasn't a major drawback to Slater enjoying a sandwich in the place. The liberal vibe of the Grace was but a minor distraction to the sheriff as she and Herb Whitefeather discussed the DeAquila case.

The big man had nodded.

"I got some inside stuff that might help you," Whitefeather replied quietly.

The basement bakery and café had been filled with college kids scantily dressed against winter; businessmen and women in expensive overcoats; and tourists bundled up in down parkas and fiber-filled ski jackets; all of whom stood in line at the lunch counter waiting to order. The sheriff and the FBI agent were seated at a small round table on the venue's tiny performing stage beneath windows looking up to Lake Avenue, the street leading to Duluth's main tourist draw, the Aerial Lift Bridge. Weak winter light filtered in through dirty glass. The officers occupied mismatched wooden side chairs; chairs obviously liberated from rummage sales. Steam escaped bowls of lentil soup resting on the distressed oak tabletop in front of Slater and Whitefeather; the bowls as divergent in pattern and style as the chairs.

Slater gulped from a glass bottle of orange juice. Whitefeather stopped talking and took a swig of cold Lake Superior water from a plastic drinking glass before continuing his revelation.

"You told me that DeAquila somehow connected the two dead Indian girls to the Mormons. Am I right?"

Slater sipped soup from her spoon, nodded, and cleared her throat.

"Fundamentalists. Don't confuse the guys that DeAquila was researching with mainstream Mormons. Much as I have my doubts about Joseph Smith finding golden plates in upstate New York, the mainstream Mormon Church, so far as I can tell, doesn't have anything to do with what DeAquila was looking into. At least not in recent history."

"Understood. Anyway, she also tapped into the fact that a social worker from Idaho, Elwood Jones, turned up missing. He was sent by his supervisor to find the young Nez Perce girl, Bethany Comes to Ride, in Montana."

"I remember those names from newspaper articles and DeAquila's notes."

Whitefeather balanced his soupspoon gently in his big right hand as he looked straight at the sheriff.

"We found the body. The M.O's the same."

"Herb, tell me something I don't know. The articles DeAquila pulled make that clear. The young Comes to Ride girl's murder mirrors DeAquila's."

"Not the Indian girl's murder, Deb. The social worker's. A group of Boy Scouts hiking in Lewis and Clark National Forest in Montana found what was left of Elwood Jones. Body had been picked apart by ravens and coyotes. But there was enough left to I.D. the body and determine cause of death."

"His throat was slit?"

"That's right. But here's the weird thing," Whitefeather's voice grew nearly inaudible. "The neck wound was likely post-mortem. He'd been shot, point blank. Through and through. To the forehead."

"Execution style."

"You got it."

"He was left naked?"

"Naked as a jay bird."

Slater paused and inhaled another spoonful of beans and broth. "Dirt in his mouth?"

"Yup. And no signs of rape. Seems sex is the last thing on this boy's mind," Whitefeather added.

Slater smiled.

"You sexist, you."

The Indian's oval face beamed, exposing straight yellow teeth.

"You said it before, Deb. How many female serial killers can you name?"

"That lady hooker in Florida. The one Charlize Theron played in 'Monster'."

"Aileen Wuornos. And that's about it, isn't it?"

"I hear ya."

Slater considered the information.

"You think there's a link between the dead Nez Perce girl, the dead social worker, a dead Indian girl in Minneapolis, my dead reporter, and some whacked out group of fundamentalist Mormons?"

Whitefeather's features had tightened.

"It's a lead pipe cinch that's the case with respect to the murders you listed. There are some minor discrepancies; Bethany Comes to Ride and Jones weren't zip tied; their mouths weren't duct taped. Jones was shot. DeAquila was tied to a tree. Julia Kingbird's murder scene, on the other hand, was nearly identical to DeAquila's, right down to the blue cord and being tied to a tree at Fort Snelling. But, yah, we think there's enough here to say a pattern exits. There's more we've uncovered, but I can't give you the details."

Slater's eyes flashed annoyance.

"Whatdayamean, 'can't give me the details?' I'm up to my elbows in a sadistic murder of a young mother and wife, with virtually no physical evidence, and you say you 'can't give me the details?' Horseshit. That's what I say, Agent Whitefeather. Horseshit."

The agent had pushed his empty bowl away from his place at the table and stared hard at the female officer.

"Look, Deb. We go back a long ways. I'm close to collecting my last paycheck from the Bureau. I didn't say I wouldn't help you out. I said I can't give you all the details, at least, not right now. You get whatever physical evidence you have to me and I'll send it on to Quantico. Maybe they can turn up something. Right now, the Bureau has zilch in the way of physical evidence from the murder scenes," the big man said, his voice cracking, emotion getting the better of him.

"Somethin' wrong?"

Whitefeather had nodded, paused, and then continued.

"Julia Kingbird was my cousin's daughter."

A tear found its way down the agent's craggy cheek as his soft brown eyes turned downcast. There was a long silence as Deb Slater closed her eyes and focused her thoughts on Whitefeather's disclosure.

"The little Lakota girl...at Fort Snelling..." the sheriff said haltingly, "was related to you?"

The FBI man had nodded slightly.

"I am so sorry."

Herb Whitefeather nodded again, the tears flowing more freely as he tilted his head and fixed his gaze upon the massive white pine beams supporting the upper floors of the DeWitt Seitz Building housing the bakery. Moments passed in silence as the officers composed themselves.

"I'll retrieve whatever we sent to the BCA and get it to you, to send to Quantico," Slater had said after what seemed to be a suitable interlude.

"You do that. I want this bastard as bad as you do," Whitefeather had replied softly, pain and hatred, disparate emotions linked inexorably to the murder of his dead relative, clear in his voice.

"I've got to hit the road. J.V. basketball game tonight in Silver Bay."

The big man had offered a weak smile.

"She any good?"

Slater deposited her dishes on a cart near the bakery's exit and turned around, her face open and smiling.

"You know it, Agent Whitefeather. Just like her momma."

The FBI agent had waved a big paw in the air as the sheriff pulled her black leather gloves tight over her hands.

"Send me whatever you have. I think I'll sit here awhile before I make my way back to the shop," the agent said.

Slater had nodded, walked to the glass entrance door, opened it, and stepped out into December's clutching cold.

●●●

"We'd like a moment of your time, Judge Prichard," Deb Slater said.

Slater and Whitefeather entered the brightly illumined corridor and stood in front of the diminutive woman. Judge Prichard was dressed in an expensive gray business suit, the skirt's hem cut slightly above her knees, and a white silk blouse.

"Is this about a search warrant?"

Herb Whitefeather extended his right hand, the fingers slightly twisted by arthritis, towards the judge.

"I don't believe we've ever met. Seems odd, given how long I've been around. Herb Whitefeather, FBI."

Prichard returned the agent's handshake with vigor. Slater extended her hand as well.

"Deb Slater, Cook County Sheriff."

The judge shook the sheriff's hand.

"We're here to talk to you about a murder up in Cook County," Slater said discretely.

"Let's go into my chambers."

The judge led the visitors down the corridor into her office. When the agent and the sheriff were in the room, the judge shut the door with precision.

"Nice digs," Whitefeather said, noting the original watercolors and other artwork displayed in the judge's chambers. "Fireplace work?" he asked, tilting his head towards an ornate oak mantle and surround that filled one wall of the room.

"Gas. Hasn't been used since the Great Depression."

"Too bad. A fire would be nice on a day like today."

The judge smiled and invited the officers to sit. Slater and Whitefeather claimed identical ox blood leather chairs in front of the judge's curiously empty oak desk. The judge noted the sheriff's scrutiny of her workspace.

"The place is pretty well tidied up. I'm taking my sons on a ski vacation to Lutsen next week," the judge offered.

Slater smiled. Lutsen Ski Area, the closest thing to mountain skiing in the Midwest, was located in Cook County, her jurisdiction.

"Snow's good right now."

"That's right. You should know, sheriff. Lutsen's on your beat, so to speak."

Slater nodded.

Whitefeather brought his eyes to bear on the judge.

"Judge, you heard about the murder up on the Gunflint?"

"The newspaper reporter?"

100

"That's the one. I'm assisting Sheriff Slater on the matter. Seems there are some similarities to cases the Bureau is working on outside this jurisdiction."

"A serial killer?"

Whitefeather demurred.

"Wouldn't go that far, at least, not yet. And whatever we discuss here, can we keep it on the Q.T.? Don't want rumors spreading that might jeopardize our investigation."

"Agreed. But how does this have anything to do with me?"

"We're interested," Slater interposed, her tone deferential, "in anything you can tell us about All Faiths Recovery Center."

There was a sudden stiffness to the judge's posture, an alertness that had not been present during the preliminary niceties. Slater observed the change and made a mental note to talk to Herb about it after the interview was over.

"Why?" the judge said defensively.

"There may be a connection between the reporter's murder and that facility. Something to do with Mormon fundamentalism," Whitefeather said, maintaining an even tone despite the judge's changed persona.

Elizabeth Prichard leaned back in her chair.

"I send young men and women to that facility. You may or may not know this: I am a woman of deep faith. Christian, yes. Evangelical to be sure. But I believe that faith-based treatment is essential. All Faiths is the only such facility in the state for juveniles."

Slater leaned forward, her arms covered by khaki shirtsleeves, and rested her forearms on the edge of the judge's desk.

"You seem to send more kids there than other judges in the district."

Prichard nodded.

"Indeed I do. Is there a problem with that?"

Slater chose her words carefully.

"Not unless there's some ulterior motive behind your using All Faiths over, say AJC or Northwoods or Woodland Hills or Thistledew," the sheriff said, listing alternatives to the All Faiths program.

Crimson erupted across the judge's face.

"This discussion is over. I'll not have you waltz into my chambers and cast false aspersions regarding my judgment in juvenile delinquency cases. Please see yourselves out."

Slater and Whitefeather stood in unison. The sheriff leaned heavily on her hands, which remained positioned on the glass top of the desk, and addressed the judge.

"I meant no disrespect, ma'am. But you have to admit, it's damn curious how young girls sent to All Faiths, particularly young Indian girls, keep turning up missing. One of them, a girl from North Dakota, is in fact, dead. And Elsie Johnson is now on the run. Doesn't that strike you as at all odd, Your Honor? Especially when no one else is sending kids to All Faiths?"

"Get out! Get out now!" Judge Elizabeth Prichard said with disdain. "Or I will call security and have the two of you thrown out."

Whitefeather grasped Slater's left elbow and gently turned the sheriff towards the door.

"Yes ma'am. We're on our way out," Whitefeather said in a conciliatory voice. "No need to get excited, just asking a few questions. We're at loggerheads is all and thought you might be able to shed some light on All Faiths and anything that might link the place to what Angelina DeAquila was looking into. She was heavily involved in researching Mormon fundamentalism and the 'bleaching' of Indians through intermarriage. Some sort of weird Mormon doctrine involving my people—the Lamanites—as the fallen. We thought you might have something to say about that."

Whitefeather nudged Slater towards the door.

"Well, I don't," the judge replied tersely. "Good day to you, sir. I can't say it was a pleasure," the judge added, her eyes narrowing in scorn.

Debra Slater broke free of Whitefeather's grasp and turned to face the judge. Prichard remained seated behind her desk. An ocean of oak separated the women.

"Just one more question."

"Deb," Whitefeather implored, "we gotta go."

"What's that, Sheriff Slater?"

Debra Slater claimed her full height as she addressed the judge.

"Does the name 'Lizzy Kittridge' mean anything to you?"

A burst of scarlet flashed over Judge Prichard's pale patrician face.

"No."

"She's lying," Slater whispered as the big Indian escorted the sheriff towards the door. "I can feel it in my bones."

Whitefeather maintained silence as he turned the doorknob, opened the glass door, and urged his companion into the common hallway.

"Did you hear what I said?"

The FBI agent stopped, cast a long glance back towards the judge through the slowly closing glass door, and nodded.

"I did. It's not every day you catch a District Court Judge lying through her teeth."

TWENTY

"She was wholly compliant on the trip from Minneapolis," The Tyler advised Obadiah Nielsen as he stood behind Elsie Johnson in the doorway of Keystone Ranch's main entrance. "Her escort from Minneapolis reports that Miss Johnson was every bit the lady on the plane ride here."

The Tyler touched the Native American girl's flowing black Ojibwe hair with his left index finger. The gesture appeared to denote genuine fondness for the girl. Elsie Johnson's short, compact frame, her hips beginning to widen with maturity, her legs turning to adult muscle, her significant bust beginning to fight gravity, was dressed in ripped Levis, a loose fitting pullover from the Gap, and a winter jacket, the sort of outfit any fifteen-year-old girl would shop for at any mall in America. She could have been someone's daughter just off the plane for Christmas, visiting relatives, dressed as she was and standing in the cavernous foyer of Keystone Ranch, her Native eyes wide with amazement and curiosity at the events unfolding before her.

"Pleased to meet you, Miss Johnson," The Prophet said in a kindly voice, reaching down from great height with his right hand, the fingers long and slender, his eyes fixed on the Indian girl's pretty round face.

The girl hesitated before reaching out with her right hand. Their fingers intertwined. Their palms met; the contrast between her brown skin and the old man's opaque flesh was obvious to anyone paying attention to detail. The gesture, at least on the part of the girl, was tentative, in keeping with her age and the strangeness of the circumstances in which she found herself.

"I hope you will find life here in Laman's River to your liking. God has blessed us by bringing you here, to join our family," The Prophet observed, retreating from the girl as he sensed her apprehension at physical closeness. "Your future sister wives will show you around the place. Evelyn, would you be so kind as to take Miss Johnson's bag and show her to her room?"

Four women stood behind the elderly man as Elsie Johnson cast a clandestine glance towards the man who was destined to become her husband. A feeling of dread overcame her as she realized that the picture Edward Big Hands had painted for her of life in The Colony had been constructed out of lies and half-truths. The counselor's rendition of the physical prowess and attributes, indeed, the handsomeness of The Prophet, had been grossly exaggerated.

He's a fucking old man, the young runaway thought as her eyes sought to escape the aging face of the man she was supposed to marry. *What the hell did I do?*

But, being a child of significant prowess when it came to deception, Elsie Johnson feigned acquiesce as Evelyn Nielsen, Jennifer Nielsen, Amanda Nielsen, and Joyce Nielsen surrounded her and began chattering in excited voices, welcoming her to the family. It was an overwhelming experience for the young girl, a circumstance that sorely tested her resolve.

There's got to be a way for me to get the hell outta here. I'll play along, comply, do whatever it is he wants me to do. Hell, I've done worse than whatever the old man can come up with. Far worse. Close my eyes. Think of that pretty little cedar grove back home. That's the way to deal with such things. Comply, Elsie. Pretend. Make believe it's not happening to you again. And when their backs are turned, I'm off, like a deer through the forest. They can't watch me 24-7. No way. At the first opportunity, I am outta this fucking nightmare.

"Welcome to our family," Evelyn Nielsen said, her sharp eyes scrutinizing the girl, looking for physical flaws, defects, anything to give her a leg up on the newest member of the clan, as she carried the girl's small suitcase through the maze of winding hallways towards the sleeping quarters of the rambling log mansion. "I hope you find God's grace, his abiding love, in the decision you have made to live The Principle."

"Yes ma'am," the girl replied, adjusting the straps of the Rage Against the Machine backpack she was carrying as they walked.

The older woman turned, stopped, and carefully placed the girl's suitcase on the pine floor. The other wives, who were following behind Evelyn and Elsie, stopped in unison.

"It's Evelyn. Or Sister. No need for formalities around here. My position as first wife gives me some marginal authority over chores and job duties but not much more than that," the woman said quietly, her voice coated with sugary reassurance. "Other than mundane, day-to-day tasks of life, we make our decisions democratically. We meet, discuss, and take an informal vote on anything of substance. And unless overruled by The Prophet, those votes, along with the Holy Spirit, are what guide our lives here at Laman's River. So, please, call me 'Evelyn'. 'Ma'am' makes me feel old."

The Indian girl kept her eyes fixed on the wide pine boards of the floor and nodded.

She's not such a bitch. I can buy myself some time by getting along with her and the others.

105

Evelyn reclaimed the suitcase. The group resumed walking and entered a curving hallway containing the bedrooms of the wives, four of which were presently occupied. An additional bedroom had been made ready for Elsie Johnson. Three bedrooms remained empty, reserved for additional wives, wives The Prophet had foreseen when the Angel Nephi came to him on the mountain.

Eight women shall ye wed and proclaim to be thine.

Everyone at Laman's River knew the prophecy; knew that the number eight was considered by The Prophet to be his lucky number.

"Here's your room," Evelyn Nielsen announced as they stopped in front of a closed door.

"Awesome hallway."

The first wife smiled.

"There's much practical about the design. Being that we are all married to The Prophet and to each other as well, we share this wing of the house. The children, whom we've sent to a friend's, but whom you'll meet tomorrow, have their own wing. It's best to keep adults and children separate, except for nursing babies, don't you think?"

The Indian girl nodded again with feigned commitment.

"You seem a bit awestruck by it all. I'm sure you'll come to understand the correctness, the divinity in our way of life, once you've been here a while. Come, let's have a look at your room."

Evelyn opened the solid six-panel pine door leading to the girl's private quarters and flicked a light switch just inside the room. The party crossed the threshold. The bedroom was not small, not large; the log walls were quaintly decorated in a pioneer theme befitting the wife of a Mormon prophet. The space was dominated by a four-post bed, the mattress and box spring covered by white sheets, a thick down-filled white comforter, and four large down pillows in matching white pillow cases arranged across the head of the bed's queen-sized frame. White Irish lace draped from maple rails above the sleeping platform provided privacy. The room also contained a matching five-drawer dresser; a vanity with a large round mirror (the edges of the glass beveled in antique style); a chair in front of the vanity; and a small table situated between the doorway and the bed. A table lamp and a mechanical alarm clock sat atop the table. The clock ticked loudly as the girl took in the details of the room. A white fan with tulip-shaped lights graced the ceiling, the illuminated bulbs casting an old fashioned glow across the space.

"I've never had my own room before," the Indian girl said reverently.

The other sister wives stood behind Evelyn as the girl leaped onto the soft mattress and box spring of the bed. There was clear joy and wonder in the girl's appreciation of her new home.

106

"I'm glad you like it," Jennifer, the second of the wives said through pouty lips. She was clearly the most beautiful of The Prophet's women; even in her thirties, her figure was near perfect in its hourglass shape; her hazel eyes remained untouched by age; and her blond hair, trussed up in a bun and golden beneath the room's light, set off her beauty in ways the other wives couldn't match. She had only given birth once; Mary, a small, sickly and cantankerous child, who was now three. Another child was expected, but not for eight months. There were no obvious signs of pregnancy about Jennifer as she spoke. "All of us have used that bed as our first one at The Colony. It's yours so long as you are the newest of The Prophet's wives. Enjoy it for it is indeed a marvelous bed, a bed which will cause you to experience wonderful dreams and visions of paradise."

The girl stopped bounding and cast a troubled look towards her future sister wives.

"Oh, no, no, child," Amanda Promise, only a few years older than Emily Johnson, and the third wife, said with compassion, her Southern dialect clear as she moved closer and placed a soft hand on the girl's shoulder. "Sister don't mean it like that. You don't sleep with The Prophet in this here bed. This bed's only for you. When and if you're called to be with him, and you know what I mean, don't you?"

The Indian girl nodded.

"Good. You know the birds and the bees. Saves us all from havin' to embarrass ourselves with our ignorance in trying to teach you some," Amanda continued. "Anyway, this here bed is for you and you alone, least wise 'til another sister wife comes to stay with us. If you're called to be with The Prophet, you go to his room. That's where you come together in bliss, not in this here little room, but in the big old master bedroom at the center of the hallway."

Elsie Johnson's eyes grew wide at the prospect of being under the skeletal body of the tall old man she had just met. It was all she could do to refrain from screaming out, "No, goddamn it, no. I will not fuck that dirty old man, a man old enough to be my grandfather. I will not. Not now, not tomorrow, not ever." But she did not cry out. She held her tongue.

Let them think I'm in agreement with The Principle. I conned Big Hands into helping me run from All Faiths: I'll work the lie a little bit longer, until I figure a way outta this place. Still, the room is better than any I've ever stayed in. The bed's soft and warm; a place to rest while I figure it out. Could be worse. I could be back in Minnesota listening to bullshit. What they never got at All Saints is that I can stop smoking weed anytime I want to. Cold turkey. Just like that. It's a matter of wanting to, is all. Now I want to. Now I want to get the hell off that shit and get a life: A life with a job, a house, a man, and babies. Not this life. But somethin' close to it. I can do this thing. I surely can.

"Come on girls, let's leave Elsie to change into more appropriate clothes," Evelyn said quietly. "Joyce, will you stay behind and help her get dressed? Undergarments and stockings are in the drawers of the dresser. Dresses are in the closet on hangers. Elsie, that's one thing we do insist on around here, conformity in our way of dress and manner. Compliance with The Principle includes dressing alike. Not identical, but in tasteful, traditional clothing so as not to provoke lust in the eyes and hearts of other men. Lust, even if never acted upon, is sin. We must not tempt other men. Joyce, will you make sure Elsie gets dressed for dinner? I'll go see about that wonderful stew you put on."

Joyce Billington Nielsen nodded. The two other women followed Evelyn into the curving hallway. The door closed behind them.

"No need to be afraid, little Sister," Joyce said in a reassuring voice.

The Indian girl noted that Joyce was the least attractive of the four wives of Obadiah Nielsen. Joyce Nielsen was extremely plain, with square shoulders, square hips, and a sturdy pedestrian build. Her bust was small and her hair was bright red. Specks of innocuous gray gave her small eyes a distant, distracted look. But there was a manner about The Prophet's fourth wife that seemed strong. Elsie Johnson found herself at peace in the woman's presence.

"Here, you'll need to take off your underclothes and slip into this," Joyce said quietly, opening a dresser drawer and pulling out a clean two-piece undergarment. "Usually, Saints are only required to wear it *after* the sealing ceremony, as witness to purity and marital sanctification. The Prophet had a revelation that all who live here at Laman's River and who are over the age of twelve should wear temple undergarments even *before* having gone through a sealing ordinance."

The girl took off her jacket, placed it on the bed, and began raising her blouse.

"Not now, silly. I'll give you some privacy to change. Do it after I leave," Joyce said with a smile as she walked to an open closet to retrieve a dress. "Let's see. I'd say yellow would look good on you, don't you agree. Not the color for the season but, since the weather outside is so dismal, might as well aspire for spring, don't you think?" The woman removed a long yellow dress in a traditional floral print, cut to just above the ankles, and held it up for the girl to see. "This one suits you."

A frown crossed the Native girl's face.

"That's fucking ugly."

108

"'Plain'. That's 'plain' ugly. If you want to get yourself in the doghouse around here with The Prophet, go about the place cursing. I found out the hard way. Ten raps across my bottom with an aspen cane the first week I was here. It took me three sessions with the cane before I caught on," Joyce said, handing the dress to the girl. "I'm a bit of a slow learner."

"Plain. That dress is plain ugly."

"Good, that's the spirit. Now there're a couple of other things I think you should know. Have a seat, right here beside me on the edge of the bed. Just hang that dress from the rail above you."

Elsie Johnson attached the wooden hanger holding the dress to the maple rail supporting the canopy and sat next to the older woman on the soft down comforter.

"Are you a virgin?"

The question, asked out of the blue, startled the girl.

"It's a question that will be asked by the First Counselor when he meets with you, and likely by The Prophet sooner than later. So I'll ask it first. Are you a virgin?"

Elsie shook her head.

"Good. Because that means you're going to be safe from a night with The Prophet for six months, minimum. I say good because, as young as you are, I sense you'll need some extra time to accustom yourself to the man, the place, and what is required of you. Six months is a long time. Things change. Circumstances," the woman said cryptically, "might alter. Just do what is asked of you and you'll survive. Understand?"

The girl's eyes widened. The internal bravado she'd used to bolster her confidence diminished as the older woman spoke.

"Yes, ma'am."

"Joyce. My name is Joyce. Though I'm old enough to be your momma, I'm not. I'm your sister now, Elsie. Call me 'Joyce'."

The Indian girl smiled, exposing straight white teeth.

"Joyce."

The older woman stared at the ceiling, composing her thoughts.

"Here's the thing," Joyce said quietly. "You been baptized?"

"As a baby. Don't remember it."

"I'd expect so. Doesn't count. Now that you're here, amongst us Saints, you'll need to be re-baptized. Full immersion at the meetinghouse. And then confirmed. The First Counselor will go over all that with you when you meet with him. You'll like him. Engaging man. Nothing to be afraid of. Once you're confirmed, being sealed to The Prophet will take at least six months. Until the sealing ceremony, which will also be done in the meetinghouse because the temple isn't built yet, The Prophet will not touch you. You know what I mean by that, don't you?"

The girl twisted the ends of her hair with her fingers before nodding.

"Good. So don't be worrying yourself silly over when he'll be calling for you to join him in the master bedroom. It will be a while, Sister Elsie, a good long while. He might stop in and pay you a visit here, in your room. He has a habit of, shall we say, 'inspecting the goods'? He'll want to see you out of your undergarment. He won't touch you. Don't be ashamed or alarmed. And God forbid, do not, I repeat, do not deny him this little pleasure. You understand? You do that, well, there's no telling what might happen. Just keep your chin up and do what he asks if and when he stops by."

The girl's head dropped in despair. Her chin quivered. Her eyes were shut tight against circumstance.

"There, there, little one," Joyce said with compassion, enveloping Elsie in her arms. "You trust me, don't you?"

Elsie Johnson opened her brown eyes but her gaze remained fixed on the wood floor. Tears formed and slowly slid off her round cheeks onto the pine planking. In a gesture that appeared to take great effort, the girl managed to acknowledge Joyce's question with a slight nod.

"Good. I will always, and I mean always, be honest with you. You can ask me anything and I will tell you what I honestly know or believe. Okay? Now, I'll leave you to slip out of those old clothes and into something more appropriate. You'll see, Sister. It isn't so bad living here with us. We'll have some fun, you and me. And I'll keep an eye on you, little one. I surely will."

Elsie Johnson drew her cheeks into her mouth, wiped her eyes with the right sleeve of her blouse, and watched the older woman close the door as she left the small bedroom.

The girl stood to undress. She was nervous, but anxiously hopeful, as she readied herself for her first meal with The Prophet at Keystone Ranch in the valley of Laman's River.

TWENTY-ONE

Christmas came and went and Sheriff Debra Slater was relegated to that most assured of all pastimes for cops; waiting. Waiting on the BCA. Waiting on the FBI lab at Quantico. Waiting to catch a break in her investigation into the murder of Angelina DeAquila. There were connections, to be sure, however slight, between the woman's tragic death on the shore of Seagull Lake, a Duluth judge, and radical Mormonism; connections that involved claimed ancient rivalries and the need to cleanse the blood of an entire race. These things, Deb Slater understood. But there was no clear-cut evidentiary link between Angelina DeAquila's death and a suspect. There was only a specter, a phantasm, of a medium height, athletically built, blond, polite, courteous, and totally enigmatic thirty-something white guy, who was likely DeAquila's killer. No name. No address. A dead end. Slater's unease increased with the passing of each day.

He's still out there, at large. He may kill again. Someone's daughter; hell, my daughter might be his next target. We need to find this guy.

The situation at home ramped up Deb Slater's angst. Rick's decline affected her concentration, her ability to think things through logically and clearly.

Her husband's mitochondrial disease was manifesting itself in serious fashion. An increase in symptoms relegated the once strapping teacher to his bed. Deb was forced to retain fulltime nursing care for Rick's daily needs, which had, in a period of ninety days, increased to the point where the sheriff and her daughter were unable to completely care for the man.

Rick's lack of vigor, caused by the buildup of lactic acid in his body's cells, had become complicated by mitochondrial encephalopathy, or MELAS syndrome, a condition that manifested in Rick Slater as dementia. Though the episodes frightened Annie to the point of hysteria and caused Deb to experience doubts that her husband would make it to Christmas, Rick's memory lapses waxed and waned without predictability. The only thing Deb Slater knew for certain, after a long and difficult meeting with Rick and Rick's neurologist in Duluth, was that the damage to the cells throughout Rick's body was lurching towards critical mass. Rick was unlikely to make it to summer. The saving grace was that Rick's mental acuity returned in time for the

111

family to take a well-deserved trip to Glenwood, Minnesota, to be with Rick's dad on Christmas Eve, and Deb's family on Christmas Day.

Debra Slater did not divulge her husband's most recent prognosis to her father-in-law, her parents, their respective siblings, other relatives, or even to Annie. She simply told family that "he's doing as well as can be expected." Despite this small deception, it was, all things considered, a wondrous Christmas in their hometown spent amongst raucous family amidst a deluge of snow that covered Glenwood in a monstrously beautiful Yuletide blizzard reminiscent of a Norman Rockwell illustration.

Immediately upon returning to the family home on the shores of Devil's Track Lake, Rick's dementia re-appeared. It was as if his brain understood the importance of remaining lucid in front of loved ones while visiting, but lost that focus once he was home. The battle Rick's mind waged, in keeping his symptoms at bay long enough to enjoy four days of peace and calm amongst family, had been taxing.

Rick Slater was, as he slept in his bed across the hall from the bedroom the couple once shared, slowly evaporating. The weight of Rick's decline, carried silently by the sheriff as she tried to unwind the twists and turns of a murder case, was nearly unbearable.

"Whatdoya have for me, Herb?" Slater asked, the receiver of her office telephone held tight to her right ear.

Debra Slater was in her office on a Saturday. As sheriff, she usually worked four twelve-hour day shifts; working weekend or evening shifts only when her deputies were out sick, or when vacations demanded that she fill a void. But the situation at home, with Rick thrashing and moaning, the dementia medication being administered by a series of LPNs (who were now his constant companions) through an IV calming the worst of the onslaught but not nearly strong enough nor miraculous enough to cure the disintegration inside Rick's brain, was untenable. Annie was off at a friend's house up the Gunflint, spending the weekend ice fishing and driving her girlfriend's sled dog team, unaware of the timetable of her father's illness but fully cognizant, without having been expressly told, that he was dying. Deb couldn't muster the gumption to stay and hold Rick's hand as he tried to fight the good fight. She'd said as many prayers as she could stomach, asked God and Jesus to relieve her husband of his malady thousands of times over the course of his illness. She was "plumb prayed out" as she confessed to Abby Smith, her best friend and the owner of a small café in Grand Marais. There was little more Deb could offer Rick, either spiritually or as his lifelong companion. So she drove into work on her day off, hoping to ease her own mind, knowing how selfish her actions might appear to someone outside her family.

112

"Quantico is good," Herb Whitefeather boasted, downplaying his surprise at receiving a telephone call from Slater in his office on a Saturday where he too was puzzling over DeAquila's murder.

"How's that?"

"Damn good, Sheriff Slater, damn good."

Deb wiped her left sleeve across her eyes. Tears had formed as she'd considered her callousness in leaving Rick at home with a nurse on a blustery January day.

Goddamn it, she thought *I'm the man's wife. 'For better or for worse', right? That's what we both promised. He'd be there for me, if it was me curled up in a ball, my muscles fighting for oxygen, my brain in turmoil. And here I am, at work, trying to forget what he's going through. Damn, I am one selfish broad.*

"Out with it, Herb. What the hell did you find?"

Whitefeather chuckled.

"I didn't find nothin' beyond love and peace in the arms of a beautiful Finnish American woman."

Slater's annoyance exploded.

"Cut the bullshit. I'm not in the mood."

The FBI man breathed deep and considered his friend's diatribe.

Somethin's eaten' her. Rick must've taken a bad turn. Cut the lady some slack.

"Sorry sheriff. We are, after all, trying to solve a homicide."

"Apology accepted," Slater said in a conciliatory tone. "What do you know?"

"We've got a name."

"The fingerprints on the Coke can?"

"Yep. That and the physical description you folks pulled out of the witnesses up on the Gunflint. I think we've found our man. At least, found his real identity. There were a lot of twists and turns in that respect. He's got friends in high places, at least when it comes to changing names and getting the necessary documents to back up new identities."

"How so?"

"He's changed his name legally at least three times in the past eight years. But Quantico was able to track him."

Slater dried the last of her tears with a tissue from a box on her desk.

"And?"

"Our man was a reconnaissance sniper with the Marine Corps. Served two tours during the First Gulf War."

"Reconnaissance sniper?"

"Think Navy Seal with attitude. Tough sons of bitches."

"Got it."

"He was born and baptized into the Mormon faith. Name's Jason Orth. Or at least it was. Looks like the name he's been using most recently is 'Allan Black'. As Jason Orth, our friend had some scrapes with the law, did some time in a Utah prison after coming back from the war. He skipped out on his parole quite awhile ago and the State of Utah hasn't been able to catch up with him."

"Do we know where he is?"

"We think so."

There was a pause as Slater considered how to prompt the agent to divulge what she was waiting on bated breath to hear.

"You gonna tell me where you think he is, or you gonna make me guess?"

Whitefeather let loose with a light laugh on the other end of the phone.

"I won't do that to you, Deb. Montana. He's somewhere in Montana. Don't know exactly where, but we've tracked him through TSA surveillance tapes taken in the Minneapolis airport. He's seen boarding flights from the Cities to central Montana, Great Falls to be specific, on a couple of different occasions over the past year."

"Timing?"

"His flights coincide with DeAquila's murder and the murder of my cousin's girl at Fort Snelling."

Slater considered the enormity of the disclosure.

"You talked with anyone on the ground?"

"We don't have agents close to where we think he might be..." Whitefeather said, his answer trailing off in hesitancy, "...at least, not in any *official* capacity."

The sheriff grew puzzled.

"What's that supposed to mean?"

The Indian sighed.

"I'm not at liberty to give you details, at least, not yet. But I can tell you there is an ongoing investigation into a fundamentalist Mormon sect, one that shares the views and beliefs about polygamy and the 'bleaching' of the Indians that DeAquila was onto. It's located in central Montana..."

Slater sensed there was some further detail, some additional point, Whitefeather wanted to disclose.

"There's more, isn't there?"

The FBI agent took a deep breath, considered his friendship with the sheriff, their past, their bond, and did the unthinkable. He divulged a detail he'd sworn to his supervisor he wouldn't reveal.

"There is. We have someone on the inside."

"Shit."

"'Shit' is right. I was sworn to secrecy; directed not to tell you we had someone undercover. But you need to know that the Bureau is thigh deep in this crap, Deb. Thigh deep."

Slater pondered the revelation before asking her next question.

"And this Mr. Black, or Mr. Orth, he's there, in this sect, living with these people?"

"Don't know that yet. It's not my case so I'm only getting this second or third hand, trading a lot of favors to get what I've gotten for you to this point."

Slater's mouth turned into an involuntary smile.

"I appreciate that, Herb. You know I do."

"Whatever. I figure I'm close to pulling the plug on this gig and running off to Cocoa Beach with Susan. You're in a pickle with a dead girl whose throat was slit, left naked in the middle of the woods, and you don't have diddly. So I think: *Why not do the righteous thing? Why not tell Deb? Who's gonna know?* Am I right?"

"You're right, Agent Whitefeather. My lips are sealed. This conversation never happened."

"One last thing."

Slater waited for a final piece of information from the big man.

"Ya?"

"You're instincts on Judge Prichard were right on. There's something fishy, some tie between her and All Faiths and this group of Mormons in central Montana. Can't tell what exactly, but we've got some agents working on the connection. May have something to do with the staff at All Faiths; or probation; or the social workers assigned to delinquency cases coming in front of Judge Prichard involving young Indian girls. Don't know as yet. If and when I get the down and dirty, I'll give you a heads up."

Slater nodded. The gesture caused the phone receiver to slide from her ear. She resituated the receiver before responding.

"I appreciate that."

There was another pause in the conversation.

"How's Rick doing? I heard he had kind of a rough spell before Christmas."

Slater composed herself before answering.

"Horseshit, Herb. He's doing horseshit. Dementia. One day he knows Annie and me, is oriented to place and time. The next day, we're strangers and its 1980. He rallied enough for us to go to Glenwood over Christmas. But now, he's worse than ever."

"Sorry to hear it. I'll say a Lakota prayer for him. For you and Annie too."

Slater wanted to tell the big man not to waste his breath, to explain the futility of her countless petitions cast into the sky over the past three years. But she held her powder.

"Thanks. I know Rick would appreciate that."

"I'll keep you posted, let you know what I can find about this 'Allan Black' character. But you keep what I've told you to yourself."

"Got it. Silence is golden."

"That's pretty cliché, Sheriff Slater. I was hoping for something more original out of you."

"Sorry Herb. I'm tired and my husband is at home, pumped full of drugs and hanging on by a thread. I should be there. I guess I'm at the office to avoid confronting reality."

Whitefeather sensed frustration in the sheriff's voice.

"Hang in there, kid. I'll pray for a miracle."

Deb Slater nodded slightly. Her thoughts focused on an old image of Rick and her, young and strong, before Annie was born, running the Skyline Parkway in Duluth, where they had lived for much of their marriage. It was a glorious September day. Autumn was prescient in the cool air, in the newly crisp leaves of the birches lining the asphalt parkway. The sky above the harbor, where the St. Louis River meets Lake Superior, was cloudless. Thousands of migratory hawks, eagles, owls, kestrels, and falcons soared high above the city, their wings set to take advantage of prevailing winds. This is what Deb Slater remembered from that run: She remembered that, despite Rick being a five minute a mile man, having run varsity cross-country for Concordia College in Moorhead, despite having placed sixth nationally in the NCAA Division III cross-country finals, which elevated him to All-American status, Rick did not run ahead of her as she struggled to maintain an eight-minute mile pace on their five-mile run. He ran with her, stride for painful stride, as she tried to get back in shape after one of the three miscarriages she experienced before carrying Annie to term.

Why am I here? I should be home, goddamn it. I should be home with the man I love.

"Thanks for the update, Herb. I gotta go."

"See you soon, sheriff. And remember, I'm praying for you and your family."

"I appreciate that. I really do."

The phone fell silent. Deb Slater hung up the receiver, stood up from her desk, and pulled a parka over casual clothes. After turning out the lights, Slater fastened buttons on her parka as she walked towards the door and remembered: *Shit. I forgot to warm up the Tahoe!*

TWENTY-TWO

"Mr. Orth, we have a problem," Obadiah Nielsen said as he met with The Tyler and the First and Second Counselors in his office in the Laman's River meetinghouse.

"Black," the ex-Marine replied confidently.

"How's that?"

"My name is 'Allan Black'. The man you knew as Jason Orth no longer exists."

The Prophet smiled.

"Sorry about that, 'Mr. Black'. I'd forgotten that little detail."

The two counselors chuckled as they followed the dialogue.

"I'm partial to 'The Tyler' myself," Ezra Pratt mused, repeating the pejorative title he'd anointed Jason Orth with at the outset of Orth's affiliation with The Colony.

Given that the title, "The Tyler", references an obscure Masonic office, and given that many non-Mormon historians and theologians believe that the temple ceremonies created by Joseph Smith were in fact lifted whole cloth by Smith from rituals he experienced as a Mason, Pratt's word choice was at best, curious, and at worst, bordered on slander. Despite Pratt's irreverence, no one in the room acknowledged his comment.

"Seems that both the FBI and the Minneapolis police, along with a sheriff from northern Minnesota, have been asking questions about Mr. Big Hands," Nielsen continued.

The Tyler smiled quixotically. He sat in a thickly cushioned chair across a massive teak desk from The Prophet. The two counselors flanked him. All the men save The Tyler wore expensive, hand tailored navy blue business suits, white dress shirts, and matching red ties. The Tyler was dressed for weather in an insulated white camouflage Carhartt jacket, matching insulated bibs, and Sorels. His white wool stocking hat and leather choppers, the wool liners wet from snow, rested on the edge of the desk in front of him.

The Tyler had driven to Laman's River from his cabin on Sixteen Mile Creek through a raging blizzard. Six inches of new powder had challenged his Dakota as The Tyler slugged his way out of the hollow, through the town of White Sulfur Springs, and into the Smith River Valley, the 4x4 plowing through drifts as high as a man's waist to make the meeting. Melting snow dripped from the assassin's shortly cropped blond hair and pooled on the cement floor of the office beneath his chair as the room's heat melted the storm's residue.

"That's unfortunate."

"We think," Second Counselor Micah Albrecht interposed, turning his dour face towards The Tyler as he spoke, "that you need to do something about the situation."

Albrecht's smallish head was framed by untamed black hair curling wildly across his forehead. His beady gray eyes were fixed sharply on the shorter, more athletic man.

The Tyler returned the Second Counselor's scrutiny before responding.

"What would you have me do?"

Ezra Pratt leaned back in his chair and snickered.

"You're the *expert*, Mr. Black. You tell us."

The Tyler's eyebrows rose as he thought through the request.

"Big Hands is an extremely loyal and valuable asset."

The Prophet nodded.

"We know that. But the FBI is investigating his role regarding the dead Indian girl at Fort Snelling and Ms. Johnson's disappearance. They're suspicious of his connection to these, shall we say, 'circumstances'. The authorities don't see the two situations as mere coincidence."

Before The Tyler could respond, Ezra Pratt spoke up.

"And it's more than just random questions being asked. The authorities are inquiring into Big Hands' finances. Word is, they've acquired a search warrant for his bank records. They'll find deposits that Mr. Big Hands won't be able to explain. Those deposits," the fat man added, "could lead back to us."

The Tyler scratched his nose with his left index finger. The heat felt good on his cold and tired body. He had shoveled snow at his cabin in the creek bottom for the better part of two hours to get the Dakota out of its garage and onto the driveway. For the moment, The Tyler was happy to be indoors, though he was annoyed that his companions weren't more astute in handling their affairs.

"You didn't just write Big Hands a check out of The Colony's bank account, did you Ezra?"

Pratt's bald palette turned red at the insinuation.

"Of course not! The money for each girl he delivered was sent in the form of a cashier's check, each drawn on a different business account from one of our many commercial concerns," the fat man blurted out with indignation.

The Tyler nodded.

"Good. Then they can't trace the money back to The Colony. At least, not quickly. That will buy us some time."

Albrecht looked at Pratt with quizzical eyes.

"How much per girl?" the Second Counselor asked, obviously having been left out of the loop.

"Fifteen thousand. Big Hands wanted twenty. We offered ten. We settled on fifteen."

Albrecht nodded in apparent satisfaction.

The Prophet folded his fingers together and stared at The Tyler.

"There's more than just Mr. Big Hands to worry about," Nielsen said softly.

The Tyler straightened in his chair.

"How's that?"

"The judge in Duluth."

The Tyler smiled enigmatically.

"Old news. Already dealt with."

•••

Though it was against his cautious nature to make too many appearances in a given place, The Tyler, upon learning that Judge Prichard was becoming a "person of interest" to both the FBI and the Cook County Sheriff's Office, had flown once more to Minneapolis, rented a car, and driven north to Duluth. Inquiries had been made by the FBI at the Montana Highway Patrol; inquiries The Tyler was made aware of by a fundamentalist Mormon working on the patrol staff as a secretary. The woman, formerly of Pinesdale and loyal to The Principle (though not a member of The Colony), had known The Tyler before his affiliation with The Prophet, and had once harbored the hope of marrying the returning Gulf War veteran. Their affair had been brief. The Tyler's path had been altered through the permanent celibacy accomplished by the bitter wound of his own hand. But they had stayed in touch through email and occasional chance meetings over the years. She had visited his cabin during a summer trip to The Colony. When the packet of documents she had assembled with clandestine precision arrived at his post office box, indicating the extent of the FBI's interest in Laman's River, Judge Prichard's name was featured prominently in the reports. The Tyler knew immediately he needed to revisit the good judge to ensure her silence.

The Tyler's first visit with Judge Prichard had taken place before the disappearance of Elsie Johnson. With Bethany Comes to Ride's unfortunate demise, The Prophet had been at his wits' end in terms of locating a young Native American girl to be his plural wife. His subsequent marriage to Joyce Billington did not fulfill prophecy; Joyce, as fine a fourth wife as she proved to be, was not Indian. Marrying her

119

did not set the example that God had ordained Obadiah Nielsen to set. It was Nielsen, who knew the details of Elizabeth Prichard's history, and who understood that a large number of Native Americans live in northeastern Minnesota, who had suggested that The Tyler pay a visit to the Duluth judge.

"Can I help you?"

It hadn't been difficult for The Tyler to find the judge alone on a sunny summer day in Duluth. She had left the courthouse at noon, walking several blocks to The Exchange, a local eatery on First Street known for its luncheon specials. The judge had been seated in the far corner of the small dining room across from a row of coolers displaying sandwiches, drinks, and assorted fresh baked cookies, bars, and pies. The luncheonette boasted simple steel tables and matching steel chairs spaced appropriately throughout the large room. Businessmen and women, county employees, and the occasional wayward tourist sat at tables, contentedly slurping soup, digging into the daily special, or munching fresh sandwiches. The judge had been alone when The Tyler approached her. He recognized her immediately from her photograph on the State of Minnesota's judicial website, though she was much more striking in person.

He had stood over the woman as she tried to read the front page of the *Duluth News Tribune*, her fruit plate empty, her napkin and fork resting on the bare ceramic surface of the dishware. A matching cup half full of coffee diluted with milk sat next to the judge's empty plate.

Judge Prichard's pale blue, nearly turquoise eyes, their color every bit as rare as when she was to be married to her uncle through an arranged marriage, stared quizzically at the stocky, well-built, handsome man who approached her table.

"Judge Prichard?"

She had nodded slowly, watching the man carefully to determine his intent. His manner was calm and deliberate; not at all agitated or excited.

"Yes?"

"Allan Black. You don't know me, but I know you."

The remark had puzzled the judge.

"How so?"

"Are you finished eating?"

She had nodded.

"Can we go for a walk? It's such a beautiful day. And what I have to say, I really do need to say privately."

His request had caused alarm to flash over the woman's elegant face.

"Judge, if I wanted to harm you, I would have done so already," the stranger whispered. "I simply want to talk, that's all. In the open, as we take an innocuous walk down a main street."

"I don't think so."

"It would be in your best interest to cooperate, Lizzy."

The use of her former name, the name she had been known by when she lived in Utah amongst her polygamist family, had shocked the judge.

"What did you call me?"

"Lizzy. As in Lizzy Joy Kittridge."

Judge Prichard balked at the reference.

"I'm sorry. You must have me confused with someone else."

The Tyler's mouth had curled.

"I don't think so, Lizzy. If you like, I can show you the birth records, temple records, and name change documents friends in Salt Lake City have accumulated on my behalf. Is that really necessary?"

The judge's eyes had narrowed and her temper had risen.

"Just what is this all about?" she asked, her words leaking out in a hiss.

"Let's take a walk."

The judge had hesitated.

"I do have a copy of the documents I referenced," The Tyler said quietly, his face absent emotion. "Perhaps the *Duluth News Tribune* would be interested in reading about your past affiliation with the Kittridge clan of the fundamentalist Mormons," he said in the same, steady voice as he tapped the banner of the newspaper sitting on the table in front of the judge. "Specifically, the paper, and the Republican Party that worked so hard to get you elected, might be interested in receiving information regarding your having been betrothed to your own uncle as a Mormon plural wife."

The judge had stood up.

"But the wedding never took place…"

The Tyler had smiled. He'd trapped the judge. She'd inadvertently confirmed that she was indeed Lizzy Joy Kittridge.

"I know that. But the documents I have, are, shall we say, extremely embarrassing," The Tyler continued, relishing the advantage he had obtained over the startled woman. "Come, let's walk together. It's a beautiful summer day."

The jurist had blown air through her thin lips, red lipstick stark and noticeable against her finely chiseled cheekbones and striking eyes.

"Alright. But only for a moment or two. I'm due back in court in twenty minutes."

They had left The Exchange, their faces immediately warmed by the noontime sun standing still and orange above industrial haze.

"It's a bit smoggy today," The Tyler had noted. "Happen often here?"

The judge wagged her head in the negative as she walked beside the man, her high heels clicking lightly against the brick sidewalk. The bricks were a reminder of a former mayor's vision of making Duluth a tourist destination by invoking Victorian charm. Instead, the bricks are a nuisance. They're unable to withstand the abuse visited upon them by snow blowers, plows, shovels, and ice scrapers used to clear the decorative walkways of snow and ice during Duluth's brutal winters.

The judge and her companion encountered chipped bricks as they negotiated the sidewalk. The pitfalls made the sidewalk dangerously uneven.

"Watch your step."

The Tyler's cautionary remark had caught the judge by surprise.

Who is this man and what does he want? One minute he's threatening to reveal my past, for what reason, I will likely soon find out. In the next instant, he's expressing concern for my welfare. Who is this man?

The Tyler had stopped and motioned for the judge to sit on an adjacent transit bench. She complied. The Tyler joined her. He shaded his eyes from the sun with his left hand as he looked downhill, towards the Lift Bridge, which had been raised to allow a saltie, an ocean going freighter, to leave port.

"I'm simply a messenger. Think of me as an emissary."

The judge had stared hard at the man's face, intent upon memorizing his features so that, when she went to the police—*if* she went to the police—she could provide a description.

"Who sent you? Was it someone from my family, from Tooele County?"

The Tyler had focused his significant blue eyes on the woman.

"No. Beyond that, I can't say who sent me. But no, this has nothing to do with the Kittridge family."

Judge Prichard's eyes had narrowed again.

"You don't believe me, do you? That's fine. You don't need to know who sent me, or why. You only need to know that the information I have about your past is available for distribution."

The judge had released a massive sigh.

"You're aware, I'm sure," the man continued softly, "that your family, after all these many years, still seeks to learn your whereabouts. They've maintained a large monetary reward for that information. An industrious Saint," The Tyler said thoughtfully, "could profit handsomely from knowing who you are and where you live."

Judge Prichard's shoulders sagged.

"There, there, Lizzy. No need to get upset or downhearted. You've done an excellent job of keeping yourself off the radar for what, over thirty years? It was only happenstance that my prophet stumbled onto a news article about you on the Internet. It was our good fortune, perhaps your bad luck, that he recognized your picture. He said he knew in an instant your true identity. He remembered you from 'the old days' when the two of you crossed paths as young Saints." The Tyler said quietly. "He says you haven't changed a bit, that you're still as stunning as you were back when he was a gangly, shy college student and you were a perky middle schooler on the path to womanhood. And you know what? He's right!"

"Look, Lizzy," The Tyler had continued, "if I wanted to make good on your family's generous offer, they would've already found you," the man said consolingly. "If you cooperate, your secret remains safe with me."

"Go on."

"Here's the thing. Many young Indian girls are struggling to make it out of poverty, to escape drugs, familial strife, and circumstances that don't bode well for them. My prophet is empowered by God to change those circumstances."

"How so?"

The Tyler had smiled.

"It's very simple, really. Once or twice a year, we want you to refer a particular young woman to the All Faiths Recovery Center in Minneapolis out of delinquency court. We will then ensure that the young women in question are well provided for once they leave that facility."

Elizabeth Prichard had swallowed hard.

"You're talking about me violating my oath. You're asking me to ignore whatever recommendations probation or social services might make regarding a child—these are children, for heaven's sake—and send them to a facility that may or may not be in the child's best interest? That's what you're asking?"

The Tyler had nodded.

"I can't do that. What if someone questions my motives? What if someone finds out? I'm afraid this is not something I can be a party to."

The Tyler smiled.

"Sure you can, Lizzy. Think of it this way: You are, as I understand it, an evangelical Christian. Forgetting your apostasy for the moment, and the fact that you are no longer able to reach Celestial paradise because you've forsaken the one true and abiding faith, you believe in Jesus the Christ and in the salvation of souls, don't you?"

"I do."

"Well, then. It's simple. As an evangelical, what better place to make your mark than with children? And what better place, as an evangelical, to send a wayward Indian girl in need of salvation, than All Faiths?"

The judge had fixed a stare on the red bricks of the sidewalk.

"Only once or twice a year?"

"That's all we're asking."

"And if I do this, how can I be assured that the girls won't end up in some worse situation, like child pornography or enslaved as prostitutes?"

"Do I really seem like the sort of person who would be involved in sin?"

Judge Prichard had considered the man with her eyes but did not answer.

"So, we have an understanding?"

Elizabeth Prichard looked into the white palms of her hands. Moments passed before she whispered her weak response.

"We do."

That had been the beginning of Judge Prichard's unsavory connection to Laman's River. In all, three Native American girls had been referred to All Faiths by the judge for treatment during the time "the arrangement" had been in place.

Two of the Native girls, Natalie Banes and Elsie Johnson, walked away from All Saints and became residents of the Smith River Valley. Cyan Blue Water, a sixteen-year-old Ojibwe girl, evinced reluctance to The Principle while at All Faiths, completed treatment, and went back to her home on the Fond du Lac Reservation near Duluth.

Natalie Banes joined Laman's River and became Natalie Towers. She eventually left The Colony with her husband, Evan Towers, a nephew of The Prophet. The couple vanished under cover of darkness after Evan determined that polygamy wasn't for him, that he was devoted to his new wife and had no interest in plural marriage. This left Elsie Johnson as the only Native girl placed at Laman's River by the judge.

No direct communication had been made between anyone from The Colony and Judge Prichard since The Tyler's meeting with the judge in Duluth until word reached The Tyler that law enforcement was interested in Judge Prichard's curious reliance on All Faiths as a treatment center for Indian girls.

This information compelled The Tyler to revisit the judge and reinforce their "understanding" shortly before Christmas, shortly after Elsie Johnson had arrived in Montana.

The Tyler had flown from Great Falls to Las Vegas, and then from Las Vegas to Duluth on Allegiant Air the week before Christmas. In doing so, he bypassed airport security in the Twin Cities. Beyond this simple deviation, he took pains to change his appearance: The Tyler shaved his blond hair to the scalp and dyed the remaining stubble jet black. He changed his eye color as well; covering the natural blue of his irises with contact lenses tinted deep brown. The man that law enforcement was looking for had once again disappeared.

Locating the judge, after The Tyler arrived in downtown Duluth in a rented Toyota RAV 4, had proven problematic. Personal inquiries made at the courthouse would have raised alarm that a stranger, someone no one had ever seen in the courthouse before, was seeking an audience with Judge Prichard. Instead, The Tyler had called the judge's law clerk, an effervescent young twenty-something former U of M hockey cheerleader, two years out of law school and still looking for a job with one of the insurance defense firms in Duluth, and claimed that he was "an old friend in town for depositions" who wanted to catch lunch with the judge. The ruse worked. Kristin Adams, Judge Prichard's law clerk, candidly told The Tyler that, "Judge Prichard is out of town, at Lutsen, with her sons Adam and Blake, enjoying a three-day ski vacation." Without prompting, Ms. Adams suggested that The Tyler "might want to call Caribou Highlands where the judge is staying" to get in touch with her.

Armed with Minnesota DMV information (acquired through his contact with the Montana Highway Patrol), The Tyler had headed north on US Highway 61 towards the Sawtooths: maple studded hills that rise from Lake Superior to a height of over two thousand feet above sea level at Eagle Mountain, Minnesota's highest point, a peak located in close proximity to Lutsen Ski Resort.

Should've guessed that she'd drive a Volvo XC 90. Nice ride. All wheel drive. Classic lines, just like the judge.

The Tyler had sat behind the driver's wheel of his rented Toyota, staking out the parking lot of the Caribou Highlands townhomes; a ski in, ski out development located next to Bridge Run at Lutsen. The Tyler read while he waited, his concentration riveted on a new Kent Krueger mystery he'd picked up at Fitger's Bookstore—a bookstore located in the hotel complex in which he'd spent the night— the same hotel where Angelina DeAquila had spent her last night on Earth.

125

Odd coincidence, that: I didn't take a room there deliberately. It was the first hotel that came to mind when I thought of Duluth. Must be God's way of reminding me of the seriousness of what I'm doing, of my true purpose: Protect The Principle; protect The Prophet; these are my simple tasks.

He had watched the judge, her natural curves accented by a one-piece blaze orange and navy blue ski suit, walk from the townhome complex to her car. He had placed the novel on the front passenger seat of the Toyota and observed the judge open the rear hatch of the Volvo, remove a ski helmet, close the hatch, and retrace her steps to the townhome. It was nine in the morning; near the time The Tyler expected the judge and her two sons to step into their skis and hit the slopes.

As The Tyler had waited for Judge Prichard and her sons to appear, he'd mused about the family's history. The boys' long absent father, Jonas Prichard, had abdicated his responsibilities when his wife rediscovered religion. Unable to deal with his wife's sanctimonious attitude, and with more than a passing interest in younger women, Jonas moved to San Diego where he established a software company and made millions; scant little of which came back to his boys as child support. Adding insult to injury, Mr. Prichard married a woman not much older than his oldest son, Adam, who was nineteen and a student at the University of Minnesota-Duluth. Wife number two was expecting the couple's first child in a month. These bits and pieces of personal information were not difficult for The Tyler to uncover, given that he'd read the entirety of the couple's divorce file at the Duluth Courthouse.

All knowledge is power but detailed knowledge gives one an advantage.

The Tyler was a thorough man. Given that he no longer felt any urge for companionship with the opposite sex, The Tyler had plenty of time to spend researching the folks who became his accomplices, his assets, and his targets. He knew everything possible about Judge Elizabeth Prichard. He'd read her LinkedIn page. He'd read her Facebook page. He'd read her profile on the 6th Judicial District website and in the online version of *Martindale Hubbell,* the national directory of attorneys and judges. In many ways, as The Tyler had watched the judge and her sons carry their skis and poles to Bridge Run, he knew more about Elizabeth Prichard than the judge's closest friends.

He had rented a snowboard, boots, and helmet from Lutsen's rental shop that morning. He bought a cheap pair of goggles to protect his eyes against the sun reflecting off snow. He had boarded a few times at Big Sky outside of Bozeman. Once or twice at Showdown near

White Sulfur Springs. Once at Big Mountain near Whitefish. Those trips had taken place before he severed his own manhood, back when he was still attracted to and desperate for female attention. Despite the interval of time and his castration, The Tyler was confident that his natural athleticism would bring him competence on the hill.

Given that it was midweek, the slopes had been sparsely populated. It hadn't been difficult to keep track of a woman wearing a bright orange ski suit and her two sons as they traversed the main hill to reach the Moose Mountain gondola. The Tyler kept his distance, following the mother and her sons, watching and waiting for opportunity

At one o'clock in the afternoon, the family stopped at the Moose Mountain chalet for lunch. The Tyler stopped as well.

"Great day on the hill," The Tyler had said to Blake, the twelve-year-old son of Judge Elizabeth Prichard as the two of them straddled urinals in the men's room of the chalet.

"Uh huh."

"Where you from?"

"Duluth."

"Unusual for someone your age to be skiing instead of boarding," The Tyler said, noting the boy's ski boots.

"My mom. She says it's better for when we go out to Vermont. Too steep for boards."

The kid had zipped up his snow pants and clambered across the tile floor in molded plastic boots. He stopped at a sink, jabbed nonchalantly at a soap dispenser, lathered his hands, and placed them under the faucet, activating cold water.

Unbeknownst to Blake Prichard as his attention was riveted on the thin stream of water, The Tyler had reached into his jacket pocket, pulled out a cellular phone, and snapped a photograph of the boy standing in front of the sink.

"You take care now," The Tyler said, zipping up his own bibs. "For what's it worth, I think your mom's wrong about boards. I grew up in the mountains. I've always used a board. Never had a lick of trouble."

The kid slid his goggles over his eyes, pulled on his ski gloves, and smiled.

"Colorado?"

"Nope. But close by. Anyway, have a good one."

The kid waved a gloved hand in the air and walked out of the restroom.

Later in the day, The Tyler found an excuse to sit next to Judge Prichard at a table in Lutsen's crowded main lodge. The Tyler's face had been concealed by the helmet, a neck gaiter, and his goggles as he approached the judge. From the woman's disinterest, it was obvious that Elizabeth Prichard had no idea who he was. Even when The Tyler removed the helmet and goggles, there had been no hint of recognition from the jurist.

The judge's sons were still skiing; taking a last run of the day as Elizabeth Prichard sipped a glass of Chablis. Her feet were propped up on a nearby chair, her boots and socks removed, the white skin of her toes wrinkled after being confined in damp wool.

"Hi," The Tyler said quietly.

The woman hadn't evinced familiarity as she glanced up from considering her wine.

"Hello."

"Judge Prichard, isn't it?"

The woman smiled cautiously.

Who's this? Some disgruntled litigant? Some upset lawyer?

The Tyler detected suspicion and smiled broadly.

"Don't you remember me?"

He stared straight into the judge's eyes.

But he had blond hair! He had blue eyes!

"What the...?"

"Now, now. Let's not cause alarm. I just came to see you, to have a little cautionary chat. Is that alright with you?"

The Tyler had maintained a calm demeanor. The judge's face had reflected upset.

"What are you doing here?" she whispered

He removed the cell phone from his jacket pocket and pressed an icon, displaying the photograph he'd taken of Blake in the restroom. The Tyler turned the screen of the phone so that the judge could see the profile of her youngest son.

"Oh my God! Where did you get that?"

The Tyler smiled brightly.

"Don't be alarmed. I took it at noon. In the Moose Mountain chalet. In the restroom. We had a nice little visit, your son and I. He's a hale hearted fellow, young Blake is."

The judge's face fell.

"What do you want?"

The Tyler closed the application on the phone and returned it to his jacket pocket.

"Your continued cooperation."

The judge's eyes widened.

"If anything happens to my son..."

128

"Elizabeth...May I call you that? Or do you prefer judge? Or Lizzy?"

She had stared hard at the man's face.

"I think we'll stick with judge. Well, judge, it's like this. Certain authorities, federal and state, will likely be around to ask questions about Elsie Johnson and perhaps, Natalie Banes and Cyan Blue Water. And I'd urge you to keep your own counsel, if you wish to see you son graduate from the sixth grade at the prestigious Marshall School. To simply say that your referrals of those young girls had everything to do with your belief in faith as a healing power for delinquent children, and nothing to do with Mr. Edward Big Hands. Understand?"

The judge had nodded.

"Good. Now you and your boys have a nice vacation. I'm counting on your discretion, here, judge. I *can* count on your discretion, can't I?"

The woman's body shuddered. She blinked her eyes as a gesture of acquiescence. The Tyler placed the helmet on his dyed hair, pulled the goggles down to conceal his eyes, and leaned in close to talk the judge.

"I pray," he had whispered into her ear, "that you do the right thing here. Or little Blake won't see his thirteenth birthday."

•••

"What do you mean, 'the situation has been dealt with'?" Ezra Pratt asked in the warm confines of the meetinghouse office.

"We don't need to know the details, of that I'm certain," The Prophet said sternly. "If the man says it's been dealt with, it's been dealt with."

Second Counselor Micah Albrecht twisted his mouth into a frown.

"We're not talking about..."

The Tyler shook his head.

"No one has been hurt. Or made to disappear. Nothing that drastic," the assassin said. "At least, not yet."

"Jesus," Pratt exploded, "Obadiah, when he talks like that, I swear we're all going to hell. I don't want to be connected with someone else being hurt, much less murdered, to protect our beliefs."

The Tyler leaned back in his chair and looked smugly at the fat bald man.

"Everything I've done has been authorized by the three of you. For The Principle. For The Colony. For the greater good. Now you want to re-invent history, to hide behind ignorance? I don't think so, Counselor Pratt. What's done is done. Live with it. I do."

129

No one spoke for an inordinate period of time.

"He's right," The Prophet finally said. "Everything he's done has been approved by us. He is our instrument. He doesn't act unless we direct him to. We can't blame Mr. Black for doing what we've asked; for accomplishing what needs to be accomplished to protect our homes, our families, our faith."

The meeting was over: The Tyler rose from his chair. He cast a last look at the other men before opening a metal service door and exiting the room.

"I don't trust that man," Ezra Pratt finally said, words sliding between teeth.

The Prophet stood up, walked over to a window, and watched The Tyler enter his Dakota, start the pickup truck, and drive away.

"You'd better, Mr. Pratt," Obadiah Nielsen said quietly. "That man is all that stands between you and a lethal injection.

TWENTY-THREE

Elsie Johnson had lived in The Colony for a week when she became friends with Brooke Talmadge, the young Crow girl sealed to Charles Talmadge as his second wife. The girls were close in age and, in meeting the other families of Laman's River as she went about learning her duties as a member of The Prophet's household, Elsie gravitated to the six other Lamanite women living in the community. She became particularly fond of Brooke. As they worked in the communal storehouse, inventorying and stockpiling canned goods, boxes of macaroni and cheese, and other non-perishable foods hoarded pursuant The Prophet's decree to stave off starvation during catastrophes, the two girls, who were naturally quiet and introspective around the white members of The Colony (including members of their own families), opened up and talked freely about their lives, experiences, and expectations for the future.

"It's not so bad," Brooke Talmadge said as the girls shuffled over the frozen ruts demarcating Zion's Way, the main road running through Laman's River.

"What do you mean?" Elsie Johnson replied, pulling a wool great coat, a hand-me-down from one of her future sister wives, tight against ripping wind.

"Being here, being part of a family, being one of many."

The girls turned off the main road onto a narrow lane. For a time, neither girl spoke.

Elsie Johnson knew what the Crow girl meant; being one of many *wives*. Though she understood the import of the words, Elsie didn't necessarily agree with the other girl. She cast a furtive glance, fixing her deep brown eyes on Brooke's protruding belly as they walked.

I don't understand how Brooke can think being knocked up by a guy old enough to be her grandfather is all that. Maybe it's my lack of faith that's the barrier to me seeing the beauty in her situation. Or maybe, this whole damn thing is just one big fucking hoax.

"Don't you ever wonder," Elsie finally whispered, cautious that any hint of skepticism might be used against her, "what it was that Joseph Smith, Brigham Young, and all those other *men* were actually after when they had their *revelations*?"

Brooke's eyes, equally haunting and deeply brown as her companion's, glanced up and down the roadway to ensure no one was

131

watching them or listening to their conversation. Brooke's foot hit a deep rut. She stumbled. Elsie reached out and steadied the Crow girl, preventing a fall.

"Thanks," Brooke said appreciatively. "I almost took a header." The pair resumed their walk. "I don't really know, Elsie. I guess, in my religion classes at the meetinghouse, I've listened more than I've asked questions. There's much about Mormonism that seems too convenient for truth. The whole bit about Prophet Smith finding the plates, translating them from 'Reformed Egyptian' using stones and special glasses, could be the greatest story of the 19th century or," Brooke said thoughtfully, "the century's biggest practical joke."

Elsie nodded as they walked, their work boots darkened from oil they'd rubbed into leather to protect against winter; their identical denim jumpers, one piece and cut to conceal the lines of their bodies, showing beneath the hems of their coats.

"I lean towards the practical joke theory myself," Elsie said through a giggle.

Brooke Talmadge's eyebrows knit together.

"I used to think that. But the more I'm around these people; the more I think they're on to something. There's so much strength of family here at Laman's River, so much belief in each other. Sure, the women have a rougher time of it; working the fields, taking care of the babies; only a very few working in town, outside The Colony. And the expectation that we all get pregnant and carry tons of little ones. That's a burden," she said, patting her bulging tummy. "But with all those souls flying around in eternity in need of a place to stay here on Earth, a place to experience mortality before they can be set free and find eternal peace, I've come to accept my role here. I love my husband, love my sister wife. If another woman joins us, I say 'great', that lessens my load in the home and I'll welcome her. I gave up dwelling on the inconsistencies in the story handed down to us; I accept what's good and decent about this place and let it go at that."

Elsie Johnson stopped in front of Keystone Ranch's covered front porch. The road they were on snaked its way from house to house, from ranch to ranch, down the Smith River Valley. Icicles hung from the eaves of the log home, the residue of water that had formed when snow, piled on the home's red metal roof, heated in the mid-day sun, melted, and then refroze during the night. Brooke stood next to Elsie and admired the ranch home.

"Did you ever dream," Brooke Talmadge asked, "growing up on the Rez, that one day you'd live in a place like this?"

Elsie took in the expansive log building, the neatly sculpted snow-covered hayfields and pastures of the ranch, the soaring yellow and gray cliffs rising across the river.

132

"No way."

Brooke patted her friend on the shoulder with a gloved hand.

"Remember that. Think about that as you consider your place here. There's plenty of time to come to an understanding with God as to what your role is. Trust in the Lord. Jesus will bring you an answer. You're part of a family here. Not just The Prophet's family but the family of all believers. Do we have doubts about the prophecies and revelations handed down to us? Sure we do," the girl said in a hushed tone. "And I expect Charles and Obadiah and all the others that came before them had doubts, from time to time, as well. But that don't change the fact that we're living something here, something good and decent and holy. Something that we couldn't have, in our wildest dreams, ever imagined being part of. Ain't that worth a bit of doubt, a few moments of spiritual discomfort? I think it is."

Elsie Johnson studied the frozen ground as she envisioned being taken to bed by an ancient man she could never love. Brooke Talmadge sensed the issue that was troubling the girl and smiled lightly.

"For chrissake," the Crow girl whispered, "it's not like you've never been with a guy before. I'm guessing there was a time or two, in the past, when things happened on a couch or in the back seat of a car that you didn't want to happen. Am I right?"

Elsie didn't respond. She simply looked up, her eyes full of anxiety as she steadied her gaze on the other girl.

"I know, I know. The Prophet, he ain't much to look at. And it's sort of creepy the way his spine is all bent and his eyebrows are growing together. But remember this: He's God's chosen minister. Whether God speaks to him directly, or The Prophet's simply inspired by God to act, I'll leave to you to figure out. But Obadiah Nielsen is a man of God; that much I've come to believe. And you," Brooke Talmadge said as she stepped back from the log mansion and began her retreat, "could do a hell of a lot worse in life than marrying a millionaire."

Elsie Johnson stood mutely, her arms wrapped around her torso, her confidence broken, her resolve in tatters, as she watched the Crow girl walk away.

TWENTY-FOUR

Agent Herb Whitefeather, Sheriff Deb Slater, and Investigator Sam Byrnes converged on All Faiths Recovery Center armed with information regarding Edward Big Hands' bank accounts.

"Thirty thousand dollars in 'consulting fees', Whitefeather had revealed to Slater via a long distance telephone call a few days before the officers visited the counselor at the treatment center. "Paid by businesses connected to a fundamentalist Mormon sect, 'Laman's River', a small group of less than one hundred practicing polygamists living in central Montana, near White Sulfur Springs on the Smith River."

Slater's mouth had broadened into a grin as she listened to Whitefeather's revelation.

"I've been reading *The Book of Mormon*, Herb," she had confided. "Learning about the River Laman. Supposedly flows into the Gulf of Arabia near where Lehi and his family left Israel for the New World. The river's named for Lehi's son, Laman, the son the Indians are named after. He's supposedly the bad seed, the unbeliever, whose line, the Lamanites, eventually wipes out the good guys, the decedents of the good son, Nephi, the Nephites."

"Impressive, Sheriff Slater. Will you be converting any time soon?"

"Not hardly. I'm a bit skeptical in the faith department right about now."

Deb Slater's veiled reference to her husband's situation had been obvious.

Who wouldn't question their faith in the face of something like what she and Rick are dealing with? Poor guy. Always liked him. Good teacher. And a great father to Annie. Should have had more, those two. Should have had a passel of little ones for Deb to take care of. Didn't work out that way. I can understand why she might've lost her faith.

Whitefeather had remained on message.

"Forensic folks at Minneapolis P.D. worked with our financial experts. The two companies that paid the 'consulting fees' appear, at first glance, to be unrelated. But digging deeper into Montana tax records and secretary of state information, we've come to the conclusion that the companies are both dummies; fronts to launder money collected by the polygamists at Laman's River from their investments, outside interests, and donations. Big Hands was getting paid handsomely for something. I think I know what it was."

Slater had listened intently, refraining from drinking the cup of hot herbal tea steeping on her desk.

Too late in the day for coffee. I'd be up all night. I'm not a 'tree hugger' or a 'tea bagger' she'd thought, considering derisive terms used by northern Minnesotans to describe tourists, fishermen, and wilderness enthusiasts from the Twin Cities, *but I'll give this stuff a try. Need something without caffeine to keep away the chill.*

"Interesting. So, when do we visit Mr. Big Hands?"

"Tomorrow morning. Pick me up at the federal building in Duluth around eight. You can drive," Whitefeather had added. "I know how much you like to be in charge."

Slater had laughed.

"I'll be there. You just be ready to go when I walk through the door."

Byrnes met the FBI agent and the sheriff on the street in front of All Faiths the next morning in Minneapolis, Hennepin County search warrant in hand.

"Herb Whitefeather, FBI."

The female detective took Whitefeather's huge paw in her small hand and returned his handshake with as much vigor as she could muster.

"Sam Byrnes. Minneapolis P.D. Homicide."

"Deb Slater. Cook County Sheriff."

The women exchanged handshakes as well.

"Whatdowegot?" Slater asked excitedly as the officers walked away from squad cars parked in front of the treatment center.

Slater was driving the department issued Tahoe. Byrnes was driving an unmarked Ford Crown Victoria.

"Search warrant for Edward Big Hands' office. All files, documents, computers, hard drives, any sort of written or digital device or record," Byrnes said between labored breaths as the officers climbed a steep sidewalk towards the center's front entrance.

"From the looks of the records we've been able to pull together regarding Big Hands' finances," Byrnes said, "he's been funneling Indian girls placed here at All Faiths by Judge Prichard to this polygamist colony in Montana. Laman's River, they call it."

"Understood," Slater said between deep draws of cold air. "Herb filled me in."

Byrnes nodded.

"Seems Ms. DeAquila was getting too close to the truth. Curious though," Byrnes said quietly as they stopped at the building's front door, "why the killer found it necessary to leave his victims, DeAquila included, in the nude, with dirt in their mouths, and their throats slit."

"I'll take a stab, no pun intended, at that one," Whitefeather offered.

"Go ahead," Slater replied, yielding to the big man.

"There's ample Mormon scripture and literature, including the *Journal of Discourses* by Brigham Young, which describe the cutting of an unbeliever's throat as a perfectly acceptable methodology to end blasphemy. I'd say," The FBI agent continued, "that the killer, Mr. Jason Orth, uses this symbolically, to invoke God in his handiwork. The clods of dirt have a similar meaning: The victim's ungodly speech is silenced."

"And leaving the victims nude?"

"They leave their mortal life the way they entered it."

"Warped perspective on the Divine, I'll give Mr. Orth that," Sam Byrnes said as she opened the ponderous door and stepped aside, allowing the other officers to enter the treatment center ahead of her.

After serving the search warrant on Ms. Meg Applewick in the facility's main office, the trio was led by the program director to Edward Big Hands' office. The door was ajar. The Native American counselor was seated behind his desk, the desk's surface covered in paperwork. Big Hands was staring at his computer screen, his back towards the door, when the director knocked once on the trim and ushered the cops into the claustrophobic room.

"Police, Edward," Ms. Applewick said quickly, annoyance at the need to be present, under such circumstances, clear in her voice.

The counselor, a much smaller man than the Lakota standing across the stifling air of the office, reached towards the keyboard of his Dell to delete the file he was reviewing. Sam Byrnes' right hand darted out and stopped the man's attempt to obliterate evidence.

"Our warrant covers the computer as well," the detective said softly, her grasp on the skinny wrist of the counselor firm yet painless. "We wouldn't want you to be deleting files before we've had the chance to take a peek, now would we?"

Big Hands grimaced but said nothing.

"Agent Whitefeather, would you mind escorting Mr. Big Hands to a chair?"

"No problem, ma'am," Whitefeather said, clearing debris from an oak side chair with a single swipe of his hand before resituating the counselor.

"Stay put, Mr. Big Hands," Deb Slater said to the suspect. "We'll have some questions to ask you as soon as Inspector Byrnes takes a gander at your computer."

"Thank you, Ms. Applewick," Byrnes said, leaning over the keyboard, her head turned so as to focus on the woman standing in the doorway. "We'll drop off an inventory of what we take before we leave."

The program director took the hint and left the cops to their work.

"Now, what do we have here?" Byrnes asked in a calm voice as she sat in front of the flat screen monitor perusing Big Hands' files.

In a folder marked "L. R. Project", Big Hands had saved all the emails he'd received from The Tyler. There were emails indicating flight numbers, times of arrival, and travel arrangements for the two girls Big Hands had turned over to a local missionary of the sect. The emails included an IP address for The Tyler that would allow forensic analysis; perhaps resulting in the revelation of the killer's physical location.

"Looks like Mr. Big Hands was saving his emails for a rainy day, am I right, Edward?"

The Ojibwe counselor sneered.

"Lawyer."

"Ah, you want a legal umbrella. Must be pouring cats and dogs," Byrnes quipped. "Mr. Big Hands will likely use these emails to play 'Let's Make a Deal' with the U.S. Attorney. Am I right, Edward?"

Big Hands swallowed hard.

"U.S. Attorney?"

Whitefeather towered over the suspect.

"That's right, Bro. This isn't a state court case anymore. Mann Act—the transporting of young women for sexual slavery. Kidnapping. And of course, capital murder."

"Minnesota doesn't have the death penalty," Big Hands blurted out. "Even I know that."

"Careful, Edward," Slater said, "you've invoked your right to counsel."

"Seems Edward thinks he knows the system, being that he's a big-wig in a treatment facility and all," Whitefeather said, studying the smaller man with his wide face and deep brown eyes. "Trouble is, Edward don't know shit."

As Byrnes disconnected cords from Big Hands' computer, Slater began inventorying the paperwork stacked around the office.

"Here's a thought, Edward," Slater said, slapping the search warrant in the counselor's lap. "You show me where your notes and other documents are regarding the girls you sent to Montana, and we'll put in a good word for you with the U.S. Attorney."

"What do you mean?"

"Well," Byrnes said, looping the power cord of the Dell around the CPU, as she stood up from the desk, "there's a chance we can save you from being indicted as a conspirator in the murder of Angelina DeAquila."

Big Hands pondered the information.

"Newspaper reporter with the *Star Tribune*," Herb Whitefeather interjected, leaning into the suspect, closing the distance between them so that Big Hands could feel the agent's warm breath on his face. "She was murdered up in Sheriff Slater's neck of the woods. And there's my cousin's little girl. Five foot three. Skinny as a rail. Barely fifteen. Her body was found at Fort Snelling," the big man continued, his words slowly grinding to a halt, choked off by emotion.

"Lawyer," the counselor whispered.

Whitefeather's temper flared. His hands grasped the shoulders of the smaller man. His rage escalated as explicit images of his cousin's daughter, helpless, naked, and exposed to the weather, rolled through his mind like frames from a pornographic snuff film. Big Hands didn't resist the assault. He simply stared wide-eyed into the broad face of the Lakota agent. It was as if the suspect was yielding to his captor's moral superiority by refusing to defend himself.

"Herb," Debra Slater said quietly, placing a hand on the agent's trembling forearms. "This isn't the way to get at the truth."

Whitefeather's mind returned from a desolate corner of Fort Snelling's sprawling complex overlooking the Minnesota and Mississippi Rivers. He slowly released his grip on Big Hands.

"There won't be any deals made," Sam Byrnes offered as she left the computer, walked to the counselor, gestured for him to stand, and, in one deft motion, removed handcuffs from a pouch on her belt and cuffed the counselor's arms behind his back, "unless you're forthright. You should talk to us. We can help you."

Big Hands remained mute. Byrnes motioned for Slater to escort the man out the door.

"No one can help me now," the counselor mumbled as he walked out of the room, Whitefeather leading the way, Slater following the suspect. "It's in God's hands."

Sam Byrnes slid through the doorway and stopped the entourage in the hallway.

"God's hands? What do you and the people you work for know about 'God's hands?'" Byrnes said with authority. "The Principle was disavowed over a century ago. It was wrong and the leaders of the church knew it was wrong. They moved to stop Joseph Smith's private transgressions; sins that Brigham Young allowed to become church doctrine. If you believe in the Mormon faith, this, above all else, you surely should know."

Slater's face evinced puzzlement.

Byrnes nodded slightly.

"Ya, I'm Mormon. A celibate lesbian practicing Mormon. Quite a mixture, eh?"

Slater wanted to have a lengthy religious dialogue with the detective but knew that it was not the time or place to explore the intricacies of faith.

""Didn't see that coming," Whitefeather offered. "So this case is personal for you as well?"

Byrnes shrugged.

"I guess so. Hadn't really thought of it in that context until I started looking at this slime ball's hard drive," Samantha Byrnes said, gesturing towards Big Hands' office. "But now that I think about, it, ya, I guess there is a personal investment in this case on my part. I was raised Mormon. I still go to the meetinghouse at least twice a month. I know that some folks think that Mormonism is just a click away from Scientology on the wacky scale. But if you're born into it, well, it's no different than being born Catholic. Or Baptist. Each religion has its own foibles," Byrnes said, resuming the trek towards the building's exit.

Slater considered Byrnes' statement and felt her assumed prejudice, her moral superiority over the other woman's faith, diminish.

"I guess that's true."

"Damn straight, Sheriff Slater. Every church has its sects and cults and hangers on who pervert the truth, change the rules, usually for some untoward motive. Polygamy was sold by Brigham Young as a way to procreate en masse, to multiply and be fruitful. But in reality, other than sealing himself on occasion to old spinsters for appearances' sake, Joseph Smith, who came up with the doctrine but kept it on the Q.T., usually sought out the best looking and most desirable women he could find. Didn't matter if they were married to someone else. Smith didn't let a little thing like marriage, even a Celestial marriage to another Mormon, subvert his lust. The revelation of polygamy was apostasy of the worst kind, a violation of the very scripture that inspired Smith to form the Mormon Church."

Byrnes used her portable radio. Within minutes, two uniformed officers arrived, secured the items subject to the search warrant, and began transferring the evidence to a squad car. The other officers and the suspect left Big Hands' office. The Minneapolis detective left a copy of the search warrant inventory with Ms. Applewick before leaving All Faiths.

As Byrnes, Whitefeather, Slater, and the suspect descended the stairs towards the Crown Vic and the Tahoe, Slater mulled over the detective's disclosure. Sam Byrnes acknowledged the questioning look on the sheriff's face.

"Mormonism, like any religion, is based upon faith and belief, not science and deductive thought," Byrnes offered as she assisted Big Hands into the back seat of the Crown Vic. The detective's small eyes narrowed as she stood up and considered the other woman. "I have doubts about my faith every day, just as I'm sure, Sheriff Slater, you have doubts, if you were raised in a particular faith, about yours. Do you, Sheriff? Do you have a particular faith?"

Byrnes slammed the rear passenger door to the squad car as she asked the question.

Slater thought for a moment before answering.

"I used to think so. Now, I'm not so sure. I was raised Presbyterian but I haven't been to a service in that denomination for over twenty years. My husband, daughter, and I attend services at a little Lutheran church up on the Gunflint Trail from time to time. My daughter Annie is in confirmation there right now. But I don't know that my faith is much larger, at this point in time, than the proverbial mustard seed."

Whitefeather gestured to the watch on his left wrist.

"Time to get this clown behind bars. Sam, maybe you can take another run at him after he's been booked, when his lawyer shows up and he's come to his senses."

The detective smiled.

"Oh, he'll crack, Agent Whitefeather. We'll invite the U.S. Attorney to meet with *his* attorney and this boy'll crack. He's just a minnow. We want the head carp in this school of ugly fish. Am I right?"

Herb Whitefeather, the vision of a dead Lakota girl lingering in his mind, nodded and walked silently towards Slater's Tahoe.

TWENTY-FIVE

Winter in the Smith River Valley relented by the first of January. The sun came out and melted drifts deposited by a succession of blizzards. By New Years' Day, the day Joyce Nielsen was due to leave The Colony, the river was cresting. There was no way for agents to drift down the Smith, land their raft on the shoreline, and ferry Joyce Nielsen to safety. The water rushed past Keystone Ranch in a torrent. It was clear to Joyce that her time at The Colony had been extended by an act of nature or God. The cause of the delayed rescue wasn't really important: Unless Joyce could gain access to a computer or a telephone to set up an alternative pick up date, the FBI agent was destined to remain undercover. The only telephone or computer close at hand was in the master bedroom of Keystone Ranch, under Obadiah Nielsen's watchful eye. Time was running out. Joyce had finally met The Tyler and she was certain that The Tyler was curious about her in ways that were unhealthy. Though they had only spoken briefly, Joyce Nielsen believed her life was in jeopardy.

• • •

The encounter took place by chance. The Tyler's visits to the compound were usually clandestine and generally occurred at odd hours. He rarely ventured further into The Colony than the meetinghouse, where the majority of his business with The Prophet, his only regular contact within the community, was conducted. That The Tyler had chanced upon Joyce while he was visiting Obadiah Nielsen at Keystone Ranch was at odds with the assassin's routine.

The Tyler had arrived before dawn and parked his Dakota in front of the mansion. He was at the ranch to meet with The Prophet privately, without benefit of the First and Second Counselors. He'd insisted on this condition when he'd texted The Prophet; just The Tyler and Nielsen, no one else.

Joyce hadn't been awake when The Tyler arrived. The sound of Obadiah leaving Evelyn's side (as the first wife snored contentedly in the master bedroom) woke the FBI agent. As the crane-necked, stoop-shouldered old man lumbered through distant dark, Joyce conjured up a vision of The Prophet's aging head; his boney skull covered in brittle red hair. Her mind recalled the knobby contours of Obadiah's knees; their prominence made more obvious by the

141

emaciated thinness of the man's stork-like legs. Curious as to why The Prophet was up so early on a Saturday, Joyce decided to follow him once he left the master bedroom.

Half an hour later, The Prophet and The Tyler sat at the kitchen table, sipping hot chocolate, talking in low tones, Nielsen claiming the proverbial head of the table with The Tyler sitting to The Prophet's right.

Joyce had donned a bathrobe and, moving with stealth, she'd entered the great room adjacent to the kitchen and sat on the couch to monitor the men's conversation.

"We've got a problem," The Tyler had begun.

"Don't we always?"

"I'm serious, Obadiah. You need to hear me out on this."

"Okay. So what is so important that you need to wake up a prophet of God at five o'clock on a Saturday morning?'

The Tyler sipped coca and studied the face of the cult leader.

"They've got Big Hands."

Nielsen leaned back in his chair.

"Who does?"

"The FBI. He was arrested in Minneapolis. Stupid fool called me on his cell phone when he was being booked. Don't know if they've traced the call to my account but it's only a matter of time."

Nielsen's upper lip had opened slightly as if to speak, but he remained mute.

"I told him, 'Buy a disposable phone with minutes. Don't call me on your regular phone'. But he didn't listen. The man's a complete disaster."

"And?"

"If he rolls over, he could jeopardize The Colony's work. He knows enough to bring the feds down on this place in a hurry."

"What's your play?"

"He's in custody, there's not much I can do now. But the judge…"

"Judge Prichard, the one in Duluth?"

"Yes."

The Prophet thought through the implications.

"You want to kill a sitting District Court Judge to keep her quiet?" Nielsen said slowly.

The Tyler had nodded.

"Why?"

"Many reasons. She can identify me. She understands the connection between what she's done and Big Hands' sending sister wives here. She'll want to protect her youngest son, who I threatened to

142

gain her compliance. She's a very credible witness. She has nothing to gain by lying on the witness stand."

Nielsen considered the issue.

"You're asking too much."

The Tyler allowed The Prophet's answer to dissipate.

"There really is no other way. She's already had one visit from the authorities."

"How do you know that?"

The Tyler had smiled weakly.

"You have friends in many places. So do I."

The Prophet nodded slightly.

"I see."

"You have to understand. There's a good possibility, really a probability that, any day now, the FBI, the ATF, the BIA, the Meagher County Sheriff, and the Montana Highway Patrol will descend upon us like locusts descending upon the crops planted by our forefathers. Armageddon, at least for Laman's River, may be just around the corner."

The Prophet had swiveled his head quickly in reaction to The Tyler's prophecy.

"The answer is still 'no'. Talmadge and the Home Guard can protect us. We have the necessary weaponry, the firepower, to give any invader pause at our gates. I do not welcome that. I do not welcome the Last Days. But if the United States of America is bent on disregarding our constitutional right to practice our faith as we see fit, then we'll have no choice. But I will not authorize the murder of a judge."

The Tyler smirked.

"She's one of the fallen. She's apostate. She, above and beyond any of the poor innocents you've 'authorized' me to dispatch, deserves consideration."

"I know these things of which you speak, Mr. Black. I understand that she has knowledge that can lead us to destruction. But there is the greater good to consider. Killing a District Court Judge gives the authorities every cause they need to commence an operation against us. No, Mr. Black, I will not authorize it."

The smaller man had studied the crooked spine and bent neck of his companion.

So be it, oh prophet of God. But when the end is near, if I have the power, I will seek out Judge Prichard and send her to her final destination. I will not wait for mortal approval; I will look only to the Lord for affirmation.

"Alright. But understand this; there is something in the wind. My contact at the Montana Highway Patrol says there will likely be an incursion before spring."

143

The Prophet had stood up and walked to a teapot simmering on the built-in commercial range, the appliance's brushed aluminum skin reflecting the kitchen lights, and poured another cup of cocoa. As Nielsen placed the pot back on the burner, he heard footsteps.

"Someone there?"

The Prophet listened intently. A door in the children's wing slammed, followed by brief silence, and the flushing of a toilet.

"One of the wee ones," Nielsen remarked, reclaiming his seat. "I think," Nielsen continued, "that the prudent course is to ensure that Charles and the Home Guard are ready. That our firearms are, as they say, 'locked and loaded', so that if intruders arrive, we can appropriately welcome them."

The Tyler fixed his gaze on the old man.

"And if that day comes?"

The Prophet had smiled wearily.

"You mean, will I hightail it out of here like Joseph Smith did before he found courage and was martyred at Nauvoo or will I stand my ground, as Brother Brigham Young did when President Buchanan sent troops to Utah? That is your question, is it not, Brother Black?"

The Tyler nodded.

"Well. That presupposes two things. One, that the authorities are audacious enough to make an attempt to disrupt our way of life, and two, that our Home Guard is incapable of stopping the attempt. I, for one, will put my faith behind the Lord. Jesus will firm up our arms and strengthen our resolve to resist and defeat the enemy. My vision affords no retreat from Zion. My legacy will bear no shame. Do I make myself clear?"

"Perfectly," The Tyler had whispered, his confidence in the leader buttressed. "I'll keep my ear to the ground. And I'll have Talmadge construct firing positions on the ridges overlooking Zion's Way. A handful of well-placed men should be able to hold the road against several hundred intruders. The walls of the canyon are steep. The Smith protects our rear. Anyone who seeks to enter The Colony by way of the road is inviting slaughter."

The Prophet smiled again.

"Don't forget the mini-guns and the RPGs."

Nielsen's reference was to two miniature Gatling guns The Colony had procured in Mexico (multi-barrel, rapid fire 7.62mm automatic weapons that were normally mounted on helicopters) and the sect's supply of rocket propelled grenades. Charles Talmadge, a federally licensed firearms dealer, had secured the advanced weaponry, along with fully automatic M-16s, from corrupt Mexican officials working with the DEA against drug cartels. No one would miss two automatic weapons, a handful of M-16s, and a crate of RPGs amongst

144

the hundreds of millions of dollars of weaponry supplied to the Mexican government by the United States in hopes of stopping the drug trade.

"I haven't forgotten them. The mini-guns will be deployed inside the front gate, one to either side. The RPGs will be strategically dispensed, to allow the Home Guard to knock out any advancing vehicles. But…" The Tyler had stopped, his mind thinking ahead.

"Yes?"

"What happens once we beat back the assault? Surely, you don't believe the authorities will let us live in peace after killing police and federal agents, if that's what it comes down to."

The Prophet hadn't considered the aftermath of a firefight.

"Well, I certainly am not going to ask my family and fellow believers to yield to the authorities in the way Jim Jones did," Nielsen had said quietly. "I have no wish to see women and children of God die like abandoned pets in an animal shelter."

The Tyler nodded.

"And I have no desire to seek God's glory so early in our effort, if that's what your insinuating," Nielsen added.

"I wasn't."

The Prophet finished his second cup of cocoa.

"I guess," Nielsen said after a significant period of silence, "we need an exit strategy; something that allows us to continue God's work."

The men had looked into empty cups and considered the options.

"Canada?" The Tyler offered.

"Plausible. We have land in Saskatchewan, not far across the border."

"There would be an issue of logistics. There's no way we can traipse eighty people into a foreign country, with the government on our heels, without being stopped at the border."

The Prophet thought further on the issue.

"The exodus would have to include only a limited number of Saints."

The Tyler concurred.

"Like when Warren Jeffs left Arizona and made his way to Texas."

"Precisely."

"You. Your wives. Your children."

"The First and Second Counselors. Their families. That would be about all we could safely transport."

The Tyler had nodded significantly and turned in the direction of footsteps approaching the adjacent great room.

"Auntie Joyce, why are you sitting there?" a child's voice asked.

The Tyler rose from his chair and walked through the archway between the kitchen and the great room. It took several seconds for his eyes to adjust to the darkness. At the far end of the room, The Tyler discerned the form of an adult woman sitting on a couch in front of a massive flagstone fireplace and a little girl standing in the shadows.

"Who's there?" The Tyler had asked.

Joyce Nielsen rose from the couch. The woman grasped Hester Nielsen's tiny hand. The woman and the eight-year-old daughter of The Prophet and Evelyn Nielsen walked slowly towards the kitchen.

"Just two little deer mice," Joyce said lightly.

The details of the woman's face and the features of the child became apparent as they advanced into light.

"Mr. Black isn't it?" the woman had guessed, extending her right hand in greeting. "Joyce Nielsen. And this is Hester."

The Tyler accepted the woman's hand, noting her grip was firm and serious and that her palm was clammy from sweat. He noted the woman's unintentional cue, removed his hand from the exchange, and tasseled the blond hair of the little girl as he bent to look into her eyes.

"And why is little Hester up so early his morning?"

"I had to go potty. And I'm hungry."

The Tyler scrutinized the woman.

"And Mrs. Nielsen, what brings you to the great room at such an early hour?"

"Couldn't sleep. I woke up and I heard voices. I thought I'd find out who was up and get an early start on breakfast."

The Tyler had followed the woman and the child into the kitchen.

"There's my little girl," The Prophet said with joy as Hester leaped onto his lap. "How is my best girl today?"

Hester giggled. The woman bent at the waist and kissed her husband's cheek. The Prophet smiled.

"And how is my wife this fine and beauteous winter morning?"

Joyce had feigned a smile.

"I'll let you know after I have a glass of cold water. My throat is parched," the woman related, opening a cupboard over the kitchen sink, removing a glass tumbler, and turning on the cold tap to fill the glass.

"Stay for breakfast?" The Prophet asked The Tyler. "Joyce is a heck of a cook. Her whole wheat pancakes are divine."

The Tyler's eyes studied the woman as she filled the tumbler, turned off the tap, and gulped water with abandon.

She's nervous. Why? How much did she hear?

The Tyler understood that it was not the appropriate time to determine how long the woman had been sitting in obscurity listening to their conversation.

Something isn't right.

His instincts were nearly always spot on. There was something amiss with respect to The Prophet's fourth wife. Her manner, her demeanor to the untrained eye, appeared normal; seemed calm and collected. But physical cues exposed a level of heightened alertness in the woman that was incongruous to the setting.

"No thank you. I'll take a rain check," The Tyler had said as he walked towards the rear door of the house.

As Allan Black passed Joyce Nielsen, she sensed a keen awareness from the man that caused her hand holding the water glass to shake.

Calm down. Play the part.

It had been all Joyce Nielsen could do to keep the glass from falling from her hand as she watched The Tyler exit the log home.

TWENTY-SIX

They walked a path between the house and the garage. Deb Slater carried her husband's portable oxygen tank. A clear vinyl hose drooped between the tank's regulator and Rick's nose. They negotiated an icy walkway Annie had chopped through significant snow. The sun and the wind had sculpted soft white powder into hard banks. A jay flitted past the couple; it's undulating flight a flash of powder blue against an overcast sky.

"How're you doing?" the sheriff asked as the couple shuffled towards the waiting Tahoe, the SUV warming outside the garage.

"It's a bitch," Rick replied, dutifully watching his feet strike slippery ground as he moved, his dementia seemingly improved, his response akin to the lucidity he's shown back in their hometown over Christmas. "But I have the world's most patient nurse to help me."

It was the Saturday after New Year's. They were on their way into Grand Marais to celebrate their wedding anniversary: "Twenty-seven years of wedded bliss," Rick had reminded her. "Doesn't look like we'll see twenty-eight."

His wife didn't appreciate Rick's gallows humor. Rick's banal pronouncement of his mortality was a facet of the mitochondria disease to which the old Rick Slater would've never succumbed.

Not in a million years, Debra thought as she considered the anger, the upset, the feeling of hopelessness such comments from her husband caused her.

"Think about that fresh lake trout you'll order at the Terrace," Debra said, changing topics as they stopped next to the front passenger side door of the SUV. "And the wonderful apple pie and homemade cinnamon ice cream I'm sure you'll insist on for dessert."

Food was one of the few pleasures Rick was still able to count on. His wife's mention of his likely dinner and dessert selections forced him to smile.

"There. That's the Rick Slater I fell in love with," Deb said quietly, planting her lips on his cheek. "Maybe you'll even have a glass of wine or two."

Rick's smile broadened.

"Some of that great Australian Merlot."

"Yellow Tail," his wife added, opening the door and helping him into the front passenger seat of the Tahoe.

148

"Yellow Tail," Rick murmured. "The only tail I'm likely to get."

Deb let out a hearty laugh as she shut the door.

"I haven't gone anywhere, you know that, don't you Mr. Slater?" the sheriff added as she opened the driver's door, slid across the leather seat, and found her place behind the wheel. "Anytime you feel up for a romp, I'm here for you, big fella'."

They hadn't made love in over a year, since their twenty-sixth anniversary. On that occasion, Rick had been eager to rekindle the passion they'd once shared. The results had been less than satisfactory. Rick lacked the stamina to complete her and his own culmination had been of minute proportions; nothing as epic as they both had hoped for given the length of time between couplings. The combination of Rick's fatigue and the aggravating intrusion of Deb's menopause made the occasion forgettable. Her reference to love making did little to heighten Rick's mood.

"I think I'll pass, darling," he said, lament clear in his voice.

Deb Slater didn't respond. There was little to be gained and incremental joy to be lost, if she continued the line of discussion.

"What do you think of the Mormons?" she asked, switching topics without segue.

Rick fiddled with the adjustment dial of the regulator on his oxygen tank before replying.

"What do you mean?"

The Tahoe swerved to avoid a balsam that wind, rushing across the flat ice of Devil's Track Lake, had toppled into the road.

"You know the DeAquila case..." the sheriff continued.

"The reporter? From the Cities?"

"That's the one. Turns out she may have been investigating a cult, an offshoot, of the Mormon Church involved in polygamy and trafficking young Native American girls."

Rick squinted. The sun sought its last hurrah before evensong. Errant rays reflected harshly off brittle snow, blinding Rick as he looked ahead.

"How can you see?"

Deb turned her head, revealing that she'd donned aviator sunglasses.

"Oh."

"The Mormons?"

"Don't know much about 'em," Rick replied, adjusting the window visor to temper the glare. "In fact, I can't think of anyone I know who *is* Mormon."

"Ben Young."

Rick's eyebrows rose.

149

"The sculptor? Up at Grand Portage?"

"Yup."

"How do you know that?"

"Heard that was the case; heard he was like a third cousin or something to Steve Young. You know, the 49ers quarterback? Drove up to the Rez and talked to Ben. Turns out it's true; they're both descended from Brigham Young, the second Mormon Prophet. Ben filled me in on differences between the mainstream Church and groups like the one that DeAquila was investigating."

Rick turned his head to watch a genderless whitetail, the time for antlers having passed, skirt the tree line and duck into forest.

"And?"

"Polygamy. That's the major difference. And then, between polygamist sects, there are subtleties as well."

Rick focused on his wife.

She's so good looking. God, how I wish I could spend one more night with her, doing what made us happy. <u>Happy</u>. There's an emotion I need a dose of. Forget the drugs. Forget the miracle cure, God. Jesus, just give me one or two more days of complete happy. Nothing else. Just happy.

"Rick?"

Her voice interrupted his silent prayer.

"You were saying…"

After a brief pause, during which Deb considered her husband's tired eyes and disconsolate profile, she continued.

"Even in Montana, where we think this thing all leads, there are differences between sects. The Mormons at Pinesdale, for example, where the folks we're looking into split off from, forbid the most egregious forms of the practice. They don't allow underage plural marriages—that's their term for it, 'plural marriage'—don't allow forced marriages, and don't allow marriages between relatives."

Rick smiled wearily.

"But they do believe in more than one wife? That sounds…difficult."

Deb laughed.

"Oh, you think having one wife and one daughter are taxing, do you? How about multiple wives and multiple daughters?"

The Tahoe came to rest at a stop sign demarcating the end of gravel and the beginning of the Gunflint Trail. The sheriff looked both ways and gunned the engine, launching the SUV onto blacktop.

"Going somewhere in a hurry, sheriff?"

The repartee between them that made their partnership a success, had, at least for a time, resurfaced.

"Just want to get to my rib eye, Mr. Slater. Now, where were we?"

"The Mormons in Montana."

"Ah yes. Well, the group we're interested in, the ones Herb and I are convinced are involved in DeAquila's death as well as two or three other murders, they don't follow the niceties like Pinesdale does."

"Underage girls?"

"Yep. And relatives. And forced marriages. That's why they're not welcome in Pinesdale. Why they founded their own colony. In fact, that's what they call it: '*The* Colony'."

Rick smiled as he watched sunlight fade under the superior weight of the sky.

"I love Montana."

Deb Slater grinned.

"Remember Red Lodge?"

Rick's lips curled upward.

"You and that teddy. How can I forget your hot little tushy in that slinky little thing."?

Deb glared at her husband.

"I was talking about the skiing, Mr. Slater."

"Oh."

"But now that you mention it..."

Inadvertently, they were back to the implausibility of intimacy. There was an extended silence, an awkward pause, as they both considered whether to continue the line of dialogue.

"What corner of Montana do *your* Mormons call home?" Rick finally asked, bringing an end to the stalemate.

"Can't tell you that. We're looking at assisting other agencies in an operation there. In the very near future."

"How near?"

"Can't tell you that either."

The SUV began its descent into Grand Marais. The frozen pan of Lake Superior stretched out before them as a pewter plain.

"These people you're after," Rick finally said in a subdued voice. "Are they militant? Militia types? Like David Koresh or that guy they just hauled to jail. The Mormon in Texas?"

"Warren Jeffs. We don't know for sure. But at least one of them has no compunction about killing reporters, social workers, and young girls."

"Slashes their throats, right?"

"Yes."

"Christ."

The Tahoe pulled into the parking lot of the Birch Terrace restaurant, the rambling building a throw-back to the days when Ma and Pa supper clubs dotted the North Shore of Lake Superior from Duluth to the Canadian border. Deb turned the ignition off and sat behind the wheel, thinking about the upcoming operation in Montana.

"You still thinking about the Mormons?"

She nodded.

"Deb," Rick said, removing his left glove and placing his bare hand on his wife's right cheek. "Be careful, Okay? I know it's your job and everything, but…"

The interior of the SUV fell silent. It was so quiet; Deb Slater swore she could hear their hearts beating over the mechanical hiss of the oxygen tank.

"But what?"

Tears welled in Rick Slater's eyes.

"This isn't just about you and me."

At that moment, Debra Slater realized how vulnerable, how afraid her husband was. Not for himself. Not for her. But for Annie.

"I know."

"You can't leave her alone, Deb. You can't."

"But…"

Rick's face turned, his eyes wet, their intensity increased by emotion.

"Don't, Deb. Don't pretend. We haven't said it in so many words, but we both know. We've heard it from more doctors than I care to count. I have a few months, Deb. A few fucking months. Then, it'll be just you and Annie. She needs a mom, Deb. She needs a mom."

The Sheriff of Cook County reached across the leather seat of the Tahoe and hugged her ailing husband.

"I know, Rick. I know."

TWENTY-SEVEN

Supervising FBI Special Agent Jeff Dugan left the United States District Courthouse in Billings, Montana, a criminal complaint and arrest warrant signed by Judge Cebull safely in hand. The complaint, its contents sworn to by Dugan and signed by the U.S. Attorney, had been cobbled together from bits and pieces of information leaked from Laman's River by Agent Corrine MacDonald, who'd been undercover in The Colony for months as Joyce Nielsen, the fourth wife of The Prophet. The facts and allegations supplied by Agent MacDonald were supplemented by far reaching investigations of FBI field offices and local law enforcement agencies from Minnesota to Utah. The complaint named Obadiah Nielsen, Ezra Pratt, Micah Albrecht, Charles Talmadge, Jason Orth (a/k/a Allan Black), and other Colony members as co-conspirators in an illegal sex trafficking ring involving underage Native American girls. The complaint also contained references to four murders that were believed to be linked to the ring's nefarious activities but the complaint did not charge the murders.

The more serious capital charges would come later, after The Colony was secure, the suspects were in custody, and the accompanying search warrants were executed.

One of the search warrants, a separate and distinct document from the complaint and arrest warrant, repeated the allegations in the criminal complaint and provided further details regarding arms purchases from Mexican interests: entrepreneurial military officers south of the border who had supplemented their meager incomes by selling RPGs, mini-Gatling guns, automatic M-16s, and ammunition to Charles Talmadge.

Talmadge, as The Colony's internal security officer (and the holder of a federal firearms license from the ATF), was named in the search warrant as the likely possessor of the weaponry. Once the village on the eastern bank of the Smith was secure, the more serious allegations, including capital murder, would be dealt with through information and complaint or grand jury indictment. But to get there, Dugan needed to enter the compound, secure its occupants, bring the principals into custody, and do so without a massacre.

Agent Dugan was assembling his team for the operation from elements of the Montana Tactical Advisory Committee, the only Special Weapons and Tactics (SWAT) organization in the state. Comprised of representatives from local police departments, county sheriffs' offices, the Montana Highway Patrol, the FBI, and the Montana Army National Guard (including its air wing located at Fort William Harrison in Helena), the SWAT force would be supplemented by additional law enforcement officers; deputies and police from the Minnesota jurisdictions involved in the death of Angelina DeAquila in Cook County and the death of Julia Kingbird at Fort Snelling; deputies and police from Idaho investigating the death of Elwood Jones (the social worker who had tracked Bethany Comes to Ride to Montana) and who were also investigating Bethany's murder; and agents from the Bureau of Indian Affairs and the Bureau of Alcohol, Tobacco, and Firearms (ATF): and ancillary federal agencies interested in the goings-on at Laman's River.

Jeff Dugan had been a young FBI field agent working out of his hometown of Salt Lake City, Utah, when the debacle at Ruby Ridge in the rugged Kootenai River Valley of northern Idaho had unfolded in the early 1990s. As a mainstream Mormon, an anti-polygamist father of three, and the husband of a wife who was a state prosecutor in Salt Lake City at the time of the Ruby Ridge incident, Jeff Dugan was not directly implicated in the ill-fated assault against the Weaver family. Nor, several years later, was Dugan involved in the disaster at Waco, Texas, where the FBI and other agencies, with slight provocation and scant legality on their side, instigated the deaths of over ninety members of the Branch Davidian sect of the Seventh Day Adventists and their leader, David Koresh.

Though he had not been at either site for the climatic results of federal intervention against these pockets of extremism, Dugan had studied the organizational structures of the Davidians and other cults in such detail that he became known within the Bureau as *the* expert regarding religious cults and the logistics of assaulting their compounds.

Jeff Dugan, who had been elevated to Supervising Agent in the Salt Lake City office of the FBI, had his expertise called upon by the Bureau in April of 2008. It was Dugan who laid out the plan to remove Warren Jeffs's polygamist Mormons from their compound near Eldorado, Texas, after authorities received an anonymous tip from a young girl claiming to be an underage plural wife of an adult member of the sect. The call triggered a massive operation, planned and implemented by Dugan, which successfully removed over 500 women and children from the Yearning for Zion Ranch with no shots fired and no loss of life.

The information to which Dugan was privy regarding Laman's River included hand-drawn diagrams of the complex smuggled out by

Agent MacDonald during her clandestine meetings with "fishermen" on the Smith River, and oral reports from the undercover agent, both of which gave the U.S. Attorney's Office in Billings probable cause to bring criminal complaints against members of the Reconstituted Brotherhood of Latter-day Saints, as well as the underlying search warrant to retrieve evidence of the cult's involvement in illegal weaponry, sex trafficking, and murder.

A simultaneous raid was to occur at Jason Orth's isolated cabin near Sixteen Mile Creek to secure The Tyler and any evidence of his involvement in the nefarious activities of Laman's River. The raids were set for the last weekend in January—on Sunday at 9:00am—when the majority of Laman's River would be gathered at the Mormon meetinghouse in worship.

Though absolute confidentiality and secrecy were imposed upon the elements coming together at Fort William Harrison, Dugan was unable to stop Astrid Yost (the clerk at the Montana Highway Patrol who had been leaking information to The Tyler) from divulging portions of the plan she overheard from her secretarial post in the Great Falls office of the Patrol to The Tyler. Her supervisor, Captain Emil Thompson, eventually discovered incriminating emails on Yost's computer after the raid; too late to warn Jeff Dugan of the woman's breach of confidentiality.

The team was to assemble at Fort Harrison in Helena the Friday evening before the raid for orientation and instruction as to the rules of engagement. Dugan had formulated a "no fire unless fired upon and cleared to return fire" approach to the operation. He was dead set against another Waco fiasco, where unverified claims of rifle fire from the Davidian compound set the massacre of unarmed women and children into motion. Only upon Dugan's direct order could officers return fire on the people of Laman's River. The indiscriminant discharge of weapons from the compound, even if directed at the incoming UH-60 Black Hawks used to ferry the team, would not be a sufficient basis for engagement. Dugan was the only officer authorized to give the order. That was the one precept he would drill into the team's collective head: "Fire your weapon without my order, and you will be federally prosecuted for assault with a deadly weapon. Period."

Joyce Nielsen (Agent Corrine MacDonald's cover) sensed Allan Black was apprehensive. Their brief meeting had convinced her that she was being watched; that he didn't trust her. Something she had done or said; some element of her disguise had slipped, revealing something about her to the man. She knew there was little time to act. She knew that, come the last Sunday of the month, January 31st, agents would be drifting down the Smith River to pick her up and steal her to safety. She did not know that her removal from The Colony would coincide with a raid on the compound. Dugan had not provided her with those details because he didn't want anything to compromise the operation. But in fact, she would be at her appointed spot along the eastern shoreline of the Smith at the exact moment Black Hawks were settling down on pasture outside the meetinghouse at Laman's River and a convoy of local police and sheriff's deputies was securing Zion's Way. Agent MacDonald had no need, in Jeff Dugan's assessment, to be burdened with information that could only cause her harm if suspicion within the sect turned against her.

However, the undercover agent possessed information that required *her* to break silence, to communicate with Dugan; the knowledge that the main entrance into Laman's River was a trap. MacDonald had no choice but to risk breaking cover to get this information into the hands of her supervisor. It was a risk that she took; a risk that proved unfortunate for FBI Special Agent Corrine MacDonald.

TWENTY-EIGHT

The Tyler was, above all things, diligent. When he finally found himself face-to-face with The Prophet's fourth wife during the early morning hours at Keystone Ranch, alarm bells went off.

There's a lack of honesty, of candor, in that woman's eyes, The Tyler had thought immediately upon confronting Joyce Nielsen. *I smell cop. I may be wrong, but there's no harm in doing a little checking up on Mrs. Nielsen. Claims to be from the Strang Clan; descended from the Beaver Island Mormons. That will be easy enough to verify. If she checks out, then, I'll chalk it up to nerves. But I don't think so. I don't think my instincts are wrong.*

The Tyler had used his assets within the genealogical records depository of the mainline Church of Jesus Christ of Latter-day Saints to research the lineage of Joyce Strang Billington. There had been such a woman, his contacts revealed; she died in 1946 at the age of ninety. But there was no record of Joyce Strang marrying Rudolph Billington and no death certificate from northeastern Minnesota regarding the drowning death of her purported first husband. The woman claiming to be Joyce Strang Billington Nielsen was a fraud.

The Tyler had received this information after his encounter with the woman but did nothing with it. He did not immediately shake a fistful of photocopied records in The Prophet's face and chastise the old man for his lapse of scrutiny. He did not alert Charles Talmadge, who, as the head of the Home Guard, was charged with the internal security of Laman's River, that there was as a spy living amongst the faithful. Instead, The Tyler had relied upon his spider-web-like network of contacts in Montana law enforcement and the inner workings of the Mormon hierarchy in Salt Lake to decipher just who Joyce Nielsen really was. His suspicions, ATF, FBI or BIA, allowed him to narrow the scope of the search. Two weeks after encountering the woman, The Tyler had his answer: Special Agent Corrine MacDonald of the FBI; an unmarried career agent with no children and no appreciable family, was the infiltrator of The Colony.

Secure in the knowledge that his hunch was correct, The Tyler telephoned Talmadge and relayed the information.

Coincidently, as Talmadge began a hurried search of the compound to find and secure the spy, Agent MacDonald was seated at the keyboard of The Prophet's computer, typing a frantic warning to Jeff Dugan.

TO: jdugan@slc.fbi.us.gov
FROM: bigmac39@fastnet.com
RE: Operation
Date: 1/28/10

Do not use the access road to assault the compound. Rifle pits and automatic weapons are in place. It's a trap. Reply ASAP.
Big Mac

Agent MacDonald assigned a high priority to the email. She was in the master bedroom, Obadiah Nielsen's private sanctuary, without permission. The Prophet was out of the house, his attention momentarily occupied with assessing steers being culled for slaughter. But Nielsen was on the premises of Keystone Ranch. MacDonald was in jeopardy of being discovered. She glanced at the digital alarm clock on the end table next to the bed. She gave Dugan five minutes to respond; after which she'd clear the message from The Prophet's account, delete it from the computer's wastebasket, turn off the CPU, and exit the suite.

A response from Jeff Dugan arrived on The Prophet's computer within the minute.

TO: bigmac39@fastnet.com
FROM: jdugan@slc.fbi.us.gov
RE: Operation
DATE: 1/28/10

Understood. Approach will be by bird. Road to be sealed but no engagement. Be at the pickup spot on Sunday no later than 9:00am.
J.E.D.

Though the message from Dugan didn't say so directly, MacDonald discerned the obvious: A raid on The Colony was scheduled for the upcoming Sunday.

"Mrs. Nielsen, what the hell do you think you're doing?" Charles Talmadge said quietly as he stood behind the undercover agent, his voice compelling the woman's fingers to frantically delete the messages.

"You gave me a fright, Brother Talmadge. I'm just looking over specials on canned goods and such at Super Savers in Great Falls," the woman lied, her right index finger selecting the "empty" icon on the computer's waste basket as the man approached her from behind.

Talmadge, a tall brooding man of advanced middle age, extended a thin wristed right hand to stop the agent. He was too late.

158

The messages to and from Dugan vanished. With a firm grasp, Talmadge lifted the undercover agent from the padded desk chair to face him. His hands locked around MacDonald's wrists in a painful grip.

"Now," Talmadge demanded, "who the hell were you contacting, Agent MacDonald?'

The woman didn't answer.

Talmadge nodded his head.

"Fine. Then we'll just have to secure you until The Tyler can see his way clear to pay you a visit and have a little chat with you."

It was the first time MacDonald had heard the term.

"The Tyler?" she whispered, straining to break the man's grip; unable to lessen the stricture on her wrists by struggling.

"You know him as Mr. Black. But you'll have plenty of time to renew your acquaintance. Sit on the edge of the bed," Talmadge commanded, shoving the woman onto the massive platform; a bed she had never shared with The Prophet.

Talmadge held her right arm tightly and produced a zip tie from a jacket pocket. With practiced precision, he bound the agent's wrists, rendering her helpless.

Why didn't I try to take him down at the legs, MacDonald thought as she watched Talmadge tighten the zip tie to its limit. *Stupid. I fucked up. Now I have no way of getting free.*

"You're committing a federal crime by doing this."

Talmadge forcefully pulled the agent off the bed and smiled as he pushed her towards the open door.

"Not the first time the U.S. Code and I didn't see eye to eye. Likely won't be the last. Start walking."

They moved through the home in silence. Talmadge used a back hallway to limit their contact with other occupants of the house.

Once outside Keystone Ranch, they made their way towards the meetinghouse. They passed by a few Saints, whose curious eyes and open mouths were greeted with a stern, "This is none of your concern, go about your business if you know what's good for you" look from Charles Talmadge. The gawkers and would-be gossips, knowing Talmadge's penchant for violent outbursts, turned their heads from the stricken woman and scurried away.

Inside the meetinghouse, Talmadge unlocked the door to the community larder and shoved the FBI agent into an enormous space lined with canned goods stacked to eternity. Provisions for Armageddon were organized neatly on plywood shelves from the room's concrete floor to its corrugated sheet metal ceiling.

Without saying a word, Talmadge escorted the woman past walls of soup, chili, stew, vegetables, and fruit, his right hand firmly

159

planted in the small of MacDonald's back. At the entrance to the compound's community freezer, Talmadge unlocked another steel door. Frigid air assaulted Corrine MacDonald's bare face. Her body began to spasm as cold wicked from her stocking-covered feet into her internal core. The FBI agent shivered uncontrollably as her eyes looked pleadingly into those of her captor.

"Don't do this," she whispered. "I pray to God that you don't do this."

Talmadge grinned.

"First off, there's nothing of God in this, Miss MacDonald. This here's the work of men. Inspired by The Prophet, that's true. Directed by The Principle; that I'll grant you. But God's involvement? Unlikely," Talmadge said, taking a breath before continuing. "And you misunderstand my intentions. I'm not going to kill you. Wouldn't be prudent. Mr. Black still needs to talk to you. He'll decide what should happen once he's had his time with you," Talmadge said, touching the woman's jugular vein lightly with his right index finger, the tip of the finger resting on her larynx. "Though, from what I understand, he's sort of partial to necks."

Corrine MacDonald trembled. Whether from cold or from fear, Talmadge couldn't discern.

"I expect he'll be by shortly. He's, as they say, 'otherwise occupied'. But rest assured, he'll be by."

Talmadge pushed the agent towards a wooden pallet. A wool blanket was folded neatly on the platform. A shiny chrome thermos and a basket of bread and cheese sat on the cement floor within reach of the pallet.

"This here will tide you over until he comes. If you need to do your business, well, that empty bucket across the way will do. There's some paper toweling on the shelf you can use for..."Talmadge smiled. "Well, you know."

Corrine MacDonald sat down on the wooden platform, leaned against the cold concrete wall, and covered her body with the Hudson Bay blanket.

"About that praying thing," Talmadge added as he grasped the knob of the steel door, closing it until only a sliver of light invaded the freezer, "now would be a good time to practice up on that. You're gonna need all the strength God can provide to deal with what comes next."

160

TWENTY-NINE

As the Mesaba Canadair jet swung low beneath the clouds on its approach to Helena, the foothills of the Big Belt Mountains manifested to the east of town.

"What lake is that?"

Debra Slater asked the question as the plane descended over a black ribbon of ice interrupting a treeless plain.

"Canyon Ferry," Herb Whitefeather said nonchalantly. "Susan and I've stayed at the campground. Fishing is great."

"Trout?"

Whitefeather nodded.

"Plenty of 'em. Rainbows stocked every year."

Sam Byrnes, who had been sound asleep, her head resting on Herb Whitefeather's right shoulder for most of the flight, awoke just as dawn was breaking.

"Where are we?" the detective asked softly.

"Helena," Slater replied in an equally subdued tone as she watched ground rush beneath plane. "Should be at the gate in five minutes."

Byrnes tilted her head away from the FBI agent, reached up with her right hand, and mussed her spiky black hair into order.

"Never been fishing myself," the homicide detective offered.

Whitefeather grinned.

"I thought you were sleeping. From the sounds of your snoring, I was sure of it."

Byrnes released a small laugh through pencil thin lips.

"Oh, I was, Agent Whitefeather. I was far away, on a small schooner somewhere off New Zealand."

"Sailing with anyone in particular?" Whitefeather asked provocatively.

Byrnes smiled broadly.

"Not gonna tell."

Slater enjoyed the interplay between her friend and the Minneapolis detective until the plane was suddenly buffeted by wind. The commuter jet lurched, dove, and rose; the plane's performance mimicking a porpoise at Sea World.

"That's not good."

Whitefeather reached between the seats in front of him and patted Slater's shoulder.

"Not to worry, Deb. We'll be on the ground soon enough."

161

Slater accepted the big man's reassurance and clenched her jaw.

As the plane sliced through drafts and zephyrs, a flock of Canada geese, late season hangers-on feeding on a stubble field just off the edge of a runway, rose as one, their black, gray, and white bodies a uniform wedge of feathers flapping beneath the descending jet.

"Hope to hell they stay away from us," Slater whispered, the memory of Nelson Davies, the son of Jack Davies, a popular family physician in Grand Marais, firm in her memory. Nelson had died in a small plane during a training flight near Eau Clair, Wisconsin, where he was going to college, when a pair of snow geese, *not an entire flock but a single stinking pair*, flew into the Cessna's blades, killing themselves and the young man and his trainer in the process.

"They're headed for open water, by the power plant north of town," a passenger seated next to Slater, a man wearing significantly thick eyeglasses in his late sixties, on his way back to his ranch west of Helena, offered. "No need to fret. They'll stay clear of us."

Slater nodded, shut her eyes, and waited for the comforting embrace of asphalt.

Fort Benjamin Harrison, the base where the team was assembling, was west of Helena on State Highway 12, the same highway that The Tyler drove to bring Bethany Comes to Ride to her destiny. A Montana Highway Patrol trooper, Ed Collins, met the Minnesotans at the Helena airport terminal, helped them find their bags and load their gear into a waiting state patrol car before whisking them through burgeoning morning light towards the assembly point. Collins offered little conversation during the short ride to the military base.

After passing through security checks at Fort Harrison, the patrol cruiser brought the Minnesotans to the aviation section of the Montana National Guard base. Lines of antiquated UH-1 Iroquois Hueys, over twenty in number, and a cluster of sleeker, more modern UH-60 Black Hawks, along with a solitary C-12R Huron fixed wing aircraft, greeted the squad car as it wheeled up to a cavernous corrugated steel hanger where other law enforcement vehicles were parked in no particular order.

Snow dusted the fifteen acres of concrete serving as the landing and takeoff platform for the Guard's air wing. An intermittent wind formed ascending columns of white under the low hanging sky as the Minnesota cops grabbed their gear and made their way through a mawing overhead door into the hanger.

An athletic looking man, his eyes covered with redundant aviator sunglasses, who'd been talking in low tones with a group of men and women in assorted uniforms, saw the Minnesota contingent disembark from the squad car. The man abruptly ended his discourse and approached the newcomers.

"Herb, it's great to see you again!" Jeff Dugan said energetically, his brown hair buzzed close to the scalp, his prominent cheekbones dimpled from smile, as he approached the big man and extended his right hand in greeting.

The Native American agent dropped his duffle bag, the name "Whitefeather" stenciled across the faded green canvas, the bag a holdover from the agent's stint in the U.S. Army Reserve, and offered a significant paw to Dugan.

"It's been, what, ten years? In Quantico. I took that class from you, remember? Something to do with the looming danger of religious extremists and how to deal with them without lighting a fuse," Whitefeather said through a beaming smile.

"I remember," Dugan replied. "One of those classes that the director thought might stop another Oklahoma City. And then 9/11 happened. A whole different equation."

Whitefeather withdrew his hand and introduced his companions.

"Deb Slater, Cook County Sheriff. She's on the DeAquila homicide. And Sam Byrnes, Minneapolis P.D. She's working the murder of my cousin's daughter," the big man concluded, emotion clear in his reference to the dead Indian girl.

"Julia Kingbird," Dugan said softly, placing a hand on Whitefeather's shoulder as if to steady the man. "Sorry to hear about that, Herb."

Whitefeather cleared his throat and nodded towards the pods of milling law enforcement, soldiers, and aviators.

"Quite a crew you've got here."

"We figure the compound has about twenty adult men," Dugan said quietly as he motioned for the officers to follow him across the blacktopped surface of the hanger. "We know they have automatic weapons, RPGs, and a couple of mini-Gatlings. But..." Dugan continued, motioning for the officers to deposit their gear near an interior door alongside a significant array of similar duffles, packs, and suitcases, "our agent on the inside hasn't witnessed much training of a military bent. They have weaponry but, by all appearances, they don't know how to deploy it."

"How we going to come in?" Byrnes asked, lowering a titanium-framed yellow backpack to the hanger's asphalt floor.

Dugan smiled.

"Detective Byrnes seems eager for this assignment. Well, I'll be briefing all of you this afternoon, one o'clock sharp, in an adjacent classroom. You'll get the details then. But the basic thought is to swing into the compound with three Black Hawks, ten officers each, mixed groups from various agencies, an FBI agent in the lead on each chopper. One Huey will carry five officers and land in a small clearing just east of Jason Orth's cabin on Sixteen Mile Creek. Their job will be to secure Mr. Orth. Rules of engagement for both phases of the operation will be clear. You'll be provided with M-16s," Dugan said as he paused and thought through what he was saying. "You all familiar with the M-16?"

The three officers nodded in unison.

"Silly me, I didn't need to ask an Army Reserve man like Herb that question, now did I? Probably hoped he'd never carry one of those plastic pieces of crap again, am I right, agent?"

Whitefeather nodded.

"You'll each get fifty rounds for the rifle. And," Dugan added as they began walking back towards the milling groups, "you can carry your service weapons and any back-ups you brought with. They just need to be inventoried so we have an accurate count and description of the weapons each officer is carrying when we go in."

Dugan introduced the newbies to the team members in the hanger. Abe Armstrong, the recently divorced sheriff of Meagher County, took a shine to Slater until he found out she was married and had a daughter about the same age as the youngest of his three girls. Armstrong, a beefy man who hadn't kept himself in physical shape after winning election to the sheriff's post, but who was quick witted, cracked wise about the women being only "along for the ride", innuendo clear in the remark. A female officer who had not yet been introduced to the Minnesotans nudged Armstrong with a sharp elbow.

"Don't pay any attention to him," Porter, a small, razor thin woman whose penchant for running marathons was clear in her physique, but whose deep brown eyes and steady gaze displayed intensity, said curtly. "Diane Porter, Great Falls P.D.," she added, extending her hand to each of the Minnesotans in turn. "Sometimes, he thinks he's funnier than he really is."

"Great Falls? How big a force?" Byrnes asked.

"Over eighty strong," Porter said with pride. "I'm deputy chief, head of our tactical response unit, and the department's rep to the state SWAT team."

"Impressive," Byrnes said thoughtfully, her notions of Montana law enforcement capabilities destroyed in one short conversation. "I guess I was thinking your department was a lot smaller than that."

Porter smiled.

"You mean, like me and two Billy Bobs with pearl handled revolvers? Great Falls isn't Minneapolis, detective, but it is over fifty thousand. And there's an active missile base in our jurisdiction, Malmstrom Air Base. Lots of shit happens in Great Falls, believe you me," the officer said with appropriate directness.

They gathered after lunch for the first of a series of lectures and exercises to prepare them for their mission. Lt. Col. Jane Emerson, a former nurse turned Army aviator who'd served in both Afghanistan and Iraq, led them through embarking and disembarking from a Black Hawk, or, in Slater and Byrnes' case, a Huey Iroquois. The groups went over and over entering and exiting the helicopter to which they were assigned until the steps were ingrained. After Emerson's instruction, each officer fired twenty rounds from M-16s on loan from the Montana National Guard.

Team members had little free time available to explore Helena: Most of the off hours were spent in Fort Harrison's barracks.

The team's final meeting, held before dawn on the tarmac of the base on Sunday, the day of the operation, was a chance for Jeff Dugan to reiterate the rules of engagement and the reasons behind their forthcoming flight.

"Each of you," Dugan began as the officers formed a formidable circle of thirty-five fully geared cops, "has had the opportunity to view the mug shots of our targets." The officers' faces were male and female, their silhouettes a variety of heights and weights, their uniforms identical military issue winter camo, including Kevlar vests fitted snugly over their fatigue jackets, their M-16s fully loaded—set to "semi-automatic" and strapped unfamiliarly across their backs—and disparate revolvers and semi-automatics secured in holsters of various styles on their belts. "The arrest warrants give us full authority to bring these folks to justice. That's what we're aiming to do: bring them in; not kill them or any of the other inhabitants of the compound. The operation will be a coordinated effort. A column of law enforcement from Gallatin County, Meagher County, Broadwater County, Helena and Great Falls, supplemented with BIA, ATF and FBI agents, some fifty strong, is already on the move and will be in place to seal off the access road to Laman's River. Given the information we've received from our agent inside, Corrine MacDonald, there will be no frontal assault. The mission of the other column is to occupy the road and prevent escape. The Air Wing'll transport us; two warrant officers per chopper. They'll fly us to Laman's River. We'll land in the pasture behind the community meetinghouse," Dugan said, taking a deep breath. "A separate flight will land near Jason Orth's cabin on Sixteen Mile Creek. Five officers will be involved in that operation. A third detachment will land by raft on the east bank of the Smith River and pick up Agent MacDonald. That unit won't participate in the raid itself.

165

We'll be in radio contact with them but their job is singular: Get MacDonald to safety."

A low murmur rumbled through the assembly.

Dugan nodded.

"Yes, she's done a hell of a job. She's been undercover for the better part of a year and she's given us virtually all the information we have about the compound's weaponry, assets, numbers, and layout."

"Remember," Dugan continued, his voice becoming emphatic, "the goal is to get this done without firing a shot, without harming civilians. The rules of engagement are clear: No one fires a shot until we are fired upon *and* I personally approve returning fire. The only exception to this is that you may return fire to prevent the imminent death of another officer or yourself," Dugan added. "The five of you that are assigned to bring in Jason Orth have more latitude: Orth may be shot on sight *if* there is credible evidence he's armed. He's already killed at least four innocent people. He likely has no compunction against taking out law enforcement when confronted. But as to the main action, the rules stand as noted. Even if the Black Hawks draw fire, until I authorize it, you are not to engage, are we clear?"

"Yes, Agent Dugan."

Dugan smiled.

"I can't hear you," the agent shouted, imitating a drill sergeant, bringing levity to a tense situation.

"YES, AGENT DUGAN!"

"Good. Now let's load up. Keep your heads low, your wits about you, and God in your minds as we take care of business."

THIRTY

Corrine MacDonald shivered in the dark. She'd explored the unlit freezer, stumbling blindly into hanging quarters of beef, mutton, pork, and the carcasses of assorted wild game, the dead animals suspended from meat hooks driven through beams supporting the building's low roof. She was relieved to find a light switch on the far wall of the room. But light afforded no escape. She pounded, kicked, and otherwise probed the exterior cinder block walls as well as the stud wall separating the freezer from the community larder. There was no way out. No means by which Corrine MacDonald could leave her prison. Exhausted from her inspection, dispirited by the situation, MacDonald reclaimed her perch on the wooden pallet and weighed her options.

She had no means of computing exactly how long she'd been kept. She'd left her wristwatch in her bedroom at Keystone Ranch. She knew it was Saturday, the day before she was to be rescued, the day before the assault on Laman's River was set to begin. Though, she had no idea what time it was, whether dusk had settled over the compound or whether the sun remained high against the distant mountains and ridges across the Smith. Her heart sank as she realized that, in all likelihood, her rescuers would find her dead body; her throat slit by The Tyler; her mouth filled with dirt; her body discarded white, bloated, nude, and lifeless somewhere in the brush and bramble along the Smith.

Got to think. Got to figure it out. I can't die without a fight. There must be something I can use here, something I can fashion into a weapon. I need to take advantage of the element of surprise when he comes for me.

She thought about what she'd gleaned from her tour of the room. Nothing seemed apparent. Her spirit waned. Had she been a religious woman, she would have prayed fervently. But she was not a person of faith. She had never been a person of faith. Corrine's parents had instilled in her their beliefs: They had been Unitarians in name but agnostics in practice. They'd passed on precious little religiosity to their daughter. Their thin belief in "a creative force", not necessarily God as a being, but some elemental formative process of nature, gave her little to call upon in her hour of desperation. She was left with her own powers of intuition and thought. She found little comfort at that hour in intellect. And so, she petitioned the unknown.

God, she began, *I have not been a person of faith. That will change; I swear to you, if you show me the way...Give me a vision, a*

167

sign, of how I can defend myself against The Tyler when he comes for me.

It was a thin prayer, built of meager hope that Agent MacDonald sent up to Heaven as she curled defensively within the slight warmth of the Hudson Bay blanket, the blanket's red wool slashed by a single black stripe.

To her surprise, the response from her Creator was instant.

The spike.

During the short inspection of her prison, MacDonald's fingers had touched the cold steel of a sixteen penny spike hammered into the wooden frame of the shelving against the freezer's far wall. Whatever had been hanging on the spike had been removed (likely as a precaution) prior to her being secured in the room.

If I can wiggle it free of the stud it's imbedded in, I can conceal it in my nightgown. When the time is right, I can strike. I can bury the nail in his neck! I'll only have one chance. It isn't much, but at least, it's something.

She stood up from the platform and allowed the blanket to pile at her stocking feet. She shuffled forward and stood before the embedded nail, trembling from fear and cold, the hum of compressors outside the block wall the only sound beyond that of her racing heart. She strained against the spike. At first, the pine stud was stubborn: The nail didn't move. But repetition forced the wood to yield. After several minutes of work, the spike pulled free of the pine's grip.

"Praise God," Corrine MacDonald whispered.

Exhausted by her effort, the agent retreated to her perch, sat down on the rough oak slats of the pallet, slipped the spike into the waistband of her nightgown, pulled the wool blanket up to her chin, and waited.

THIRTY-ONE

Deb Slater and Sam Byrnes flew in a Huey, an UH-1 Iroquois; an antiquated model developed for the Army's use after the Korean War and relied upon by the 101st Airborne Division and other units to transport them from conflict to conflict in Vietnam. Modified Hueys equipped with guns or rockets also flew ground support during the war. Though the Huey is slower and less maneuverable than its successor, the Black Hawk, a few of the old choppers remain in service with select Guard and Reserve units into the 21st century.

FBI Agents Whittaker and Walker accompanied Slater and Byrnes. Meagher County Sheriff Abe Armstrong joined these four. Armstrong looked uncomfortable riding on the steel bench behind the two female officers; his rotund body crammed into a Kevlar vest, his girth in competition for space with the two angular FBI agents sitting on either side of him as the Huey "thwop-thwopped" its way across the early Sunday morning sky.

"You don't look so good," Walker noted.

Agent Walker was nearly identical in size, weight, and physique to his companion, Agent Whittaker, who sat on the opposite side of Sheriff Armstrong. The two physically fit agents functioned as bookends and held the robust Montana sheriff in place during the turbulent ride.

Sam Byrnes turned her head and noted that the color had drained from Armstrong' face.

The fat man didn't respond to Walker's observation. He simply bowed his head and willed himself not to puke.

"He's turning green," Byrnes said over the roar of the rotors.

"Here," said Warrant Officer Jeremy Graves, seated in the observer's seat next to Warrant Officer Amanda Otis, the chopper pilot, handing a plastic barf bag to the Minneapolis police officer.

Byrnes couldn't hear the words but discerned Graves' intent from his actions.

"Thanks," Byrnes said, accepting the bag and passing it back to Walker.

Walker in turn handed the bag to the sheriff. Armstrong convulsed. Streams of partially digested scrambled eggs, bacon, and toast regurgitated into the sack Armstrong held with trembling hands.

"Gross," Byrnes remarked, turning her head to avoid upchucking her own breakfast.

Armstrong emptied his stomach as the Huey flew a southeast course between peaks of the Big Belt Mountains towards Sixteen Mile Creek.

Sixteen Mile Creek flows west from its source in the Lewis and Clark National Forest east of Ringling through the northern corner of Gallatin County and the tiny hamlet of Maudlow, finally joining the Missouri River just above Toston. The waters of the Missouri, the Gallatin River, and Sixteen Mile Creek are confined a few miles north of Toston to form Canyon Ferry Lake, the reservoir Deb Slater had commented upon as the Minnesotans flew into Helena. Though Jason Orth's cabin was actually in Gallatin and not Meagher County, Abe Armstrong had been selected by Jeff Dugan to accompany Agents Whittaker and Walker to arrest the assassin because Armstrong professed a keen knowledge of the creek basin from his forty plus years of fishing the stream for elusive Cutthroat trout.

"We'll be putting down in a few minutes," Warrant Officer Otis said over the intercom, her voice distorted by the whirring of the chopper's main blades. "Shouldn't be too bumpy putting 'er down. Recon has it that the meadow we're using as a LZ is fairly flat."

Armstrong closed the barf bag and placed it between his feet.

"We'll get rid of that once you clear," Graves said loudly, sympathy for the fat man in the little Kevlar vest evident in his tone.

"Here we go," Otis announced, tilting the chopper into the wind, bringing the whirling bird in for a landing in the inky darkness of the Sixteen Mile Creek Valley just a stone's throw from The Tyler's cabin.

The chopper settled gently. Significant snow cushioned the landing. Dawn announced its presence by accenting the foothills of the Big Belt Range in gold. Slater, Byrnes, and Walker removed their seat belts, grabbed their M-16s, and slid across metal seats to exit the Huey. Graves reached back to assist Armstrong as the big man moved gingerly across the bench, his eyes woozy; his breath smelling sour. Whittaker waited patiently for the sheriff to disembark before joining his comrades on the snowy field.

"You gonna be alright, big fella?" Graves asked, concern for the sheriff evident in the warrant officer's tone.

Armstrong nodded and stood precariously alongside his companions in the cold morning air.

"We'll be here if you need us," Amanda Otis said softly, the whirling blades of the chopper thinning as the aircraft powered down. "Bring that asshole Orth back alive, will you Sheriff Armstrong?"

Otis and Graves watched as the five law enforcement officers trudged west. Armstrong led the little column into a bank of morning fog leaking from the creek bottom. The rising sun provided scant light. Armstrong picked up the pace. The officers entered the cottonwoods, and, within moments, struck Sixteen Mile Creek.

Abe Armstrong surveyed the cabin site. An unlit incandescent bulb hung from wire strung over the rear stoop of the cottage. The cabin's steeply pitched cedar shake roof was dusted with new snow. The Tyler's Dodge Dakota wasn't visible. The banks of the cabin's driveway were piled high; the snow stacked neatly by the bucket of the ancient Oliver tractor.

"Maybe his truck's in the garage," Armstrong whispered to Agent Walker as the two men lay in snow a few hundred feet to the north of the cabin. Slater and Byrnes were spread out to the left of the two men and similarly concealed. Whittaker was posted across the creek bottom.

"Could be," Walker agreed. "Or he might not be home."

Armstrong nodded.

"I'll slide on up to the rear door, using those trees as cover. You take the front porch."

Walker nodded.

The sheriff motioned with his gloved right hand for Slater and Byrnes to cover the two men as they advanced.

Armstrong rose to his knees using a significant spruce as cover. As the sheriff regained his feet, nausea returned. He steadied himself against the evergreen's gray trunk and waited for the sensation to pass. Walker noted the man's discomfort.

"You okay?"

"I'll be fine," Armstrong whispered. "Follow that line of scrub aspen into the front yard."

Walker touched his right index finger to his wool watch cap and skirted the trees.

"Hope that sonofabitch is sleeping like a baby," Debra Slater whispered.

Sam Byrnes was to Slater's right, prone behind a fallen cottonwood, the barrel of her M-16 resting on snow-covered wood. Byrnes's rifle was trained on the front door of the cottage.

I hope the asshole fires first, Byrnes thought. *I'll put one right in his forehead from here.*

Armstrong waddled forward. His approach, though cumbersome, was stealthy. He made no noise as he carefully placed one booted foot in front of the other and cautiously made his way towards the rear stoop of the cabin. As he neared the clearing, where he would be exposed to The Tyler's fire, he stopped in his tracks.

Crash.

171

A mangy coyote burst from its snowy lair and skedaddled through underbrush. The animal's sudden appearance sent the fat man's heart into his throat.

Fuck.

Armstrong allowed his breathing and heart rate to normalize as he watched the brush wolf evaporate. The sheriff looked back. Slater and Byrnes remained in position. Walker was at the limit of the aspen grove. The FBI man waved. Both men broke simultaneously for open space.

Lumbering towards daylight, Abe Armstrong suddenly felt tension against his right shin. Though the sheriff hadn't served in the military, he knew what encountering a trip wire meant.

THIRTY-TWO

The Tyler drove towards Laman's River in his Dakota secure in the knowledge that he would be able to break Agent MacDonald and learn what the FBI had planned in store for The Colony. "My Lady", one of The Tyler's favorite Mountain ballads, played over an iPhone connected to the truck's MP3 player. The phone was a trophy taken by The Tyler from Angelina DeAquila's Subaru as a memorial to her death.

Jason Orth was clear in his mind as to what was happening: Corrine MacDonald had embedded herself in The Colony and learned its secrets. She had, in her time with the community, discerned the strengths and weaknesses of the defenses erected by Charles Talmadge and the men of Laman's River. She was a spy whose intellect and memory needed to be plied before she was dispatched. The Tyler had advised Talmadge concerning the details of the FBI agent's apprehension and confinement. Her hands and feet were to be bound; she was to be gagged, chained to a post, and locked in the community freezer until The Tyler could make his way to The Colony. The Tyler was unaware that his instructions had been short-changed by Charles Talmadge.

The Dakota remained in two-wheel drive as it sped north on U.S. Highway 89. The pavement was clear of snow. New Bridgestones (tires The Tyler had purchased in Great Falls) held the road as rubber screamed over asphalt. He was not adhering to normal patterns: He was no longer cautious. The truck's speedometer hovered at ninety miles an hour as the Dakota roared down the highway. There was little time for him to make The Colony, interrogate the woman, kill her, and prepare for the FBI agents on the raft who would appear later that morning.

Though he knew the day and the approximate time when agents would come for MacDonald, The Tyler did not possess similar details as to when invaders would appear at Laman's River seeking to bring the Saints to secular justice. His contact at the Montana Highway Patrol had been unable to fill him in as to when the incursion would take place.

"Ms. Yost is on vacation," was what he'd been told when he called the Great Falls office of the state patrol to pry further details about the operation from the woman. "She's on a cruise, won't be back for two weeks."

The Tyler hated going into the fray blind. His nature demanded planning but there was no time for such niceties. Agent MacDonald held key information that could save The Principle. If he knew the date and time of attack, he could spirit The Prophet, the First and Second Counselors, and their collective families away from Montana, to the vast wheat fields the Reconstituted Brotherhood of Latter-day Saints owned in Saskatchewan.

Three identical black Denali's crossing the border in convoy would alert the authorities that something was amiss. Three black Denali's crossing at three different border stations would not raise suspicion. But flight would mean the end of the dream; the end of Laman's River. For The Tyler to countenance retreat, he had to know the details of the invasion. Those details eluded Jason Orth as his Dakota entered the town of White Sulfur Springs.

As the assassin's pickup truck idled at a stop light (waiting for the town's only semaphore to change from red to green) The Tyler made a startling discovery: Assembled in a parking lot adjacent to the town's main intersection were dozens of squad cars.

"Jesus," the Tyler whispered, unable to stop the invective. "They mean to take Laman's River today!"

The light changed. The Dakota crept through the intersection. The Tyler's mind raced as he calculated the number of law enforcement vehicles assembled in the parking lot.

"Thirty at least!" The Tyler exclaimed as he pushed the accelerator of the Dakota towards the floor. "Maybe more. At least fifty cops Hell-bent on doing Satan's work, I'll wager."

As the pickup truck cleared town and sped north, Jason Orth's mind wandered. He sought to reconcile the imminent collapse of Zion with his own personal history, his fervent dedication to The Principle.

His transformation from man to eunuch, inspired by the example of Boston Corbett, the slayer of John Wilkes Booth, and fueled by Mormon fundamentalist zeal, had been an attempt to mimic the legendary exploits of The Destroying Angel: Bill Hickman.

A steadfast soldier in Brigham Young's war against Mormon apostates, Hickman had killed Saints at odds with The Principle and had done so without remorse and with scant evidence of backsliding by the unfortunate victims.

Hickman did what needed doing.

The Tyler had realized, before his self-emasculation, that he could not, if he maintained his sexual drive, focus on doing the Lord's

174

work. This revelation was clear in his mind that day in a seedy hotel room where he contemplated desecrating himself for Jesus. Though the knife had stung but a little, his senses dulled as they were by self-injected morphine, there had been much blood. Jason Orth had not researched the story of Boston Corbett intimately enough to understand the amount of blood that would be lost once his testicles were dissected. The compresses he applied in hopes of stemming the fountain of red as he sutured the wound with coat thread were ineffective. Only the hotel owner finding The Tyler passed out in the inn's common bathroom had saved Jason Orth's life.

A miracle. God works in mysterious ways.

From that day forward, The Tyler had dedicated his life to Obadiah Nielsen and The Prophet's vision of converting Lamanites to the one true religion through the bleaching of their blood. Though he had been forced by duty to dispatch four souls to God, The Tyler still believed. Not a shred of doubt remained in his mind that Obadiah Nielsen was a great prophet of God.

The time was not right. We were not ready to implement The Principle. We can begin anew in Canada. There will be a new chapter to our story.

The Dakota roared down Zion's Way before skidding to a stop at the gated entrance to Laman's River. A steel livestock gate poised between stone towers blocked the road. Log guard shacks stood on either side of the stone columns, the words "Welcome to Laman's River: A Community of God" displayed on a wooden sign suspended between the towers. The words of the sign were stenciled in black lettering edged in gold across a white background. A floodlight illuminated the message. Two additional floodlights shone on the entrance gate.

The Dakota idled. Two sentinels, M-16s strapped across their winter jackets, handguns holstered to their hips, left the warmth of their posts and approached the truck.

"Evening, Mr. Black," a young boy said, his face red from cold, pimples of adolescence pock marking his forehead and chin.

"Kevin Ganzt. My, how you've grown. How are you boy?"

"Excellent, sir. The Lord has provided."

The Tyler nodded.

The other sentry, a short, inconsequential man of middle age, his eyes black as ink, scrutinized the visitor.

"What brings you to The Colony so early on a Sunday?"

The Tyler's authority exceeded that of anyone at Laman's River except for The Prophet and the two Counselors. The man's impertinence annoyed the assassin.

175

"Look, Josephs, security is about to be breached. I need to see The Prophet immediately."

The man stared wide-eyed.

"The Final Judgment?"

The Tyler fixed his eyes on the man,

"Nothing so serious. Let me pass so I can see The Prophet," The Tyler lied.

Josephs motioned for the boy to open the gate.

A faint line of blue became apparent in the eastern sky as the Dakota rolled to a stop in front of Keystone Ranch. The Tyler opened the driver's door, slid off the seat, slammed the door shut, and walked quickly towards the covered front porch of the mansion. He pounded on the front door. Porch lights illumined. The door opened to reveal Evelyn Nielsen in a flannel nightgown, a terry cloth robe pulled tight around her square figure, her eyes still full of sleep.

"Mr. Orth."

The Tyler pushed his way past the woman.

"I need to see Obadiah."

Evelyn nodded.

"Have a seat in the great room and I'll go wake him."

The Tyler shook his head.

"Can't wait. I'll follow you back to the bedroom."

The Tyler didn't allow questions. He grasped the woman by the elbow and moved her towards the master suite.

"Obadiah," the woman said in a firm yet quiet voice as they stood over the slumbering old man.

The Prophet, his sparse red hair splayed across the pillow, stirred beneath the bedcovers but did not wake.

"Obadiah," the woman pleaded, shaking her husband's exposed shoulder with her right hand.

The Prophet shot up in bed as if he'd seen a ghost.

"What in God's name is it, Evelyn?"

Nielsen immediately noticed The Tyler.

"Oh, it's you, Mr. Black."

The Tyler nodded.

"What is it? It's...." The Prophet looked at his alarm clock, "only six-thirty. It's Sunday. What could possibly be so important that you'd wake me as I was conversing with the Lord about this morning's worship message?"

"They're coming."

Obadiah rubbed his eyes with his hands.

"Who?"

"The FBI. The ATF. The BIA. Local sheriffs. Cops. They're all coming."

Nielsen tossed aside the quilt and sheets, revealing his two-piece temple undergarment, and stood in front of the smaller man, his great height bent from age, his spine as crooked as a cooked green bean.

"When?"

"Now."

The old man's eyes widened but he didn't say a word.

"You, your family, the Counselors, and their families must leave. There's only enough time to pack a small bag and make haste. Each family in one of The Colony's Denali's. Take different routes once you're on the highway. Don't head towards town. That's where they're assembling. Work your way north, to the Canadian border. Cross at different exit points, at different times. Give yourselves two hours minimum between crossings. Coordinate with Pratt and Albrecht. Here," the man said quietly, handing The Prophet three fictitious passports. "These should get you through customs. The kids and your wives should be all right. Security between Montana and Saskatchewan is fairly loose."

"Evie, get the children and the sister wives ready," Nielsen said gently.

The first wife didn't move.

"Woman, did you not hear me?" Nielsen asked with force.

Evelyn Nielsen refused to budge.

"What about Joyce?"

The Tyler grasped the woman's arm and turned her towards the door.

"I'll handle Joyce," the assassin said firmly. "You take care of getting the others ready to leave. The way I figure it, you have maybe a half-hour before the road is sealed off and you're trapped here."

Obadiah Nielsen watched the woman compliantly leave the room.

"We could fight," The Prophet said as he opened the closet, pulled out a suitcase, and tossed clothing into the luggage.

"To what end? Martyrdom doesn't suit you, Obadiah. Better to flee with The Principle intact and live to do God's work another day."

The old man stopped to consider the admonition.

"The traitor is in the community freezer waiting for you."

The Tyler's hand reflexively slipped to the wood handled fillet knife secured in the leather scabbard on his belt.

"I'll deal with her soon enough."

"Blood atonement?"

The Tyler nodded.

177

"After she tells me what I need to know."

The old man slipped out of his Celestial underwear; the impressive length of his powder white manhood exposed without shame. The Prophet stepped into a clean pair of temple undershorts and slid them to his waist. He pulled a clean temple T-shirt over his head before dressing in freshly pressed blue jeans and a navy button down shirt.

"Be quick about it. We're going to need your services in Canada," Obadiah Nielsen said as he zipped up his fly.

But The Tyler was already gone.

THIRTY-THREE

Abigail Talmadge peeled potatoes in the kitchen sink of the small log home she shared with her husband Charles, her Lamanite sister wife Brooke, and the family's four children. Brooke had given birth two weeks prior to Raven Ruth Talmadge, a beautiful little girl. Charles's attempts to follow the revelation of The Prophet and "bleach" the sins of Laman out of Brooke's line were a clear failure as witnessed by the Native skin tones of the offspring they'd created. Despite the child's sinful complexion, Abigail was delighted by the infant's birth: Raven's arrival signaled the beginning of Brooke's productiveness as a child-bearing woman and the end of Abby's duty to carry children of her own. After seven pregnancies (but only three successful births) Abby was worn out. She still enjoyed intimacy with Charles but she'd surreptitiously taken to using birth control pills prescribed by an OB/GYN in Great Falls to forestall pregnancy. She could not countenance further loss. She could not watch another child be brought through her loins stillborn, or find another infant dead in its crib. Four dead was enough. God would have to satisfy His need for mortal bodies to carry immortal souls through Brooke's young womb. Abby, though only thirty-seven, was through with the business of conception and birth.

The first wife heard the padding of bare feet on ceramic tile as she readied Sunday breakfast. As Abby turned her head, her long black hair (free of the traditional Mormon bun that usually kept the strands in order) shifted against the terry fabric of her bathrobe as she moved.

"Morning, Brooke."

"Morning, Abs."

The Crow girl retrieved a leather covered stool from behind the breakfast counter and sat down heavily, the weight of pregnancy not completely dissipated after Raven's birth; residual folds of loose skin draped over the girl's normally flat stomach and boney hips; the excess clear under the thin fabric of her silk pajamas, a gift from Charles for birthing their daughter.

"I need some bacon from the community larder," Abigail said absent-mindedly.

Abby focused on frying slices of potato. She dripped cooking oil from a plastic bottle into a hot skillet as she spoke.

"I'll throw on my coat and walk over and get some. Two pounds enough?" Brooke asked.

179

"Make it four. I might want to make BLTs for lunch when we come back from service."

Brooke nodded, clambered off the stool, and was gone.

It wasn't until the girl was out the door and out of sight that Abigail Talmadge remembered her husband's admonition.

The evening before, as they lay exhausted in each other's arms, their desire sated, the husband misled so as to believe that he was planting his seed within his first wife for the eighth time, Charles had mentioned that Joyce Nielsen was no longer to be trusted. That she had been found out to be a spy, an FBI informant, and that she was awaiting judgment. Charles had cautioned Abby not to go to the community larder because the room was being used to hold the woman until Mr. Black, the mysterious agent of The Prophet who was seldom seen but known by reputation, could deal with the situation. Charles had made his message clear: Under no circumstances was Joyce Nielsen to be disturbed.

"Oh, no!" Abby Talmadge exclaimed, having remembered the prior evening's dialogue. "What have I done?"

The Talmadge cabin was one of the closest homes in Laman's River to the community larder. Brooke Talmadge, her silk finery concealed by an overcoat, her feet protected by mukluks, her shimmering black hair curled neatly beneath a stocking cap, raced through crisp winter air to the meetinghouse, the plastic tab attached to the larder keys cold in her bare hand. She'd forgotten to wear gloves against the morning.

The meetinghouse rose from whitened ground to meet creeping daylight as Brooke selected the key for the service door, placed it in the lock, opened the door, and entered the building. Once inside, she turned on the lights and walked down a long corridor towards the community food larder. At the end of the corridor, she unlocked another steel door, found another light switch, and illuminated the warehouse. She passed aisle after aisle of cans and boxes stacked from floor to ceiling on plywood shelving, each container free of dust; the result of the fastidious diligence of the women of Laman's River.

At the door leading from the larder to the community deep freeze, the girl selected the appropriate key, turned the lock, opened the door, and entered the room. Her breath was taken away by intense cold as she entered the freezer.

"Brooke?"

The Crow girl stopped dead in her tracks.

"Is that you?"

180

Brooke Talmadge stood as still as a pillar of salt in an Old Testament verse.

A figure shrouded in wool stood up. A disheveled and disoriented Joyce Nielsen emerged from the folds of the Hudson Bay blanket. The revelation was akin to a butterfly slithering free of its cocoon. Joyce's scarlet hair was a mess. Her eyes blinked nervously. Her lips appeared parched and dry.

"Help me," the woman whispered, extending her hands in front of her nightgown-covered body, a white zip tie securing her wrists.

"What the hell...?" Brooke asked, an angry inflection to her voice as she moved quickly to the woman's side. "Who did this to you?"

Joyce fought emotion.

Be strong. Remember the time you spent with Brooke. She's a friend. Just stay calm and she'll come through for you.

One day, while Brooke was minding children on the playground next to the meetinghouse, her eyes riveted on *Wide Sargasso Sea,* the only book she owned, one of the only possessions she took with her when she ran away from her mother and her mother's abusive boyfriend, Joyce had chanced upon the Crow girl and commented on the elegance of Jean Rhys's prose. The off-hand remark had sparked a friendship and prompted Joyce, whenever she was in Great Falls, to buy new novels or short-story collections for the girl. They would share whatever literature Joyce picked out and discuss the books over herbal tea and lunch. Due to the slender nature of Rhys's collected work, they'd exhausted the author's writing in short order. Then they dove into *The Bluest Hour*, a heady biography of Rhys's life, her loves, and her infatuation with her home (the Caribbean island of Dominica). When they finished reading Jean Rhys and *about* Jean Rhys, Joyce introduced the girl to the works of Minnesota Ojibwe author, Louise Erdrich on the premise that Brooke, who loved Rhys because of her exotic upbringing, would come to appreciate the beauty of the modern Native American narrative found in Erdrich's stories. A connection had been made between the FBI agent and the young Crow girl; a bond created of written words.

Brooke Talmadge reached into the pocket of her coat, removed a red handled Swiss Army knife, and opened the blade. The older woman held her arms in front of her body. With a swipe of hardened steel, the girl snapped the zip tie in half. Joyce drew the Hudson Bay blanket around her like a cloak.

"There. That's better. Now, you mind telling me what the hell this is all about?" Brooke asked, folding the knife carefully and returning it to the depths of her coat.

The FBI agent pushed the girl ahead of her with a firm hand towards the open door.

"No time. We've got to move. I'll explain as we go."

They sped through the warehouse at a near run. They didn't bother to close doors behind them. The urgency in Joyce Nielsen's movements was contagious. Despite being out of shape from her recent pregnancy, Brooke Talmadge kept up with the older woman with ease.

Outside the meetinghouse, the women entered a grove of cottonwoods; the twisted gnarls of the great lowland trees bulging like ogre faces from a fairy tale. Dawn angled above the surrounding hills and bathed the woody phantasms in golden light. Beneath the barren branches of the cottonwoods, the women stopped and drew deep breaths.

"Charles discovered that I'm not who I say I am," Joyce offered, her teeth chattering as she stood on the cold ground in her stocking feet, her eyes locked on the girl.

"What the hell does that mean?"

"I'm an FBI agent."

Brooke's face contorted.

"No way!"

"It's true."

"But why? Why are you here?"

The agent looked around furtively.

"Too long a story to tell. There've been some murders. Young Indian girls like you. We think The Colony is involved. Not everyone. But some of the leadership."

"Charles?"

"The details aren't important right now," the agent said quietly, searching the rapidly brightening landscape for evidence that The Colony had been alerted to her escape. "I need you to do something for me," she added, her eyes locked on the young Native girl's face.

"Anything."

"Under my mattress, there's a handgun and a clip. I need you to bring them to me. Mr. Black… you know who he is, right?"

The girl nodded.

"Well, he's not who he seems. He's coming back to Laman's River. He's coming here to kill me. I need that gun, to defend myself."

The girl thought for a moment.

"On one condition."

"Sure, I'll take you with me."

"No, that's not it. I can't leave now. This is my home. I have a baby and, though I don't love Charles, he's not the worst I could do. No matter what he did to you, he's a hell of a lot kinder than that asshole my mother took up with."

Joyce's eyes blinked.

"Then what?"

"Tell me."

"Tell you what?"

The girl grinned shyly.

"Tell me your real name."

The agent hesitated.

"No name, no gun."

The older woman relented.

"Corrine. Corrine MacDonald."

The Indian girl extended a bare hand, the skin warm from being concealed in the cuff of her coat.

"Pleased to meet you, Corrine. You stay here. I'll see what I can do about getting that gun. It's a good half-mile back to Keystone Ranch. It'll take some time. You best take shelter while you wait," the girl said, pointing to a loafing shed full of alfalfa at the far end of the tree line. "You can hide there. The hay'll keep you warm."

Corrine MacDonald's eyes studied the ground.

"We're leaving tracks in the snow. It won't be long before they find me. Hurry, will you? Agents are on the way. They should be here..." the woman paused. "Do you know what time it is?"

"About six forty-five," Brooke said, puffs of moist air exiting her mouth like steam from a teakettle.

"They'll be here by eight. Hurry up girl, get me that gun."

Brooke Talmadge nodded, drew her coat tight to her body, and broke into a run.

THIRTY-FOUR

Precious little was left of Abe Armstrong. By the time Agent Walker made the man's side, the sheriff was gone. Armstrong's lower torso had been ripped apart by seven hundred pellets ejected by a Claymore mine. The man's right leg remained intact; his black boot on his foot, but his left leg had been completely sheared off at the hip. And where there'd once been a face, there was only blood. Steel shot had peeled away Abe Armstrong's features, rendering him unidentifiable.

"Christ," Walker said as he knelt by the side of the fallen officer. "Jesus fucking Christ."

Conscious that other booby traps might be in place, Slater gingerly made her way to the dead man.

The sheriff of Cook County had seen her share of dead bodies during nearly three decades of law enforcement work. Two old men shot to death by a Yugoslav secret agent. A-seven-year-old child burned in a fire pit by her rapist after strangulation; her tiny body charred beyond recognition. Folks felled by heart attack, suicide, or other causes; bodies young and old dispatched by evil, nature, or poor choices. A serial rapist killed in a gas line explosion by a resourceful victim in a cabin on a remote island in Lake County.

That last one is the closest I've ever come to something like this, Slater thought as she studied what had once been Meagher County Sheriff Abe Armstrong.

Agent Walker's hand grasped Armstrong's right wrist. The FBI special agent could not check Armstrong's left wrist for a pulse. The dead man's gloved left hand and wrist lay a few feet from the cooling body; scarlet spattered the snow covered ground, witness to the trajectory of the severed hand. Slater looked at Walker. The agent's eyes were shut tight.

"Walker," Slater said quietly. "He's dead. We need to move on."

The agent released Armstrong's wrist and stood up. Before Slater could utter a word of caution, Walker broke through the bramble at a full run, M-16 locked, loaded, and pointed in the general direction of the cabin's back door.

Samantha Byrnes steadied the muzzle of her assault rifle on a kitchen window overlooking the rear yard of the place, her left eye closed, her right eye fixed on the gun's sights.

Slater rose from the ground. Snow and soggy leaves slid from her winter camouflage fatigues as she followed Walker's furious run.

Agent Whitaker made for the front porch of the cottage, his rifle held fast by its sling; a 9mm Glock in his right hand. There was no sound, no movement, no activity inside the cabin as the officers surrounded the place.

Walker and Slater took positions on either side of the rear door and pressed their backs against the log wall of the cottage. Walker cradled his rifle. He nodded to Slater. The sheriff reached across her torso, M-16 in her left arm, and opened the rear door to Jason Orth's home.

"FBI," Walker yelled as the door creaked on its hinges.

There was no response. Whitaker skirted the open space of the cottage's front yard. By gestures, he redeployed Byrnes behind a lodge pole pine. Byrnes aimed her rifle at the front door. Whitaker sped over loose snow, vaulted up the stairway, opened the screen door to the three-season porch, and posted himself to the right of the front door.

"FBI," Whitaker shouted as he tested the front door knob with his gloved left hand while holding the Glock in his right. The knob turned. The door was unlocked.

Inside the cabin, it was clear to the four officers that The Tyler wasn't home. There were no dirty dishes in the kitchen sink; everything was in its place. There was no fire in the soapstone fireplace or the cook stove, making the cabin nearly as cold as the outdoors.

"He took his laptop," Slater said, her eyes riveted on a table in the cabin's living room. "The docking station is empty."

"He knew we were coming," Sam Byrnes said after checking the bedroom. "My guess is that he packed himself a bag," the detective continued. "Left this behind," Byrnes added, scooping up a solitary white athletic sock with a gloved hand from the wood floor. "Must've been in a hurry."

Slater sniffed the air. Her nose picked up a familiar scent. The sheriff's eyes were drawn to an ashtray on an end table next to the sofa. She slung the M-16 over a shoulder, bent down to examine the contents of the ashtray, and retrieved a turquoise wrapper with black lettering.

"You're right, Sam. We must have just missed the bastard," Slater said, removing the Black Jack gum wrapper from the ashtray, turning the paper over and over in her hand.

"Shit," Walker said, the despondency in his voice clear as he sat on the sofa, the plastic butt of the rifle resting on the freshly washed pine floor. "Abe died for goddamn nothing."

THIRTY-FIVE

Brooke Talmadge made her way towards Keystone Ranch. Toothy promontories and sandstone ridges, still in shadow and waiting for the sun's touch, encircled the Smith River valley like enormous black fingers as the Crow girl moved with stealth, her boots unsettling weightless snow as she scurried towards the hidden gun.

She's in trouble, Brooke thought. *She's my friend. But what about my duty to Charles? To Abby? To our family? Maybe Joyce, or Corrine, or whatever the hell her real name is, isn't telling me the truth. She didn't show me a badge. How do I know who she really is? Maybe she means to harm us. I should just turn back, go to Charles, tell him where she is. He's my husband. There's been precious little good in my short life; he's been, despite the fact I have to share him with Abby, the best of it. He never forced me into this. Now we have a child together. Now, we are a family. Maybe not the sort of family Momma would recognize. But one that replicates the family structure of my ancestors: Prominent Crow warriors sometimes had plural wives. I need to think. I need to do the right thing.*

As the girl moved into the shadow of the Keystone Ranch mansion, the sun climbed above ridges to the east. A pink glow enveloped the valley. Brooke stopped short of the kitchen door to Keystone Ranch and questioned herself again.

Elsie. I'll ask Elsie what I should do. She's new here, has a fresh perspective. And she's Native, like me. Not Crow; Ojibwe. But she'll understand. If she says I should tell Charles, then that's what I'll do. If she tells me to bring the gun to the woman, then I'll do that. Elsie's been around. She'll know what to do.

Brooke knocked tentatively on the door. Jennifer Nielsen answered.

"Brooke, what are you doing up at this time of the morning running around in your PJ's?"

"I need to talk to Elsie."

"She's packing. We're getting ready to leave. Something's come up."

The Native American girl detected urgency in the other woman's voice. She noted that Jennifer, despite the fact that Sunday worship service wouldn't start for another hour, was already dressed for church.

"Somethin' wrong?"

Jennifer shook her head.

"No. The Prophet just got called away is all. You know how busy he is. He wants the family to come with, to keep him company," the woman lied.

"It'll only take a minute," Brooke pleaded. "I really have to talk to Elsie."

Elsie Johnson appeared from behind the older woman.

"Hi, Brooke. What's up?" Elsie asked.

The Ojibwe girl was fully dressed. She was wearing a denim skirt cut to below her knees and a print blouse, the ridge of buttons in the center of the rose colored fabric decorated with lace and bows. She wore winter boots. An unzipped jacket hung loose across her shoulders.

"Looks like you're getting ready to leave too," Brooke observed as she entered the house.

Jennifer Nielsen closed the kitchen door.

"We don't have much time," the older woman said nervously. "I'm gonna get the kids in the Denali. When I come back for you, Elsie, you better be ready to go."

The Ojibwe girl nodded.

"Come on, we can talk while I pack."

The girls headed down the hallway. Sounds of scurrying and thumping emanated from distant reaches of the mansion.

"Evelyn is getting the kids packed," Elsie confided. "What gives?"

"Joyce."

They entered Elsie's bedroom.

"What about her?"

Brooke Talmadge looked back, over her shoulder, towards the master bedroom.

"He's not here, if that's what you're worried about. He's waiting for us in the Denali," Elsie advised, referring to The Prophet. "He was ready to go before I even got out of bed. Why are you so jumpy? And where the hell *is* Joyce? I haven't seen her in a couple of days. Obadiah says she went to Great Falls for a medical appointment. But that's not like her. She would have said something to me before she left. What the hell is going on?"

Brooke closed the solid pine door to the room.

"Charles."

"What about Charles?"

"He tied Joyce up and put her in the community freezer!"

The Ojibwe girl's face twitched.

"What the hell's going on?"

The Crow girl pursed her lips.

"Joyce isn't her real name."

188

In the hallway, Evelyn called for Elsie.

"What the fuck," the Ojibwe girl said quietly.

Brooke frowned.

"Whatever," Elsie shrugged. "Get to the point. We don't have much time."

"She says she's with the FBI; that her name is Corrine MacDonald. Says that Mr. Black, that spooky dude who hangs around The Prophet, is coming back here to kill her."

"You're shitting me!" Elsie gasped.

"That's what she told me no more than fifteen minutes ago."

"You saw her?"

"I found her tied up in the freezer and cut her loose. She's in the hay shed across the community pasture. There's more…"

The voice of the first wife got louder and closer.

"Get to it," Elsie whispered.

"She has a gun. She wants me to get it from underneath her mattress and bring it to her."

"No way!"

They heard Evelyn's labored breathing on the other side of the door.

"Elsie? Are you in there?"

"I'll be right out!"

"We have to leave now!"

"I had a small accident. I'll be right out," the girl lied, using her monthly cycle as a ruse, knowing that Evelyn, as first wife, was privy to such information.

"Two minutes. If you're not in the car in two minutes, we'll leave without you."

"Yes, ma'am."

The girls listened to the older woman's footfalls recede.

"What should I do?" Brooke Talmadge whispered. "I want to do what's right by Charles. If he thinks this woman is a threat to us, shouldn't I turn her in?"

Elsie stared at her friend.

"There's more, isn't there?"

Brooke nodded.

"She's a friend. A good friend. At least, I thought she was."

"Uh huh."

"What should I do?"

Elsie Johnson stood quietly in the warm air of the bedroom and thought for a moment.

This is my chance to get the hell out of this place.

"I'll do it."

Brooke's eyes widened.

189

"Do what?"

"I'll bring her the gun. You go back to Charles. Don't tell him anything."

"But your family is leaving."

Elsie smiled enigmatically.

"They ain't my family. I'm not like you. I never really wanted this," the girl motioned with her arms, meaning to encompass the entirety of Laman's River with the gesture. "I just wanted to get away from where I was, is all. This place is just a rest stop on the way to somewhere else."

Brooke opened the door.

"The hay shed… in the meadow…behind the meetinghouse."

"I know."

The Crow girl left the room.

Outside the mansion, the Denali idled. The Prophet, agitated by the unforeseen delay, cursed an epithet, pounded his fists on the leather dash, cursed again, and shoved the SUV's gear shift into 'drive."

THIRTY-SIX

"There's the LZ," Jeff Dugan shouted above the roar of the Black Hawk. "Set 'er down in the pasture."

Warrant Officer Jack Green nodded, maneuvered the joystick of the old chopper, adjusted the blades, and positioned the helicopter to land. Behind the first chopper, a second bird, piloted by Warrant Officer Gil Jamison, followed the course of the lead Black Hawk and descended beneath the tree line. A third Black Hawk was a minute off the lead chopper's pace.

The flight had gone smoothly. It was nearly eight o'clock, time for the Sunday morning services in the meetinghouse to begin. Dugan had planned the assault for an hour when nearly every man, woman, and child in Laman's River would be at worship. There would be little resistance to the intrusion. Warrants would be served. The three principals, Charles Talmadge, and their co-conspirators would be arrested. As for The Tyler, Dugan hoped that he was home snug in his cabin on Sixteen Mile Creek.

If that's the case, the FBI man thought as a blanket of snow rose to meet the Black Hawk, *Walker and Whitaker will take him into custody and that chapter in this little adventure will be over.*

Dugan didn't entertain any other possibility. He was reasonably certain that Jason Orth would be caught napping.

"Let's go," Dugan shouted over the din of the rotors.

The FBI agent unslung his M-16 and leapt from the chopper, his boots unsettling new snow as they claimed frozen ground.

Herb Whitefeather struggled to rise from the bench seat in the second helicopter. The big Lakota jerked and thrashed about like the Tin Man as he stood up, grabbed his rifle, and stepped out of the chopper.

"Come on, old man," Dugan chided, "get a move on."

"Damn B-Ball's finally caught up with me," the Indian complained as he joined the other officers. "Never thought I'd be one of those broken down old wrecks you see signing autographs at the mall," the agent quipped. "But I guess that's about all I'm good for."

The first and second Black Hawks disgorged their teams. The third chopper landed and did the same.

"Gentlemen and ladies," Dugan said as thirty federal agents, police officers, and deputies assembled in the gathering morning; pink waxing to blue as the sun rose in the sky; "lock and load one round.

Make sure your safeties are on. No discharges unless I authorize you to fire or a life is in danger, you all understand?"

The group nodded sullenly, the reality of their mission clear. They were invading an American community. The constitutional and legal implications of their actions would likely be debated for years. It was Dugan's goal to preclude loss of life. He was duty bound to keep a rein on his team and to apprehend their quarry without firing a shot, without creating martyrs.

•••

A yellow Zodiak floated down the Smith towards its rendezvous. The boat landing was a mile from the helicopter LZ. The team in the raft was to pick up Corrine MacDonald and spirit her away. The rescue team was not to engage the citizens of Laman's River.

Special Agent Bob Plesha, his bald dome covered with the winter camouflage hood of his jacket, M-16 resting in his lap, sat in the front seat of the inflatable. Special Agent Todd Stevens, his massive girth confined in a set of winter fatigues one size too small, occupied the second seat in the raft, his rifle held at port. Special Agent Tracy Gibbons, Corrine MacDonald's direct supervisor, sat next to Stevens. Ellis Carlson, a guide who'd been born and raised on the river, manned the sweep.

As the Zodiak floated downstream, a solitary figure descended a ridgeline high above the Smith. The Tyler, a high powered .50 caliber sniper's rifle slung across his back, his face painted white, his body covered in white Carhartt bibs and jacket, his feet protected from the snow by white Red Wing trapping boots, moved into position. His intent was to pick off the FBI rescue team from elevation. He found a protected perch behind a line of gray limestone boulders, debris left by centuries of weather assaulting soft rock, unslung his weapon, and waited for the Zodiak to appear.

The Tyler had filled his Dakota with gear and personal items before setting up the Claymore, after which he'd driven away from his home, confident that he would never see his little slice of paradise again.

Possessions, The Tyler mused while waiting for the yellow raft to arrive, *aren't important. The Principle. The teachings of The Prophet. The Bible. The Book of Mormon. Nephi's Letter to the Lamanites. These are the things that one needs to cherish and value; not goods or wealth.*

The Tyler slipped off his left glove, slid his bare hand into the open pocket of his jacket, and removed a stick of Black Jack.

A small pleasure that does no harm.

192

He unwrapped the gum and popped it into his mouth.

Once I dispatch the agents in the boat, I'll head down the hill and take care of MacDonald. I'm uncertain as to the hour of the main assault but I should have enough time. God is, after all, on my side.

The raft came into view. The Zodiak squeezed between rocky spires, bounced over a treacherous cascade, and shot into a small pool like a wad of tobacco spit by a logger. The Tyler placed his left index finger in the trigger guard of the rifle and trained the scope on the first agent in the boat. With his right thumb, The Tyler snapped the safety to the "off" position and took aim. The crosshairs of the scope rested on the right cheek of Agent Plesha as the raft drifted towards shore.

Snap.

The Tyler turned away from his target. His eyes scanned the steep slope above him for the source of the noise but he saw nothing.

Jumpy. I better calm down or I'll miss the shot.

The assassin returned his attention to the river.

Snap.

The Tyler spit out his gum and turned around a second time

What is that?

A guttural rumble echoed behind the sniper's position.

What in blazes is that racket?

The assassin stared at the winter landscape. His pupils adjusted to shadows caused by an overhanging ledge. Tawny fur emerged from the white and yellow escarpment. A cougar was crouched beneath the overhang, its eyes locked on The Tyler. The cat's haunches vibrated with excitement as it considered its prey.

The Tyler pointed his weapon in the general direction of the cougar. The lion's tail twitched. Its nose sniffed morning air. Without warning, the animal leaped high, intent upon landing paws down on The Tyler. There was no time for the assassin to aim.

Crack.

"What the hell was that?" Agent Gibbons asked.

"There, up on the ledge," Plesha said, his eyes squinting through a set of binoculars he'd drawn to his face at the sound of the rifle's discharge. "Goddamned sniper," Plesha whispered, watching the man and his rifle tumble down slope. "Looks like he's tangled with a wolf or something,"

"Cougar," the river guide said, as the bow of the Zodiak met shore. "The hills are crawling with 'em. Usually only run into them at night. But they'll take a swipe at you, if you're in their territory alone, even in broad daylight."

"We best get the hell out of this boat and into some cover," Stevens said, urging his overweight torso out of the Zodiak. "Make for the swale. That should shield us from whoever's on that hill."

The agents and the river guide scrambled out of the Zodiak. The men made the safety of the woods before The Tyler emerged victorious from beneath the carcass of the dead cat.

"Shit."

Jason Orth studied the valley through his riflescope. He'd lost track of the enemy. They were concealed by thicket and unavailable as targets. With no clear shot, there was no reason to hang around. He had no more business at the landing. He left the dead cougar, a single .50 caliber round through its heart, and retreated into the pines.

THIRTY-SEVEN

It was ten minutes to eight when The Tyler noted, from a position high above Zion's Way, three black Denali's leaving The Colony in great haste.

Down in the valley, The Tyler hurried past residents dressed for church; their bodies bundled against the weather, their faces red from winter and exertion. He'd stashed his rifle up slope. His Dakota waited for him at a U.S. Forest Service parking lot on the other side of the ridge. The Tyler knew that Zion's Way was about to be sealed off, that there was scarce little time for the leaders of The Colony to escape.

The Prophet had better get a move on, the assassin thought as he joined the churchgoers moving towards the meetinghouse.

Few people in Laman's River knew The Tyler. Those living in The Colony who'd met him felt there was something unsettling about the man. The community members who'd encountered The Tyler did, of course, ask questions of the First and Second Counselors and The Prophet about the stranger. Folks were reassured that the man was harmless; that he was simply a friend of those in power and that they need inquire no further. The responses of the men in charge were curt and authoritative; their demeanor made it clear that such queries shouldn't be repeated.

Consequently, as The Tyler made his way towards the meetinghouse, no one offered a greeting. No one tried to engage him in small talk. Folks parted and kept their distance from The Tyler as if he was a leper.

"Charles," The Tyler called out as he neared the main entrance to the church.

Charles Talmadge stood tall against the new morning, his best suit pressed to natty perfection, a yellow tie clasped to his prim white dress shirt by a gold tie clip in the shape of a beehive, the symbol of his faith.

"Mr. Black," Talmadge replied in a near whisper as The Tyler joined him in front of the meetinghouse.

"Can we talk?" The Tyler asked.

"Holmes," Talmadge shouted to one of the other elders of the church standing nearby. The man advanced towards Talmadge and The Tyler dressed in an ill-fitting discount store sports jacket, white shirt, and blue tie. "Take over greeting the folks, would you? Mr. Black has need of my counsel."

Edward Holmes, a diminutive man of middle age, his chin a mass of cuts from shaving, his blond hair wild and untamed, nodded and replaced Talmadge as the greeter at the front door of the meetinghouse.

"What's the problem?" Talmadge asked as the men stood apart from the crowd.

"Three things you must know. One, law enforcement is in the process of blocking the exit from Laman's River. Fifty or sixty officers are moving into place up the road. I doubt they're going to make a move anytime soon but they're here to arrest us."

"Well, then, it's Armageddon, isn't it? They won't come waltzing in here to disrupt what we've worked for without a fight. I'll get the men in position and break out the automatics, the RPGs, and whatever else we've got to give them a warm welcome."

"I doubt they're interested in causing a blood bath," The Tyler said softly, his eyes scrutinizing the tall man. "More likely they'll wait us out. Like Waco, but without the messy ending. The FBI and the ATF learned from that disaster. They don't want pictures of dead kids plastered across the front page of the *Billings Gazette*."

Talmadge placed a boney hand to his significant chin.

"You said there were three things."

The Tyler's face tightened.

"So I did. The second thing you need to know is that three FBI agents and a guide landed at the boat landing moments ago. They're here for MacDonald."

Talmadge's nose twitched as he stared hard at the man.

"If you know that, they must be dead," Talmadge whispered.

The Tyler smiled weakly.

"Tried to accomplish that. Failed at it, I'm afraid. Cougar spooked me. I missed taking them out as they landed. They're hunkered down in brush along the river as we speak."

Talmadge made a move to leave but The Tyler, though much smaller, restrained the taller man with a single hand.

"Not to worry. I'll take care of them."

Charles Talmadge stopped in his tracks.

"The third thing I need to know?"

"The time is at hand for you to show leadership. The Prophet, the First and Second Counselors, and their families, have left Laman's River. As the leader of the Home Guard, you're now in charge."

Talmadge's head bowed in reverence to the disclosure.

"They've left? Left Laman's River?" he asked in a carefully modulated tone. "Why would our leaders do that when our way of life is threatened, when The Principle that Obadiah Nielsen was given by an angel of God is now challenged? Why would The Prophet not stay to rally his people, to stand with us against the unbelievers who seek to destroy the truth?"

The Tyler smiled weakly.

"Do you know your history?"

"What?"

"Do you know the story of Leonidas?"

A puzzled look descended over the tall man's features.

"Leonidas was a Spartan king. One of two. The war king. He stood his ground against the Persians at Thermopylae so that the Greeks could rally and defeat the invaders. Sacrificed himself and his men for principle. That's what you're being asked to do, Charles. Make the ultimate sacrifice for The Principle. The Prophet, his ideals, are more important than you. Than me. Than any single member of Laman's River."

Charles Talmadge thought for a moment.

"I understand. The die is cast. It falls to me to make ready the people," Talmadge said quietly.

"Get your men in position. I'll take care of the four intruders," The Tyler said as he turned towards the distant silver line of the Smith. "Use the barricades you built along Zion's Way. Catch any approaching vehicles in a cross fire. Make *them* pay for thinking *they* can defy the Word of God," The Tyler said before retreating.

The congregation was waiting for the tall man inside the church. The snow-covered parking lot was quiet. As Charles Talmadge turned the doorknob to enter the building, a resonant vibration disrupted the morning's quiet. Talmadge turned his head and watched in utter disbelief as three Montana National Guard helicopters circled The Colony, hovered like a trio of hawks hunting mice over an open meadow, and settled to Earth.

THIRTY-EIGHT

Deb Slater rolled the remains of Sheriff Abe Armstrong onto a blanket retrieved from the Huey. Sam Byrnes wrapped the dead man in soft green wool. Agents Walker and Whitaker hoisted the heavy bundle and began to walk through sunlit forest towards the waiting Huey.

"We need to secure the place," Slater said softly as she watched the agents carry the dead sheriff over uneven terrain.

"Then let's get to it," Sam Byrnes said quietly.

The homicide detective entered the cottage. Slater followed. The two officers scoured the interior of the log dwelling and noted items of interest, including computer disks, a 4Gig USB drive that Slater found taped to the bottom of The Tyler's desk (obviously missed in the man's hurry to evacuate) along with other written notes, file folders, papers, and documents. The search was over in moments. They left the cabin as the familiar sound of the Iroquois warming up, its rotors beginning to spin behind the thick wall of cottonwoods and brush, announced their ride was ready to leave. They placed police tape, "Crime Scene: Do Not Cross!" emboldened in black lettering across yellow vinyl, over the front and rear entrances of the cottage. Forensic investigators would arrive later to evaluate the premises and inventory its contents. Slater and Byrnes' job was nearly done. Once they were back at the Huey, they would radio Dugan and advise him that The Tyler was not at his cabin. Then they would bring Abe Armstrong home.

As the chopper climbed above the trees and followed Sixteen Mile Creek, Slater held the dead sheriff's cold hand.

Dear Jesus, Slater prayed silently. *Take Abraham Armstrong into your arms. Make him one of your flock, a sheep of your own fold. Amen.*

Slater's eyes scanned the landscape flitting beneath the chopper as it claimed sky; but her thoughts were not fixed upon the white pastureland passing under the Huey.

Not much time left for us now, the sheriff thought. *Rick's in the last stages of the disease. I could ask for more time; ask God for another remission. But that would be for me, not for Rick. That would be selfish. He's done. He has no more strength left for the fight.*

Slater's eyes watered as the aircraft made altitude. The noise inside the helicopter was deafening but created privacy. No one around

Deb Slater could hear the soft whimpering she made as tears paraded down her downy cheeks. She averted her eyes from the dead body placed carefully at her feet but retained her strong grip on the dead man's hand.

It's for the best, Dear Lord. For the best that you let Rick find peace before the spring. It'll be hard on Annie. She's too damn young for this, God. Jesus...Christ...this is so unfair! Get a grip, Debra Marie Slater. Get a fucking grip. No one said it would be fair. No one made you any promises. Take what is given, make the best of it. That's what Daddy always says. He's right. Dwell on the good. Ignore the bad. You need to live your life for Annie. Maybe, Slater thought, *it's time to hang it up. I've got my years in. My pension is vested. Maybe it's time to retire, find some part-time work at the Casino in Grand Portage as a security officer and get to know my daughter.*

"Whatya' thinkin'?"

Sam Byrnes had to nearly shout for Slater to hear the question.

The sheriff didn't answer. She simply tucked Abe Armstrong's cold hand inside the woolen blanket and stared straight ahead.

THIRTY-NINE

Dugan's command split into three columns of ten each. Two columns, a total of twenty officers, were to move in choreographed fashion on the meetinghouse where their intelligence indicated that the entire community of Laman's River, save two men posted on the front gate, would be worshipping. After surrounding the church, Dugan would enter the building through the main door with two other officers, their M-16s locked, loaded, and ready.

Herb Whitefeather was given command of the remaining column. His objective was to capture the sentries defending the entrance gate to Laman's River.

Whitefeather strategically placed the seven men and two women under his authority and kept a sharp eye on The Colony's front gate. The advantage of surprise was on the intruders' side. The sentries, whose view of the helicopter landing zone was limited by trees, buildings, and distance, would not be looking inward for an assault: Their eyes would be glued to the east, on Zion's Way, in expectation that law enforcement would be arriving by way of the road.

So long as we don't alert the sentries to our presence, Whitefeather thought as the column deployed around the entrance gate, *we should catch them unprepared.*

When Charles Talmadge heard the choppers, he lost his bravado. There was no time to rally the men of Laman's River to retrieve their personal rifles, shotguns, and side arms; certainly no time to break out the more onerous weaponry from The Colony's armory located a quarter-mile from the meetinghouse.

Talmadge had argued with Nielsen on this point. Argued and lost. He had argued that the meetinghouse was the focus of The Colony; that the food larder, community freezer, and offices of the sect were attached to or inside the building; that locating the armory in close proximity to the worship space made sense. The Prophet would have none of it. He would not countenance (to use a Biblical phrase Obadiah Nielsen was fond of uttering) weapons being stockpiled at or near the church.

"God has seen fit to reveal to me," Nielsen had said plainly, "that the weapons must be no closer to our house of worship than a quarter-mile. No closer, you understand, Charles?"

200

No, I don't understand, Talmadge remembered thinking at the time. But he was not about to incur the wrath of the founder of Laman's River. The leader of the Home Guard was not about to offend God. And so, the armory was built into the hillside, in a style reminiscent of a settler's root cellar, off a shoulder of Zion's Way between the meetinghouse and the main entrance to the community.

It was a decision Talmadge lamented as he stood before the congregation, The Colony's members packed tightly in the sanctuary's wooden pews. Families worshipped together: First wives were seated next to their husbands; sister wives sat alongside the first wives in order of marriage; the children were next, arranged by descending age.

Some prominent seats were vacant, a circumstance which was noticeable and, to some degree, puzzling to the congregation. In addition, three high backed wooden chairs on the stage behind Talmadge (usually occupied by the three leaders of the church) remained empty.

From the podium, Charles Talmadge located his family in the third row of pews to his right. First wife Abigail, sister wife, Brooke, the baby Raven Ruth suckling at Brooke's bosom, and three other children birthed by Abigail sat completely still, their eyes riveted on their husband and father. Members of the Home Guard, the men and boys charged with protecting Laman's River, sat beside their wives and their families, their eyes fixed on the tall man.

Charles Talmadge knew he had only a few moments before officers would enter the church hell bent on his arrest. Wagging his head, Talmadge began to preach.

"They say," Talmadge orated, his coarse voice thundering across the room, "that we follow a false prophet. That our ideals—family, plural marriage, Celestial bliss, the bleaching of the Lamanites, the Word of the Angel Moroni, the prophesy of Obadiah Nielsen—are for naught. They say that we are foolish and misguided in our dream of a place, this place, where The Principle can be practiced and kept alive until the coming of Jesus as foretold in both the *Bible* and *The Book of Mormon*. For did not King Mosiah say to his people, in the time of judges:

Therefore choose you by the voice of this people, judges, that ye may be judged according to the laws which have been given you by our fathers, which are correct, and which were given them by the hand of the Lord...

And if the time comes that the voice of the people doth choose iniquity, then is the time that the judgments of God will come upon you; yea, then is the time He will visit you with great destruction even as He has hitherto visited this land. (Mosiah 29: 25-27).

201

"Unholy power is about to be visited upon us," Talmadge continued, "not because of our following The Principle. Not because we believe The Prophet. But because of the iniquity of people who do not know or understand the words of Obadiah Nielsen. They cannot comprehend that we are prescribed by God to do the bidding of our prophet as to the Lamanite people; some of whom sit here as members of our community today as sister-wives so that their blood may mingle and mix with our blood; so that future generations shall fulfill the words of the great Nephi:

And then shall they rejoice; for they shall know that it is a blessing unto them from the hand of God; and their scales of darkness shall begin to fall from their eyes; and many generations shall not pass away among them, save they shall be a white and delightsome people (2 Nephi 31: 6).

Charles Talmadge suddenly stopped preaching. Every head in the place turned in unison towards the sound of entry. Murmurs of disbelief rose amongst the Mormons as the doors to the sanctuary opened. Jeff Dugan strode into the church with two other officers. The three men, carrying M-16s and wearing winter camouflage, stomped irreverently into the church and stood brazenly amongst the congregation with their rifles held at the ready. Talmadge nodded to the intruders.

"They are here, my brothers and sisters. They are here to arrest me, to pillory me. They will say," Talmadge offered thoughtfully, lowering his voice, "that The Prophet, the First and Second Counselors, Mr. Black, and I have engaged in crimes, crimes of the most heinous and vile nature. Do not believe them, my fellow citizens of God's chosen city. Do not listen to their lies. They are most corrupt and untruthful in their speech. They are willing to sacrifice paradise to ensure that The Principle dies with us. Do not let it be so," Talmadge warned as Jeff Dugan walked athletically towards the podium, his rifle cradled in his arms; his two companions posted at either side of the main aisle. "For it has been written, for it shall be. Amen."

Dugan stopped next to the sect leader.

"Brother Talmadge," the Mormon special agent said in a firm but quiet voice, "do not make a scene. Come willingly and no one in this church will be harmed."

The preacher nodded acquiescence. Dugan gestured with the barrel of the rifle for Talmadge to begin walking towards the open doors of the church. The air inside the building was moist and warm. Snow slid off the agent's boots and melted on the cement floor as

Dugan followed the taller man down the main aisle of the sanctuary. At the third row of pews, Charles Talmadge stopped, bent at his waist, embraced Abigail, and whispered in her ear. He stood up, moved closer to the pew, touched the almond colored cheek of his infant daughter with his right index finger, kissed Brooke on the lips, and resumed walking.

"Where are you taking him?" an elderly sister wife of one of the seventies screamed, standing in excitement as the two men passed her seat. "Why are you doing this to us?"

Dugan didn't engage the woman. When she attempted to grab the sleeve of Dugan's winter jacket, Talmadge blocked the effort with his right hand.

"Don't, Sister Mary. Don't make a scene. It will do no good and will only excite the children."

The woman retracted her arm, covered her plump white face with her hands, and wept inconsolably as Talmadge continued walking.

Dugan and Talmadge stopped at the open doors. One of the officers urged the prisoner's arms behind his back, placed handcuffs on his wrists, and secured the shackles in place.

"Take him outside," Dugan said calmly.

The officer motioned with the barrel of his rifle. Talmadge exited the church. With a wave of his gloved hand, Dugan deployed additional officers inside the sanctuary. The FBI special agent walked deliberately into the center of the worship hall, stood with his back to the podium, and addressed the congregation.

"All of you will, in good time, be interviewed and processed by officers under my direction. What happens to you once Mr. Talmadge and the others we're here to arrest are in custody, I can't say. Likely any young women who have been forced..."

Dugan's oration was greeted with hisses and boos from the congregation. A young man in the last row of the sanctuary started to rise, his fists clenched in anger, upset clear on his reddened face.

An officer walked up behind the young Mormon, placed a firm hand on the man's shoulder, and forced the protester back into his pew.

"...into marriage and who are under the age of sixteen, under the age of consent, will be removed, along with their children, from Laman's River. Those men who have had relations with underage girls will be arrested and prosecuted in state court. Those who brought young girls into sister wifery from across state lines will be arrested and prosecuted in federal court. Any illegal weaponry found on the premises will be seized and the owners, or the individuals found to be responsible for the same, will be charged with violations of federal law. And," Dugan concluded, "your leadership, Obadiah Nielsen, Ezra Pratt,

Micah Albrecht, Charles Talmadge, and Jason Orth, the man you know as Allan Black, will be detained on other, more serious charges that I cannot, at this moment, divulge. What happens to your property, your homes, your children, will depend upon your level of criminal involvement. Now," Dugan urged sternly, "please remain seated while officers under my command identify and process you."

Five additional officers entered the building armed with notepads and pens; rifles secured on their backs by slings, the business of investigation now a priority. The men and women under Dugan's command started at the front of the church, their effort supervised and watched closely by armed guards posted throughout the sanctuary.

Dugan, his words having caused women and children in the congregation to wail and sob, left the building. As the special agent stepped outside, he heard gunfire in the distance.

"Shit," Jeff Dugan muttered as he moved quickly towards the sound of battle. "Shit."

FORTY

Elsie Johnson sprinted over snow, the burnished steel of the magazine and the gun cold against her bare hands, as she made her way towards Corrine MacDonald. The girl sought concealment in shadow as she moved stealthy through Laman's River, escape from a life of bondage, servitude, and procreation with a man she could never love central to her motivation. Her speed was restricted by her dress. She felt the sting of morning's touch. She could see the three-sided shed, square bales of alfalfa stacked from the ground to the building's galvanized steel roof visible through the shed's open front. She could not see Corrine MacDonald but Elsie knew the woman was there, waiting for her.

Without warning, Allan Black stepped out from behind Alfred Sloan's cabin and blocked the Ojibwe girl's path. Twenty feet separated Elsie from the assassin. He'd made his way from the meetinghouse to the community freezer, intent upon extracting information from Agent MacDonald, only to find her gone.

"Sister Johnson," The Tyler said calmly after his sudden manifestation, "why aren't you at worship?"

The Tyler's eyes fixed on the young Indian girl's face. He noted the tenseness in Elsie Johnson's jaw, the surprise in her eyes, as he spoke. He took note of the automatic clutched in the girl's right hand and the extra magazine pressed firmly against her left hip.

"What have we here?" The Tyler asked, nodding towards the gun. "Where ever did you get that?"

The girl's throat became as dry as a Montana arroyo in summer. The sounds of distant gunfire drew the man's attention. He turned his head towards the noise. Without warning, the girl bolted into a nearby alder thicket and vanished. The Tyler drew an automatic from his belt and moved into the underbrush in pursuit of the girl.

Something's up. She's likely headed for a rendezvous with that apostate agent. The gun. I need to stop the girl before she gives MacDonald the gun.

The snow gave The Tyler an advantage: Elsie Johnson could run, but, with each footstep leaving a roadmap, she could not hide.

The girl moved with surprising vigor. She found sanctuary in the cottonwoods beneath the escarpment defining Laman's River. She understood the need to create distance. The girl redoubled her effort. Her exhalations formed small clouds as she dodged between the massive trunks of hundred-year-old trees. Her movement was silent; time spent on the Grand Portage Reservation gathering berries and

205

walking forest trails reinforced an innate stealth that cannot be taught. She knew advantage lay in the trees. She knew that The Tyler was close behind. But she also knew that if he could not see her, if he could not hear her, he could not harm her.

Whoosh.

A covey of Hungarian partridges burst from cover. Ten birds rocketed through tight forest.

Damn it!

Crack.

A shot rang out behind Elsie Johnson.

Thwip.

A bullet cleaved a branch next to her head.

Shit that was close.

The girl's boots chafed her shins. She felt blood seep into her athletic socks.

Crack.

Thwip.

Another bullet sailed harmlessly above her head. Elsie knew she was not presenting the man with a viable target; that he'd guessed her location from the flight of the partridge.

The loafing shed was fifty yards beyond the last cottonwood. She pumped her arms, her hands clenched bloodlessly tight around cold steel. More gunfire.

Not him. Too far away.

The Tyler was no longer taking chances. He was, she knew, waiting for her to make the open field. He was smart, this man who was seeking to end her young life.

But I am Ojibwe. The forest is my people's home. Gichi-manidoo, give me the strength to run faster. Protect me as you protected warriors of old. Like Crazy Horse, who could not be brought down by the Blue Coats' bullets. A Sioux, to be sure, but a brother all the same. Let my lungs fill with air and my feet fly like those birds that were nearly my undoing.

The Mormon scripture that she'd heard recited in the meetinghouse one Sunday morning, a reading from Alma 18, which postulated that the Mormons had convinced her grandfathers and grandmothers, the Lamanites, that the Hebrew God was the Great Spirit, stuck in her craw as she ran. The hypocrisy, the arrogance of the people she had come to live with, enraged her and propelled her through the forest. Though Elsie Johnson did not know how to spell "hypocrite", she understood the meaning of the word. Her rage at the Mormons' chauvinism brought her to the place where cottonwood forest gave way to pasture meadow.

She stopped to listen. She heard the faint sound of boots moving over snow. She held her breath and listened intently. The man was closing the distance.

Gichi-manidoo, make me invisible. Bring me safely across the pasture to where the woman hides.

Elsie inhaled deeply. The exhalation of her last breath caused her shoulders to shrug. She lessened her grip on the magazine and the pistol to allow blood to resume flowing into nearly frozen fingers.

Snap.

The breaking of a twig caused her eyes to pop open.

Shit. He's closer than I thought.

Her eyes located the shed across the white field and focused on the yellow bales of last summer's hay stacked in orderly fashion beneath the shed's silver roof. Grip tightened on steel. Elsie gulped a last bit of winter air and sprang from behind the protective wall of trees, her boots slapping awkwardly as she sought to make speed across the frozen meadow.

Crack.

The Tyler's first shot hit snowy ground behind its target. Elsie struggled against the weight of exhaustion as she zigzagged over open terrain.

"Keep moving," Corrine MacDonald yelled as the agent stepped from shadow into light.

MacDonald watched the steady progress of the Ojibwe girl.

God protect her.

MacDonald watched helplessly as The Tyler emerged from the distant tree line, raised his pistol, and snapped off another shot.

Thwack.

The bullet caught Elsie Johnson in the left thigh. The impact spun the girl around but the Indian girl did not yield her precious possessions. She clutched the magazine and the automatic as she twisted in pain and fell to the ground.

"Shit, he shot me! The fuckin' asshole shot me!" she screamed.

The girl's thrashing ceased as she descended into shock. The Tyler broke into a run. MacDonald had little time to choose a course of action: flee, leaving an innocent girl to a horrendous fate, or take a chance, make a move for the gun and hope that her training would allow her to get off a shot before the assassin could drop her.

Here goes nothing.

Corrine MacDonald, her feet frozen solid, frost bite having taken hold through the thin cotton of her socks, darted out from behind the alfalfa. The Tyler stopped, took aim, and squeezed off another round.

207

Ping.

The bullet hit the steel roof of the shed just above the agent's head.

MacDonald's quickness caught the man off guard. The Tyler was unable to get a solid bead on the woman as she dove next to the stricken girl and pulled the .38 free of Elsie's clenched fist.

Stay low. Use the girl for protection.

Corrine MacDonald steadied the muzzle of the .38 on the left hip of the unconscious girl. She was about to fire the weapon, when, inexplicably, The Tyler retreated towards the cottonwoods. MacDonald compensated for the distance, took aim, and pulled steadily against the cold trigger with her right index finger.

Crack.

The bullet grazed the back of The Tyler's right calf but did not bring the assassin down. Killer merged with forest and the man was gone.

Why the hell did he turn tail and run?

The agent rolled Elsie Johnson onto her back and examined the girl's wound. The bullet had passed clean through. Though blood saturated the girl's silk pajama bottoms, it was clear the bullet had missed the femoral artery.

Thank God.

Corrine MacDonald ripped a strip of cloth from the hem of her nightgown and bandaged the girl's wound. As she worked to save Elsie Johnson, Special Agent Corrine MacDonald discovered the reason for The Tyler's retreat: Three FBI special agents and a river guide were headed her way.

FORTY-ONE

The boy watched his partner confront the intruder. Unexpectedly, the older sentry placed his M-16 on the ground and surrendered to the intruder without firing a shot.

That coward! Kevin Ganzt thought. *What the hell is he thinking? We're the first line of defense, or, in this case, since the threat comes from within, the last line of defense. Why did he not fire on the Lamanite? Why did he not take the man's life in preservation of The Principle?*

The boy slipped out of his guard shack and crouched low. It was full morning. Winter birds danced across the sheltered fields and meadows of the valley, their flights fanciful and desperate against the barrenness of the season. Ganzt began to sweat. Perspiration formed inside the collar of his parka as he released the safety of his assault rifle and slid his trigger finger into position. He did not have a clear shot at the big Indian as the man patted down the other guard, slid handcuffs over the man's wrists, and bent over to retrieve the sentry's discarded rifle. Ganzt waited patiently, controlling his breathing as his father had taught him hunting elk in the mountains. The boy knew the intruder would turn at some point, exposing his broad back to the teenager. Ganzt would only need one shot to take out the cop.

He'll never know what hit him.

As if scripted for a movie, Herb Whitefeather turned on his heels and exposed his back. Kevin Ganzt brought the muzzle of the M-16 up slowly, so as not to give away his position. He concentrated all of his energy and attention on the scene in front of him. He did not see the other officers closing in on his position.

"Son, put down the weapon," a woman's voice called out.

The command caused the boy to spin on his haunches.

"Don't do it son," a male voice added.

Officers materialized. Ganzt was surrounded.

Armageddon.

The boy fingered the trigger of his rifle.

The Lamanite or the woman?

Nerves trumped thought. Ganzt accidently squeezed the trigger of his rifle and sent automatic fire into the hillside above the woman's head.

"Return fire," Whitefeather shouted as he pushed his prisoner to the ground. "Return fire at will."

Crack.

A round slammed into the wooden siding of the guard shack near Ganzt's right shoulder. The boy regained his composure, flipped a lever on the M-16 to semi-automatic and leveled the rifle barrel on the woman.

Thwack.

Whitefeather's shot was dead on. The bullet caught Kevin Ganzt square in the forehead.

Crack.

A round discharged from the boy's M-16 as he collapsed but the bullet ripped only empty sky.

"Stay down," Whitefeather commanded his prisoner. "Stay the fuck down!" the Lakota repeated.

The big Indian sprinted over gravel. By the time he reached Kevin Ganzt's side, the boy was already dead.

"Ah, Christ," Whitefeather moaned, removing his white stocking cap as he took a knee beside the dead teenager. "He's just a kid."

Detective Betty Hastings of the Billings P.D., the woman who'd been Ganzt's target, joined the agent alongside the dead boy.

"Good Lord," she whispered. "He can't be more than fifteen."

Herb Whitefeather looked at the female cop with troubled eyes. He was searching for answers he knew the woman did not have.

FORTY-TWO

Montana shares a five-hundred-and-forty-five mile border with three Canadian provinces: Saskatchewan, Alberta, and British Columbia. Fourteen roadways pierce the international boundary between the countries; entry points where both nations maintain border and customs agents. One of the crossings, I-15, which heads north from Great Falls and enters Canada near Sweet Grass, Montana, is a major highway. The remaining entry points are accessed by less traveled paved and unpaved roads.

Ezra Pratt made a mistake. The First Counselor believed he and his family should flee north on I-15. Pratt thought that speed, not stealth, would be his protector as he sought to make the Saskatchewan property owned by The Colony. He was apprehended by the Canadian Border Service just north of Sweet Grass, and detained, along with his family (which included two underage sister wives) until United States Customs and Border Protection agents could take custody of Pratt and his family. The fake passport provided by The Tyler didn't fool the new security scanners in service on the Canadian side of the border.

Second Counselor Micah Albrecht, who's Denali was identified by a Montana State Trooper just outside Harlem, Montana on US Highway 2, died as the result of a high-speed chase. As Albrecht, his three wives, and his seven children careened down a gravel road between Hogeland and Turner in the big SUV, the astute trooper and a Blaine County sheriff's squad in pursuit, the right front tire of Albrecht's Denali struck a pothole. The vehicle left the roadway and collided with a power pole at ninety miles an hour. Only the youngest Albrecht child, Deseret, a three-month-old girl strapped into a child seat, survived. The child's mother, Amelia Talks Aloud, the fifteen-year-old concubine of Albrecht, and one of the underage Lamanite women taken by the men of Laman's River as a sister wife, died of massive head trauma in the crash.

In the aftermath of the assault on Laman's River, three other young Lamanite girls were taken into protective custody: Brooke Benson Talmadge, the seventeen-year-old Crow girl who had given birth to Raven Ruth Talmadge after being sealed in Celestial marriage to Charles Talmadge; Elsie Johnson, who had been destined to become

211

The Prophet's fifth wife; and Audrey Blue Water, a quiet, introspective, chubby Cheyenne girl of fourteen who had been sealed to Edward Johannson, one of The Colonies' seventies. Audrey was six months along with another of the sect's "experiments" in the bleaching of the Lamanites when she was removed from Laman's River.

Talmadge and Johannson were indicted by a Billings federal grand jury for trafficking minors for sexual purposes. Talmadge was also indicted for federal firearms violations; and for false imprisonment, assault, and kidnapping relating to his confinement of FBI Special Agent Corrine MacDonald. Both men remained in custody while awaiting trial.

Other adult members of The Colony were charged with lesser crimes including child abuse, child endangerment, statutory rape, and the like in Montana state court. Most of the state court defendants were released on their own recognizance or on bail. They returned to their homes in Laman's River to await trial or plea.

Of the three principals of The Colony named as defendants in the U.S. Attorney's complaint (based upon a grand jury's indictment) following The Tyler's killing spree, only Ezra Pratt was arrested. He alone faced trial on four counts of capital murder for the execution-style slayings of Angelina DeAquila, Bethany Comes to Ride, Elwood Jones, and Julia Kingbird.

Three months after the assault on Laman's River, Pratt remained in the Yellowstone County Jail in Billings, his lips sealed, his resolve firm. He was uncooperative with the authorities on the subject of the whereabouts of The Tyler or The Prophet. Despite repeated interrogations by Jeff Dugan and other federal agents, Pratt revealed nothing. He would neither confirm nor deny the rumor that The Prophet and his family had escaped to Canada.

Attempts by Agent Corrine MacDonald to loosen the lips of her friend and fellow Jean Rhys aficionado, Brooke Benson (who had dropped "Talmadge" from her name) were similarly unsuccessful. The young Crow girl and her child left Laman's River to live in a Native American foster home on the Crow Reservation. Though the girl wanted nothing more to do with the Reconstituted Brotherhood of Latter-day Saints, she refused to engage Agent MacDonald in anything other than literary discussions, which continued for a while, and then ended with the agent having learned nothing about the cult beyond what she'd personally observed. The Crow girl offered no new insights into the inner workings of The Colony and didn't divulge the whereabouts of the wanted men, either because she didn't know where they were hiding, or because she didn't care to share that information.

•••

The rancher stood in shade created by an ancient barn, the weathered Manitoba maple of the structure visible through peeling red paint. A June sun, high but not yet achieving the intensity of deep summer, warmed the stoop-shouldered man's face as he considered the land. Three thousand acres of wheat had sprouted since the old man and his family arrived on the banks of the Wood River, a small Saskatchewan meander flowing into Old Wives Lake southwest of Moose Jaw. The derelict farm house had been constructed of native maple cut and planed at the end of the nineteenth century when a settler by the name of Ian McTavish founded Wood River Farm. It was a paradise to the immigrant Scot who had left behind a dismally cold sheep fold located in the highlands of Scotland, trading up, in McTavish's view, for space, peace, and quiet, not to mention endlessly generous soil and an optimistic growing season.

As The Prophet studied his new surroundings, he concluded that he had invested The Colony's tithes wisely. Here, on the desolate plains of Canada, The Principle could begin anew. Obidiah Nielsen appreciated that his remaining wives and his children were disappointed by their new surroundings. Gone was the privacy that the wheel and spoke arrangement of the big log house in Laman's River afforded. Gone were the beautiful setting, the verdant pastures and the high craggy limestone cliffs enclosing the contented denizens of The Colony. A few stragglers had joined them in Canada. But the remnant congregation of the Reconstituted Brotherhood of Latter-day Saints that established a toehold in Saskatchewan, less than two dozen strong, was unable to attract new membership from the suspicious Scots-Irish stock of the surrounding communities. With the history of Laman's River looming clear in their past, the members of The Colony remained cautious. No new Lamanite girls were procured to become sister wives. No underage local girls were enticed into plural marriages with the half-dozen Mormon men who now called the banks of the Wood River home.

Content in the moment, The Prophet turned his back to the steady sun and strode towards the barn, intent upon assisting his wife Jennifer with the castration of two barrows. Nielsen's lanky stride seemed to defy his age and his past troubles. But seeds of doubt had been sown in The Prophet's mind.

Someday, Nielsen thought as his eyes focused on Jennifer waving to him from the open door of the barn, *they will come. Though it will be Canadian Mounted Police and provincial officers instead of the FBI, the BIA, and the ATF, the result will be the same. But until they come,* the old man mused, *I will live The Principle as God intended to the best of my ability. Until they come, I will be true to the*

213

Angel Moroni, to the Angel Nephi, to Prophet Smith, and all the other Saints. Until they come…

•••

The USB drive retrieved from The Tyler's cabin cinched the case. The names, telephone numbers, and email addresses of every contact that Jason Orth had relied upon in his attempt to carry out the instructions of The Prophet and the First and Second Counselors, including The Tyler's connection with the Mormon genealogical center in Salt Lake City; his connection to Astrid Yost (the secretary at the Great Falls office of the Montana Highway Patrol); his contacts with Joseph Buckanaga, (the social worker in Duluth who had no difficulty recommending the placement of young Indian girls in the All Faiths Recovery Center when asked to do so); and The Tyler's extensive relationship with Edward Big Hands (the Native American employee of All Faiths who had no compunction against leading troubled Indian girls into the arms of fundamentalist Mormon men at least twice their age); were all memorialized on the USB device.

The drive also contained details used to build a case against Judge Elizabeth Prichard, who, once the net was pulled tight around her, confessed the details of her involvement in the scheme to Herb Whitefeather, Deb Slater, and Sam Byrnes. By the time the contents of The Tyler's USB drive were leaked to the press, Judge Prichard was on hiatus from the bench, awaiting professional discipline by the Minnesota Board of Judicial Standards.

The judge would also face trial in Duluth on the federal conspiracy charges pending against her; though given the coerced nature of her involvement in the plot to bleach the Lamanites, the judge had been spared any charges relating to the murder of Angelina DeAquila.

Deb Slater returned to her job as the chief law enforcement officer of Cook County. She also returned to a husband battling an insidious disease and a daughter at risk for paralyzing sadness. But a ray of hope shone upon the Slater home on the shores of Devil's Track Lake as winter's ice melted and snow retreated.

Rick Slater underwent a last-ditch regimen of stem cell implantation at the University of Wisconsin Hospital Stem Cell Research and Regeneration Center in Madison. The protocol, one that treated the specific genus of mitochondria disorder with which Rick had been diagnosed, had been developed at Columbia University in New York and was being applied selectively to "at risk" patients in three trials across the country. After six treatments involving costly stays in Madison (which caused the Slaters to incur medical, hotel, and ancillary expenses not covered by insurance) Rick Slater was no longer confined to bed, was off oxygen three hours a day, and was eating Deb's bad cooking like a pig at a feeding trough. They had no guarantees that the early success of the trial would do more than buy Rick extra time. But Debra Slater was convinced that the telephone call from the university hospital (prompted by Rick's doctor reading about the study in a medical journal) was indeed God's answer to her less than diligent faith and fragile prayers.

"You guys be careful," the sheriff called out as she stood on new grass and watched Rick, Annie, and Duke walk down the gravel drive leading away from the Slater home. "Take it easy on the old man, Annie. He's had a hell of a winter," Deb Slater added. "He's not up to par. Rick, slow down. You're gonna give yourself a heart attack!"

Rick Slater threw a dismissive hand into the spring air.

"I'm okay. Stop being so protective."

"He's doing great, Mom," Annie added. "Don't be such a pain."

Deb Slater watched the panther-like gait of her daughter, the girl's burgeoning womanhood clear in the sway of her slender hips; her adolescent energy controlled so as to remain alongside her father; and drew a deep breath.

The air is so clean. The sun feels so good. I've had enough winter, enough cold. I hope this summer is one to remember, she thought. *Thank you, Lord,* Sheriff Deb Slater added as she watched her husband, daughter, and winter-fattened Lab disappear around a bend.

AFTERWORD

Elizabeth Prichard lost it all. Her license to practice law. Her position as a District Court Judge. Her place in the world. With the criminal charges against the judge set for trial in Duluth during the upcoming term of federal court, Prichard retreated to the one place she knew held solace and solitude.

There would be a plea bargain. Prichard would, in the end, be spared the indignity of a public trial; a spectacle that could drag her improprieties out into the bright light of scrutiny. She had been a fool by not going immediately to the FBI when The Tyler had first approached her. Elizabeth knew this and understood that her fall was due to her pride, her foolish vanity, her self-assured belief in her own importance. She had no one to blame for her demise but herself; though, in the big scheme of things, she had fervently hoped that Herb Whitefeather and Debra Slater would find the man who had wrecked havoc on her life.

The Tyler.

That's what he was called; at least in the newspaper articles she'd read concerning the raid on Laman's River. Jason Orth was his real name. Or was it Allan Black? In her current state of disoriented self-pity, she lacked the certainty that she'd held to her breast as a concise and swift judge of circumstance and character. He could be either. Or neither. Or both. But she knew that, somewhere, in some article, she had read that his title amongst his people, those deluded fundamentalist Mormons who followed Obadiah Nielsen, folks a lot like the sect that she fled Utah to escape, was indeed "The Tyler."

Her sanctuary, at least until it was confiscated by the authorities to satisfy whatever civil judgment would be won against her by the family of Elsie Johnson, floated easily alongside a pier in the tannin stained waters of the St. Louis River. Across the teak and mahogany stern of the fifty-two foot 1949 Chris Craft Conqueror, the name of the vessel was painted in bold black lettering outlined in white.

The Bountiful.

It was her wicked sense of humor that had caused Elizabeth Prichard to pick an inglorious reference to her former religion as the name for the boat. Her ex-husband, with whom she bought the sedan cruiser as a derelict hulk of rotting wood and disabled machinery before their ugly and protracted divorce, had objected to the name. He favored *Kittiwake*, a shore bird of gentle grace and swiftness, as the boat's title.

But Elizabeth had won the battle of nomenclature as she won most contests of wills between them. Her inflexible nature was one of the reasons she and Jonas divorced; that and her evangelical zeal and his predilection for younger women. She had, in the end, prevailed upon her unfaithful husband to give her the boat in the divorce. She was, after all, the one who spent two years, with the assistance of her sons, friends, and assorted tradesmen, rebuilding the old tub into a gleaming showpiece that won awards at antique boat shows. Jonas took little interest in the rebirth of *The Bountiful*. In the scheme of their breakup, he had little claim against the wooden cruiser and yielded it to his wife without protest.

It was late August. Elizabeth Prichard sat on a folding canvas chair on the back deck of her boat. *The Bountiful* was docked at the Riverside Marina in the far western reaches of Duluth. The brown water of the St. Louis River flowed past the old boat launching facility like an immense expanse of unsettled butterscotch pudding. The marina was a remnant of a shipyard that had once been home to Captain Alexander MacDougal's whaleback empire. The slender cigar-shaped vessels built in the late 19th and early 20th centuries at the shipyard had disappeared from the Great Lakes, save one: The *S.S. Meteor*, the last of its kind, served as a tourist attraction across the bay in Superior, Wisconsin.

Elizabeth Prichard knew the history of the marina. She chose to keep her boat docked in Riverside, not out of sense of nostalgia, but because the fees charged by the seat-of-the-pants operation fit her budget. Jonas was often late with his child support payments. The fallen judge, even before her legal troubles, was something of a spendthrift. The Riverside Marina, though not up to her high standards, provided a safe place to dock the old boat between runs up and down the river and the occasional foray onto the big lake.

The woman propped her feet on an empty lawn chair and sipped a piná colada through a straw. An early autumn sun hung just above the hillside to the west, its descent imminent, its intensity all but exhausted. No sounds echoed across the water. Beyond the limits of the marina, sport fishing boats bobbed silently on the wide expanse of Spirit Lake, a broadening in the river that holds a plethora of game fish: walleye, pike, sturgeon, pan fish, perch, bass, and muskie. The disgraced judge removed her sunglasses; the dark lenses redundant at dusk, and hooked the frame in the neckline of her T-shirt. She wore her mousy brown hair short. Her face was newly tightened: The surgery, a vain attempt to conceal the affects of her most recent troubles. She rose from her chair, drink in hand, and stepped through a doorway into the main salon of *The Bountiful*.

Before mixing the piná colada, Elizabeth had visited the marina office to buy ice. Upon her return to the boat, she'd dumped the ice cubes into a Coleman cooler on the aft deck of the boat. She had not been back into the boat's salon since leaving to buy ice. As she walked through the ornate cabin (intent upon retrieving a dish cloth from a drawer adjacent to the small stainless steel sink in the galley) something seemed amiss. There was a faint odor reminiscent of childhood wafting delicately in the cool shadows as she descended the narrow stairway from salon into galley.

Licorice?

"Hello, Judge Prichard."

A tremor shook the woman. Her eyes adjusted to dim light. He sat quietly on a bench seat at the galley table against the far wall. His square shoulders occupied all the available space as he leveled a wicked looking automatic at the judge. Elizabeth stood very still.

The Tyler.

"Mind having a seat, judge?" the man said quietly.

The Tyler's face was perplexing. He displayed a Cheshire smile, but, with the pistol aimed at her, the smile seemed duplicitous. The woman's right hand began to shake and she spilled froth onto the varnished wood floor of the galley.

"Please join me," the man said between chews of gum. "We have much to talk about."

Elizabeth Prichard slid into the booth opposite the assassin and placed her drink on the table's mahogany surface.

'What do you want?" she said weakly.

"Justice."

A confused look claimed the woman's face.

"What?"

"Well, you are a judge, aren't you? I simply want your take on something that has been bothering me since I left Montana."

Silence.

"I see you don't understand. Let me explain. You talked. To the big Lamanite and his friend, the sheriff. You told them what they wanted to know. About me. About The Principle. About Laman's River."

"I did no such thing," the woman whispered unevenly.

The Tyler smiled.

"Look, Lizzy," he said, the reference to the judge's former name recalled easily despite the passage of time. "I know what you did. You know what you did. All I am asking is that you fess up, admit your mistake."

The judge gulped air.

"No one has called me by that name since I left Utah. Except you," the woman whispered, a hint of desperation invading her speech. "I haven't gone by that name in years."

The Tyler considered the woman's face.

"I like what you've done with yourself. A little lift to the eyes. Some elevation to the tip of the nose. A bit of structure to the cheeks. Very impressive. Costly, I'd suppose."

The woman looked down at her drink but did not respond.

"Well, that's neither here nor there. What I need to hear, what the Lord God needs to hear, from you Lizzy Joy Kittridge, is your admission of sin. Not confession. That's something the Catholics insist upon. I'm not that rigid. I'll accept, as would be proper in front of a jury, your admission that you caused the destruction of Laman's River. That you, and you alone, led the authorities to my door at Sixteen Mile Creek. Can you do that, Lizzy? Can you admit your wrongs? It will do you good, you know. There's little hope that you'll get another chance to make amends."

The judge placed her head on the wooden surface of the small table and began to sob.

"I'm... a... mother. I... have... two... boys... to raise," she said haltingly.

"I'd like to be sympathetic," The Tyler said. "But you see, I have a duty too. Don't you see that, Lizzy? I'm just like you. You have a duty to your boys but that's an earthly obligation. My obligation is to God. I am his angel, his disciple here on Earth. Granted, my job, at times, is disheartening. Understand, I do not relish what I am about to do. But you will be in a better place. Your sons have a father. Things will work out. Perhaps not in your time, but in God's time. You'll see. Now, don't you think you should let go of the burden of carrying these lies? Isn't it better to meet Jesus with a clear conscious and the knowledge you've admitted your wrongs?'

The woman raised her teary eyes from the table and looked into the killer's calm face.

"But I tell you, I did not do what you say I did. I did not give the officers what you think I did."

The Tyler shook his head slowly and stood up. He walked over to a radio plugged into the wall near the sink, opened the CD drive, removed a disk from his shirt pocket, placed the disk in the changer, and closed the drive door.

The strumming of an acoustic guitar filled the room. The Tyler turned up the volume on the Mountain tune, "Because You are My Friend" as loud as the little radio would allow, placed his handgun on the teak surface of the counter surrounding the steel sink basin, and

219

removed the fillet knife from the sheath on his belt, its slender blade shining in migrating light, before moving towards the stairway.

As The Tyler stood in the narrow entry and lifted his right hand to secure the door, the sound of footsteps, followed by the appearance of an enormous shadow, caused The Tyler to pause.

The Lamanite.

Crack.

Before he could turn towards the sound and raise the knife in his left hand, a 9mm slug struck Jason Orth at the base of his skull. Blood exploded across the room. The bullet exited the assassin and clattered through a cabinet full of pots and pans on the far wall of the galley before coming to rest in the thick mahogany hull of *The Bountiful* with a thud. The killer toppled face first to the floor and did not move.

The galley door swung open. Light reclaimed dark. Herb Whitefeather, his height compressed by the low ceiling, nudged The Tyler's body with his right shoe as he stepped into the galley.

Elizabeth Prichard was speechless.

"The story you will tell..." the big Indian said as he tucked his 9mm automatic into the waistband of his khaki Dockers and knelt to feel the carotid artery of The Tyler with his left index finger, "...is that Jason Orth drew his weapon..." Whitefeather continued, casting his eyes towards the pistol on the counter, "...and that I had no choice but to shoot the man."

The judge nodded hesitantly.

"I need to know that this will be your story, judge. Tell me how it happened," Whitefeather said in the same concise tone. "Tell me what you're going to say to the Duluth Police when they arrive."

"He had his gun on me... He heard you coming in... He took aim..."

Whitefeather nodded.

"And?"

"And you shot him... to save my life."

A grin spread over the agent's craggy face.

"I did, didn't I?" Whitefeather said, wrapping a paper towel from a dispenser in the kitchen around the handle of the fillet knife before replacing the blade in the sheath on the dead man's belt. "I saved your life."

The agent removed another paper towel from the dispenser, wrapped the towel around the dead man's automatic and placed the pistol in The Tyler's limp left hand.

"There. Story complete," Whitefeather said with satisfaction, shoving the towels into a pocket of his slacks.

The woman stood. She held her head imperiously so as to avoid acknowledging the dead man lying at her feet. "Never in My Life", a boisterous Mountain song blared from the CD changer. Whitefeather reached over and turned the music off.

"Much better," the agent said as quiet reclaimed the galley. "Let's get you out of here."

Herb Whitefeather held the narrow teak door open for the judge. They exited the boat's cabin and stood on the aft deck as the sun declined and the marina became cloaked in shadow. A crowd had gathered near Whitefeather's rusty Toyota Land Cruiser parked adjacent to the boat slip.

Whitefeather and Prichard watched as police squads turned off Grand Avenue onto the marina's access road in hell-bent-for-leather fashion. Sirens echoed across the water. Lights revolved in cascading dark. The squads skidded to a choreographed stop on the loose pit-run of the parking lot adjacent to *The Bountiful.*

Judge Prichard began to shiver. Herb Whitefeather re-entered the salon, retrieved a wool throw from the back of a sofa, exited the cabin, and covered the woman with the blanket.

"How did you…?"

Whitefeather raised a hand.

"Border Patrol. Mr. Orth came through Thunder Bay. Crossed at the Pigeon River just north of Grand Portage. They missed him there, some sort of snafu. By the time they realized who he was, he was already headed down the shore. Border Patrol called DPD. Local cops found his car ditched on a side street in downtown Duluth. Must have taken a cab to the marina. He was likely going to do what needed doing," the agent said softly, "and then hightail it out of here. Don't know why he risked coming back for you, though."

The woman thought carefully before responding.

"He believed that I'd given you information."

The big man smiled.

"Shit, Judge, you didn't give me nothin'. I would have told him that, had he asked."

The woman stared hard at the Indian.

"But why did you kill him? You could have taken him in."

Herb Whitefeather looked towards the dusky sky.

"My cousin's kid." There was a pause in the agent's disclosure. "He murdered my cousin's little girl."

Elizabeth Prichard looked at the big man.

"Funny," she said softly. "He came here seeking justice and he got it; just not in the way he envisioned."

A gang of uniformed patrolmen exited their marked squad cars and scurried towards the boat.

"You got our story straight?"

Elizabeth Prichard nodded.

"But what if it unravels? I'll keep to the company line. But what if DPD goes all CSI and starts poking around? The truth could end your career."

Herb Whitefeather didn't respond. His eyes were focused on a sign taped to the rear window of *The Bountiful's* salon.

For Sale by Owner. Inquire at Marina.

"You selling her?"

"I am."

"How much?"

"It's on the market for one fifty-five."

"Nice boat for that price. It'd look good down in Fort Lauderdale."

The woman missed the import of Whitefeather's comment.

"You interested?"

"I might be. I just might be," the agent said in a reflective tone.

The big man scrutinized the freshly painted canvas of the sedan cruiser's roof and studied the boat's classic lines with a practiced eye. He touched the brass of *The Bountiful's* finely polished aft railing with tawny fingers before fixing his eyes on the judge.

"Tomorrow," Agent Herb Whitefeather said calmly as a cadre of uniformed police officers hustled towards *The Bountiful*, "tomorrow is my last day with the Bureau."

The End

Sources

Books

Bigelow, Christopher Kimball, and Riess, Dr. Jana, *Mormonism for Dummies.* Hoboken, New Jersey: Wiley Publishing, 2005.

Brodie, Fawn M., *No Man Knows My History; the Life of Joseph Smith.* New York: Vintage Books, 1973.

Krakauer, Jon, *Under the Banner of Heaven; a Story of Violent Faith.* New York: Anchor Books, 2003.

Laake, Deborah, *Secret Ceremonies.* New York: William Morrow, 1993.

Munger, Mark. *The Legacy.* Superior, Wisconsin: Savage Press, 2000.

Smith, Joseph, Jun., *The Book of Mormon.* Salt Lake City, Utah: The Church of Jesus Christ of Latter-day Saints, 1971 and 1981 editions.

Stenhouse, T.B.H. *The Rocky Mountain Saints.* Salt Lake City, Utah: Utah Lighthouse Ministry (Photomechanical Reproduction), 1873.

Tanner, Jerald and Sandra. *The Changing World of Mormonism.* (Online version).Website: www.utlm.org/onlinebooks/changecontents.htm (Accessed March 25, 2010).

The Road Atlas, '04. Skokie: Illinois: Rand McNally, 2004.

Werner, M.R.. *Brigham Young.* New York: Harcourt, Brace and Co., Inc., 1975.

Worrall, Simon. *The Poet and the Murderer.* New York: Plume Books, 2003.

Websites

"Adam-God Theory." Wikipedia en.wikipedia.org/wiki/Adam-God. (Accessed November 10, 2009).

"A New Candidate in Arabia for the Valley of Lemuel" by George D. Potter. *Journal of Book of Mormon Studies,* Vo. 8, No. 1, 1999. (Web version; date of access unknown).

"An Inside Look at the 1,000 Member Kingston Clan." www.childpro.org/1998%20meida/1998%20meida%2004.htm. (Accessed December 28, 2009).

"Apostolic United Brethren." Wikipedia en.wikipedia.org/wiki/Apostolic_United_Brethren. (Accessed November 10, 2009).
"Apostolic United Brethren." www.abosoluteastronomy.com/topics/Apostolic_United_Brethren. (Accessed November 10, 2009).

"A Second Wife's Tale." www.beliefnet.com/Faiths/Christianity/Latter-Day-Saints/2006. (Accessed October 1, 2009).

"Author's Acknowledgements: The 19th Wife." www.19thwife.com/acknowledge.htm. (Accessed February 17, 2010).

"Beaver Island (Lake Michigan)." Wikipedia en.wikipedia.org/wiki/Beaver_Island_(Lake_Michigan). (Accessed October 2, 2009).

"Book of Mormon Word Change." www.equip.org/articles/book-of-mormon-word-change. (Accessed September 30, 2009).

"Booth Confirms 'Bleaching' of The Lamanites." www.utlm.org/newsletters/no.36.htm. (Accessed November 11, 2009).

"Bountiful, B.C.." www.rickross.com/rference/polygamy65.html. (Accessed October 2, 2009).

"Canadian Border Patrol." www.cbp.gov. (Accessed February 15, 2010).

"Canada-United States Border." Wikipedia en.wikipedia.org/wiki/Canada_%E2%80%93_United_States_border. (Accessed February 14, 2010).

"Extasea." www.unitedyacht.com. (Accessed 2008)

"Felix Pappalardi." Wikipedia en.wikipedia.org/wiki/Felix_Pappalardi. (Accessed November 26, 2009).

"Fort William Harrison." www.montanaguard.com/trainingsite/html/fort_harrison.cfm. (Accessed January 14, 2010).

"Genetics and the Book of Mormon." Wikipedia en.wikipedia.org/wiki/Genetics_and_the_Book_of_Mormon. (Accessed September 30, 2009).

"In His Own Words: FLDS 'Prophet' Warren Jeffs." www.splcenter.org/intel/intelreport/article/jsp?sid=342. (Accessed September 30, 2009).

"Jonestown." Wikipedia en.wikipedia.org/wiki/Jonestown. (Accessed January 14, 2010).

"Julian the Apostate." Wikipedia en.wikipedia.org/wiki/Julian_the-Apostate. (Accessed September 30, 2009).

"Laman." http://eom.byu.edu/index.php/Laman. (Accessed October 1, 2009).
"Laman and Lemuel." Wikipedia en.wikipedia.org/wiki/Laman. (Accessed October 1, 2009).

"Lamanite." Wikipedia en.wikipedia.org/wiki/Lamanite. (Accessed October 12, 2009).

"Latter Day Church of Christ." Wikipedia en.wikipedia.org/wiki/Latter_Day_Church_of_Christ. (Accessed December 28, 2009).

"Letters from a Man who Comes from a Polygamist Family."
www.exmormon.org/mormon/mormon218.htm. (Accessed November
10, 2009).

"Linguistics and the Book of Mormon." Wikipedia
en.wikipedia.org/wiki/Linguistics_and_the_Book_of_Mormon.
(Accessed February 17, 2010).

"Mark Hoffman." Wikipedia en.wikipedia.org/wiki/Mark_Hoffman.
(Accessed December 15, 2009).

"Meagher County, Montana." Wikipedia
en.wikipedia.org/wiki/Meagher_County,_Montana. (Accessed January
14, 2010).

"Meet Mark Hoffman." www.mormoninformation.com/hoffman/htm.
(Accessed December 15, 2009).

"Minigun." Wikipedia en.wikipedia.org/wiki/Minigun. (January 14,
2010).

"Mitochondrial Disease."
www.myclevelandclinic.org/disorders/Mitrchondrial_Disease/hic.
(Accessed November 25, 2009).

"Montana Sheriff and Peace Officers Association Tactical Advisory
Committee's Report: Montana Special Weapons and Tactics (SWAT)
Standards." August 18, 2005. (Online version, date of access
unknown).

"More about the Fundamentalist Church of Latter Day Saints."
www.feniste.us/blog/archives/2008/04/28/more-about-the-
fundamnetlaist-mormons. (Accessed September 30, 2009).

"Mormon Fundamentalism." Wikipedia
en.wikipedia.org/wiki/Mormon_fundamentalism. (Accessed November
10, 2009).

"Mormonism."
www.wrestedscriptures.com/a02mormon/polygamypreliminary.
(Accessed February 17, 2010).

"Mormonism." http://thenarrowgate.net/mormons.html. (Accessed September 30, 2009).

"101 Reasonable Doubts about Mormonism." http//packham.n4m.org/101.htm. (Accessed December 17, 2009).

"Origin of Latter-day saints Polygamy." Wikipedia en.wikipedia.org/wiki/Origin_of_Latter_Day_Saint_polygamy. (Accessed February 17, 2010).

"Pinesdale Polygamy Fears." http//missoulanews.bigskypress.com/Missoula/pinesdale-polygamy. (Accessed November 10, 2009).

"Polygamist 'Underage Sex Cult' Case Descends into Farce." www.dailymail.co.uk/news/article-559808/Polygamist-underage. (Accessed September 30, 2009).

"Polygamy Charges in Bountiful." www.theglobeandmail.com/news/national/article963758.ece. (Accessed October 2, 1009).

"Progress in Understanding Mitochondrial Disease." www.meajo.org/article.asp. (Accessed November 21, 2009).

"Putting Polygamy in the Spotlight." www.philly.com/mld/inquirer/news/special_packages/sunday_review/1 4241453.htm. (Accessed; unknown date; posted 4/2/06).

"Ruby Ridge." Wikipedia en.wikipedia.org/wiki/Ruby_Ridge. (Accessed January 14, 2010).

"Science Challenges Mormon Beliefs." www.rickross.com/reference/mormon/mormon182.html. (Accessed September 30, 2009).

"Special Agent Frequently Asked Questions" www.fbijobs.gov/114.asp (Accessed February 19, 2010).

'Stem Cells for the Treatment of Mitochondrial Disease." www.brighthub.com/science/medical/articles/23612.aspx. (Accessed February 15, 2010).

"Texas Polygamists May Recant." www.msnbc.com/id/24084663. (Accessed January 14, 2010).

"The Doctrines and Covenants of the Church of Jesus Christ of Latter-day Saints." scriptures.lds.org/dc (Accessed February 17, 2010).

"The Mormon Church: Is it Christian?" www.pnc.com.au/~fichrist/momon1.html. (Accessed November 11, 2009).

"The Polygamy Cults of Southern Utah." www.childbrides.org/excuses_CP_plig_cults_Southern_Utah.html. (Accessed September 30, 2009).

"The Spaulding Research Project." http://solomonspaulding.com/SRP/saga2/sagawt0i.htm. (Accessed September 30, 2009).
"The United Mitochondrial Disease Foundation." www.umdf.org. (Accessed March 14, 2002).

"Tyler." Wikipedia en.wikipedia.org/wiki/Tyler_Masonic. (Accessed November 26, 2009).

"UH-1 Iroquois." Wikipedia en.wikipedia.org/wiki/UH-1_Iroquois. (Accessed January 14, 2010).

"UH-60 Black Hawk." Wikipedia en.wikipedia.org/wiki/UH-60_Black_Hawk. (Accessed January 14, 2010).

"Utah Saints and Sinners: Mormons and Outlaws." www.uiweb.uidaho.edu/sepcial-collections/papers/utah.htm. (Accessed September 30, 2009).

"Waco Siege." Wikipedia en.wikipedia.org/wiki/Waco_Siege. (Accessed January 14, 2010).

"Warren Jeffs and the FLDS." www.npr.org.templates/story/story.php?StoryID. =4629320. 9Accessed October 1, 2009).

Other Works by the Author

The Legacy (ISBN 0972005080 and eBook in all formats)
   Set against the backdrop of WWII Yugoslavia and present-day Minnesota, this debut novel combines elements of military history, romance, thriller, and mystery. Rated 3 and 1/2 daggers out of 4 by *The Mystery Review Quarterly*.

Ordinary Lives (ISBN 97809792717517 and eBook in all formats)
   Creative fiction from one of Northern Minnesota's newest writers, these stories touch upon all elements of the human condition and leave the reader asking for more.

Pigs, a Trial Lawyer's Story (ISBN 097200503x and eBook in all formats)
   A story of a young trial attorney, a giant corporation, marital infidelity, moral conflict, and choices made, *Pigs* takes place against the backdrop of Western Minnesota's beautiful Smokey Hills. This tale is being compared by reviewers to Grisham's best.

Suomalaiset: People of the Marsh (ISBN 0972005064 and eBook in all formats)
   A dockworker is found hanging from a rope in a city park. How is his death tied to the turbulence of the times? A masterful novel of compelling history and emotion, *Suomalaiset* has been hailed by reviewers as a "must read."

Esther's Race (ISBN 9780972005098 and eBook in all formats)
   The story of an African American registered nurse who confronts race, religion, and tragedy in her quest for love, this novel is set against the stark and vivid beauty of Wisconsin's Apostle Islands, the pastoral landscape of Central Iowa, and the steel and glass of Minneapolis. A great read soon to be a favorite of book clubs across America.

Mr. Environment: The Willard Munger Story (ISBN 9780979217524: Trade paperback only)

A detailed and moving biography of Minnesota's leading environmental champion and longest serving member of the Minnesota House of Representatives, ***Mr. Environment*** is destined to become a book every Minnesotan has on his or her bookshelf.

Black Water: Stories from the Cloquet River
(ISBN 9780979217548 and eBook in all formats)

Essays about ordinary and extraordinary events in the life of an American family living in the wilds of northeastern Minnesota, these tales first appeared separately in two volumes, *River Stories* and *Doc the Bunny*. Re-edited and compiled into one volume, these are stories to read on the deer stand, at the campsite, or late at night for peace of mind.

Sukulaiset: The Kindred
(ISBN 9780979217562 and eBook in all formats)

The long awaited sequel to *Suomalaiset*, this sprawling historical novel portrays the journey of Elin Gustafson from the shores of Lake Superior to the shores of Lake Onega in the Soviet Republic of Karelia during the Great Depression. A tale of love, war, the Holocaust, and human dignity.

Other Books from Cloquet River Press

Back of Beyond: A Memoir from the North Woods (ISBN 9780979217500: Trade paperback only)

The debut effort from Minnesota author Susanne Kobe Schuler, this memoir of building and working at a family style Minnesota resort during the 1940's is a sure- fire winner. Come, meet the Kobe family, their friends, their relatives, the guests of the resort, and join them for a trip back into a kinder, gentler time set in the deep woods of Northeastern Minnesota.

About the Author

Mark Munger is a District Court Judge serving four counties in northeastern Minnesota. When not on the bench, Mark lives on the banks of the wild and scenic Cloquet River with his wife René and one of their four sons. You can email Mark with your comments about this book or his other writing at: cloquetriverpress@yahoo.com.

SmileTrain
Changing The World One Smile At A Time.

10% of all gross sales of CRP books are donated by CRP to SmileTrain in hopes of helping children born with cleft lips and palates across the world. Learn more about SmileTrain at http://www.smiletrain.org/.

Visit us at:
www.cloquetriverpress.com
Shop at our online store!

53426207R00142

Made in the USA
Charleston, SC
10 March 2016